W9-CLG-888

THE POSTMODERN NOVEL IN LATIN AMERICA

Politics, Culture, and the Crisis of Truth

Raymond Leslie Williams

St. Martin's Press
New York

In memory of Germán Vargas

THE POSTMODERN NOVEL IN LATIN AMERICA

ISBN 0-312-12081-8

Library of Congress Cataloging-in-Publication Data

Williams, Raymond Leslie
    The postmodern novel in Latin America : politics, culture, and the crisis
of truth / Raymond Leslie Williams.
        p. cm.
    Includes bibliographical references (p.) and index
    ISBN 0-312-12081-8
    1. Spanish American fiction—20th century—History and criticism.
2. Postmodernism (Literature)—Latin America. 3. Politics in
literature. 4. Literature and society—Latin America. I. Title.
PQ7082.N7W55 1995
863—dc20   95-13163
                                                  CIP

Book design by Acme Art, Inc.

First Edition: November 1995
10 9 8 7 6 5 4 3 2 1

Contents

Also by Raymond Leslie Williams

The Colombian Novel, 1844–1987, 1991

Una década de la novela colombiana, 1981

Gabriel García Márquez, 1984

Mario Vargas Llosa, 1987

The Novel in the Americas (editor), 1992

La novela colombiana contemporánea, 1976

Preface

The subject of this book is the postmodern novel in Spanish America, with focus on the fiction written from the 1970s to the present. Given the range of postmodern cultural activity in the Americas in recent decades, I often use the plural postmodernities in recognition of the heterogeneity that I will explore in each chapter. One theorist recently published a book titled *Against Postmodernism* because of (as he himself admitted from the outset) the "irritation" of the omnipresent discourse of and about postmodernism in academia today.[1] My study has been written with a full awareness of the irritation many scholars feel about the term *postmodernism* and, in a minor way, as a response to my own irritation with the proliferation of articles and books on postmodernism today. In particular, I am responding to the looseness and vagueness surrounding the term *postmodernism* in the context of Latin American literature.[2] The most notable critics who write against postmodernism tend to be critical theorists with a relatively weak background in contemporary fiction, such as Alex Callinicos and Fredric Jameson. I am a scholar of Latin American literature writing—I will be clear about my position from the beginning—in favor of postmodernism.

I am fully aware that there is no common agreement on the exact definition of the *postmodern novel* and that several critics have questioned the appropriateness of using the term *postmodern* when speaking of Latin America. On the other hand, others have argued that Latin America, in fact, set the precedent of postmodernity long before the notion appeared in the North Atlantic regions.[3] Theorists such as Callinicos and Jameson have simplified the concept of what contemporary postmodern fiction writing is, and then, in turn, questioned the political function of this supposedly simple and popular fiction.[4] One of my several interests is to reveal and hopefully elucidate the political in the Latin American postmodern: I will argue that the postmodern novel is as political as its more traditional (realist-naturalist) and modern (modernist) predecessors in Latin America.

My point of departure is the assumption that Latin America is concurrently a region of premodern, modern, and postmodern societies, a fact supported by numerous scholars.[5] Many of its rural areas, small communities, and villages are still premodern; most of its major cities have been undergoing an intense process of modernization since the 1930s and 1940s, and some urban sectors of Latin American society are as postmodern as Los Angeles, Boulder, Miami, New York, and Paris. In this book, I am concerned primarily, of course, with the fiction produced under the sign of the postmodern, but, rather than entering yet another inevitably futile (and perhaps ideologically or aesthetically limiting) exercise in defining postmodern fiction, I will discuss a broad range of the postmodernities that correspond to the different nations, regions, and conditions in Latin America.

This book was born in 1989 for several reasons. On the one hand, I had completed a book, *The Colombian Novel, 1844–1987*, in which the last chapter offered a brief, schematic view of modern and postmodern fiction in Colombia. This chapter left me with an interest in expanding and refining those ideas in a broader, Latin American context. In the fall of 1989, I offered a graduate seminar at the University of Colorado on the postmodern novel in Latin America, which forged beyond the schemes introduced in the book on the Colombian novel. In that seminar (and several similar seminars that followed), we read a variety of contemporary Latin American fictions within the context of the ongoing critical and theoretical dialogue on postmodernism, beginning with the writings of Ihab Hassan, Brian McHale, Jameson, and others. At the end of that semester, in December of 1989, I went to Mexico City and found myself explaining my recent seminar at a dinner in Carlos Fuentes's home to a group of Mexican intellectuals. After listening patiently to my brief description of the seminar, the Mexican cultural critic Roger Bartra lamented that the Mexicans were still concerned about becoming modern, and here the *gringos* were already teaching seminars on postmodernity. Later that evening, while watching U.S. troops invade Panama on CNN in the Hotel Maria Cristina, I decided to write this book. I thought of the project then as a logical culmination of my readings in postmodern theory, as a response to the many Roger Bartras in Latin America (and the United States, too), and as an outgrowth of my own postmodern experience in Latin America over the past two decades—including watching CNN in numerous hotels throughout Latin America while I skimmed Gabriel García Márquez novels or read the local press.

Most scholars of Latin American literature and culture, including my friend Roger Bartra, are far less skeptical about postmodernism in Latin America today than they were a decade ago. Recent Latin American cultural and political magazines have published numerous articles related to issues of postmodernity, such as *Nuevo Texto Crítico* and *Boundary* 2, which have dedicated special numbers to this matter.[6] There have been a broad range of responses to these issues in Latin America. Some critics, such as the Chilean Nelson Osorio, consider it a foreign importation and sign of cultural imperialism, just as the nationalist intellectuals of the 1920s resisted the modern novel of the avant-garde writers who were hidden in small (and often elite) pockets of Buenos Aires, Mexico City, Havana, and a few other cities. Given the cultural interaction that Europe has always maintained with the Americas, beginning with the Spanish language, this nationalist argument seems as questionable now as it was in the 1920s.

Several social scientists and cultural critics have set forth much more substantial arguments against the postmodern in Latin America. Two prominent Latin American voices, the Chilean cultural critic José Joaquín Brunner and the Mexican philosopher Adolfo Sánchez Vásquez, both arguing from Latin American perspectives strongly influenced by Jürgen Habermas, are highly critical of the postmodern. For Brunner and Habermas, postmodern culture is one of mass media manipulated by the dominating classes. Sánchez Váquez argues that postmodern culture is essentially conservative in that it reproduces the cultural forms of the dominant ideology. Brunner, Sánchez Vásquez, and some other Latin American intellectuals, such as Fredric Jameson in the early 1980s, find little to recommend the postmodern, although none of these critics makes specific reference to contemporary Latin American fiction in their generalized condemnation of the postmodern. Certainly the recent work of Linda Hutcheon, particularly *The Politics of Postmodernism,* has done much to find value in the postmodern, including its critical political practices. Jameson's recent *Postmodernism or the Cultural Logic of Late Capitalism* also recognizes politics in postmodernism that the followers of Habermas have been reluctant to see, including Jameson himself in early writings on postmodernism.[7]

"Is there a story?" the narrator of Ricardo Piglia's *Artificial Respiration* (1980) asks at the beginning of the novel, and one narrator of Carlos Fuentes's *Holy Place* (1967) asks "Is there another place?" The possibilities of telling a story and of telling it in *this* place are questionable in Latin America today, after Jorge Luis Borges, Julio Cortázar and Gabriel García Márquez, for very different reasons. It was also problematic to tell a story under the military regimes of the 1970s and to fix the locus of the telling of these stories. These are all issues of the postmodern writings of José Emilio Pacheco, Ricardo Piglia, Carlos Fuentes, and others.

A lively debate on postmodern culture and society has arisen in Latin America over the past decade. Young writers, such as the Venezuelan José Balza, the Colombian R. H. Moreno-Durán and the Chilean Diamela Eltit, consider themselves postmodern and politically progressive, despite the positions of the neo-Marxists Brunner and Sánchez Vásquez. In another postmodern direction, the Cuban Severo Sarduy, a key figure of these Latin American postmodernities, has found his artistic roots in Jacques Derrida and Roland Barthes, and has searched for a divorce between ideology and writing.

In Santiago de Chile, on the other hand, an impressive group of young intellectuals between the ages of 35 and 50, who for the most part survived the Pinochet dictatorship (1973-1988) living in Chile as underground resistors, have surfaced as Chile's leading writers, cultural critics, and artists. The young novelist Diamela Eltit, who has published four books, heads the group symbolically and collaborates on their new journal *Revista de Crítica Cultural*, directed by Nelly Richard. They conceive of their work in literature, criticism, and the visual arts as their space in *una escena de la escritura* (a scene of *écriture*).

A different "scene of *écriture*" has arisen out of complex cultural and political contexts in Argentina, Colombia, and Mexico. During the early 1980s, a phenomenon of marginality in Buenos Aires similar to the situation in Chile resulted in the publication of such diverse texts as Alejandra Pizarnik's violent rewriting of a vampire legend (an underground and subculture best-seller throughout the 1980s), Ricardo Piglia's experimental literary and historical fiction, and in Argentina the cultural speculations of various critics on postmodernism. Colombian intellectuals have organized several public discussions on postmodernity in Bogotá over the past five years (in some of which I have participated), and Colombian novelists such as Albalucia Angel and R. H. Moreno-Durán have numerous affinities with foreign postmoderns.

The scene with respect to postmodern culture is very complex in Mexico City, where Jameson is well known, Octavio Paz has questioned the very concept of postmodernity, and one of several feminist groups has begun publishing a journal called *El debate feminista*, with collaborations of writers such as Diamela Eltit and Albalucia Angel.

These discussions and, above all, the Latin American literary production of recent decades, suggest that there has been an epochal break in Latin America that took place in the late 1960s. From the late 1960s, as I will demonstrate in the upcoming chapters, a change in attitudes toward fiction and a change in novelistic production is evident. These changes correspond in many ways to what is currently being identified as *postmodern* in First World or North Atlantic academia.

Concepts of postmodern society and a postmodern fiction began to appear in Latin American intellectual circles in the mid-1980s, for both in Latin America and among First World academics actively engaged in the study of Indo-Afro-Iberoamerican culture. By the late 1980s, lines of division had been demarcated, as the "debate" had begun between critics and proponents of the postmodern. Since then, numerous social scientists, cultural critics, and academics have taken positions on postmodernism in Latin America, including (in addition to those already mentioned above) George Yúdice, Santiago Colás, Neil Larson, and John Beverly in the United States; Hernán Vidal, Martín Hopenhayn, and Norbert Lechner in Chile; Fernando Calderón from Bolivia; Ernesto Laclau; the Brazilians Luiz Costa Lima, Renato Ortiz, Heloisa Buarque de Holanda, and Silviano Santiago; Jesús Martín-Barbero; the Venezuelans Celeste Olalquiga and Luis Britto García; Ricardo Gutiérrez Mouat; the Uruguayan Jorge Ruffinelli; Ticio Escobar in Paraguay; Antonio Benítez Rojo from Cuba; the Colombians Alonso de Toro and Carlos Rincón; the Argentine Beatriz Sarlo.

My approach to the numerous and heterogeneous Latin American postmodernities is to discuss a group of the most representative, innovative, and postmodern novelists writing today. In chapter 1, I offer a general introduction to the development of Spanish-American modern and postmodern fiction, beginning with the origins of both the modern and postmodern in Borges, within several contexts, including the context of truth claims. I refer briefly to the historical discussion of truth claims as articulated by Hans-Georg Gadamer and Paul Ricoeur, and then address this question within the context of modern and postmodern fiction in Spanish America. In chapters 2 through 5, I analyze the production of novels from four regions: Mexico, the Andean region (Venezuela, Colombia, Ecuador, Perú, and Bolivia), the Southern Cone (Chile, Argentina, and Uruguay), and the Caribbean (the Spanish-speaking islands of Cuba, the Dominican Republic, and Puerto Rico). In each of these four regions, I offer a brief introduction to the postmodern cultural scene in general, and then analyze three or four texts of writers such as Severo Sarduy, Manuel Puig, José Donoso, Ricardo Piglia, Luis Rafael Sánchez, Diamela Eltit, Salvador Elizondo, José Balza, Jorge Enrique Adoum, and R. H. Moreno-Durán. Hardly any of the novelists I study are "popular" writers (with the exception of Puig and Donoso), although each has a respectable readership in Latin America and, in most cases, a substantive body of work consisting of at least three novels. Chapter 6, "In the Margins," is dedicated to writers who have been marginalized, such as women writers, or who write about marginalized groups. I include commentary on both modernist and postmodern writers, as well as on the fiction of the two countries most frequently marginalized in discussions of Latin American culture, Brazil (linguistically marginalized in Latin America) and Paraguay (geographically marginalized from the West). This chapter also deals with Central American fiction, gay and lesbian writing, and the *testimo-*

nio. Much of this fiction does not fit easily into most concepts of postmodern-ism; rather than forcing them into a category, I will discuss their affinities and differences with the variety of postmodernities described in the previous chapters.

I would like to thank the Council on Research and Creative Work of the University of Colorado at Boulder, which provided a semester research leave to advance this project. I would also like to express my appreciation to the Dean's Fund for the Humanities. Institutions in Latin America have kindly afforded me the opportunity to present and discuss ideas in this book at their early stage of development, including the Universidad Javeriana and Biblioteca Luis Angel Arango in Bogotá, the Universidad Central in Caracas, and the Universidad de Caldas in Manizales, Colombia. Several groups of graduate students were extremely helpful to my finding coherence in this project, particularly the participants in that 1989 seminar, which included Guillermo García-Corales, Laura López Fernández, Sandra Garabano, Yolanda Forero-Villegas, María Dolores Blanco-Arnejo, Alicia Rolón, Gina Ponce de León, and Alicia Tabler. I would also like to thank graduate assistants Jana DeJong, Michael Buzan and Jennifer Margit Valko. I appreci-ate the opportunity I had to speak formally and informally with numerous writers about the state of Latin American culture and literature, including their own; writers Carlos Fuentes, Gabriel García Márquez, Ricardo Piglia, Diamela Eltit, R. H. Moreno-Durán, José Balza, José Emilio Pacheco, Severo Sarduy, Luis Rafael Sánchez, and Federico Patán have been both generous and helpful, and have affected this book in a variety of ways, directly and indirectly. John Brushwood, Howard Goldblatt, George McMurray, and Donald Schmidt have made useful suggestions on the manuscript in its different stages. The ideas set forth in this book, however, are mine, as are its inevitable errors in fact and critical reading.

1

Introduction to the Spanish American Modernist and Postmodern Novel

There is growing acceptance of the idea of a modernist and postmodern novel in Latin America, but the characteristics, definitions and chronologies are in the process of discussion and debate.[1] The literature of Latin America was mostly ignored by scholars and general readers alike until the 1960s, when the now much-acclaimed Boom of the Latin American novel arrived. Until then, this entire body of literature was typically relegated to a small and usually secondary sector of the Spanish departments in First World academia, and only occasionally mentioned (usually in the context of "magic realism") among general readers. The rise of the modern novel in the 1950s and 1960s, in addition to several other factors, has radically changed the situation.[2] The entrance of postmodern fiction from Latin America into the consciousness of scholars and readers, however, has been a far more complex issue. In one of the early chapters of Gabriel García Márquez's *One Hundred Years of Solitude*, José Arcadio Buendía places a sign at the entrance to Macondo that reads "God exists"-in response to its inhabitants' loss of memory. In the early 1950s, before García Márquez had published any novels, Diego Rivera painted a mural that stated just as boldly *Dios no existe* (God does not exist). These two affirmations bring to bear a central issue of this study—truth claims.[3] Can we establish truths in writing? Under what conditions can we speak of truth in contemporary Latin American premodern, modern, and postmodern society? I will refer briefly to the historical discussion of truth claims as articulated by Hans-Georg Gadamer and Paul Ricoeur, and then address this question within the context of Latin American modern and postmodern fiction. In the process, I will attempt to clarify my understanding of the concept as it may be used in reading contemporary fiction in Latin America. The characteristics and chronologies of this fiction will be of some concern.

The problem of "truth claims" has its historical origins in the philosophical discourse of hermeneutics, phenomenology, and phenomenological hermeneutics. Gadamer has recently articulated this hermeneutical tradition, which he, in turn, inherited from Friedrich Schleiermacher, Wilhelm Dilthey, and Martin Heidegger. Since Schleiermacher, the problem of interpretation has been historicized. Dilthey also conceived of hermeneutics within a historical context: he saw himself as a historical being and maintained that there is no such thing as a universal subject, only historical individuals.[4] Citing Hegel, Gadamer points out in *Truth and Method* that the truth that lies in every artistic experience is recognized and at the same time mediated with historical consciousness.[5] Reading this philosophical tradition, Gadamer views the development of hermeneutics in the modern period as the culmination of the rise of historical consciousness.[6] Gadamer concludes that "Understanding is, essentially, a historically effected event."[7] *Truth and Method* has been appropriately described as one of the most serious attempts in contemporary theory to recover history for textual interpretation.[8]

For Gadamer, the hermeneutical problem is not a matter of method, but of knowledge and of truth. In the foreword to the second edition of *Truth and Method*, Gadamer explains that the purpose of his research is not to offer a general theory of interpretation and an account of its methods, but to discover what is common to all modes of understanding and to show that understanding is never a subjective relation to a given "object" but to the history of its effect. In other words, according to Gadamer, understanding belongs to the being of that which is understood. Gadamer's position on hermeneutics depends to a large degree on the concepts of horizon and prejudice. He describes horizon as the range of vision that includes everything that can be seen from a particular vantage point. Returning to Dilthey, we find that he argues that the prejudices of the individual, far more than its judgments, constitute the historical reality of his being.[9] Citing Heidegger, Gadamer states that "the important thing is to be aware of one's own ideas, so that the text can present itself in all its truth against one's own fore-meanings."[10]

Tradition is another important concept for Gadamer's understanding of interpretation and truth, and tradition grows out of the senses of historicity and the concept of horizon. Interpretation includes our sense of historical past and our own present situation. As such, Gadamer approaches the text as a speaker in a tradition. In addition, our ever-renewed fusion of ever-changing horizons is crucial to the understanding of ourselves—as interpreters—as part of a tradition.

For Gadamer, the text may present itself in all its newness and thus be able to assert its own truth.[11] He argues that the phenomenological return to aesthetic experience (*Erfahrung*) teaches us that this aesthetic experience is real truth.[12] Gadamer's conclusion demonstrates his profound faith in the truth to be found in the operations of hermeneutics, a discipline that, for him, guarantees truth through its processes of questioning and inquiry.

Ricoeur concurs with Gadamer on many positions concerning language and has developed numerous positions with respect to truth: in *History and Truth* he has argued for the pluridimensional nature of truth. Ricoeur has noted our historical temptation to unify the truth by violence and has proposed a differentiation of the orders of truth in our cultural history. Like Gadamer, he returns to a sense of tradition in his discussion of truth:

> At a first glance, nothing is simpler than
> the notion of truth. Tradition defines it
> as an agreement, an agreement at the level of
> our power of judgment (of affirmation and
> negation), an agreement of speech with
> reality, and, secondarily, an agreement among
> ourselves, an agreement of minds. Let us
> note the features of this definition of
> truth: it is a manner of disposing ourselves
> "in conformity with, in the same way as."[13]

Gadamer and Ricoeur have exercised an enormous influence, of course, on literary studies and theory in recent decades. Gadamer's positions relate to connections in literary studies between society and literature, and Ricoeur's writing—emphasizing the plurivocity of texts and the multiplicity of readings—corresponds to some aspects of poststructuralist theory. Jameson favors Gadamer's historicism and agrees with what Gadamer calls "prejudices," which Jameson calls "class habits" and ideological thought modes inherent in our own concrete social and historical situation.[14] Jameson also points to Ricoeur's "negative hermeneutics," which are a demystification and are at one with the most fundamental modern critiques of ideology and illusory consciousness associated with Nietzsche, Marx, and Freud. According to Terry Eagleton, hermeneutics sees history as a living dialogue between past, present, and future, and seeks patiently to remove obstacles to this endless mutual communication.

Nevertheless, Habermas and some other critical theorists have raised serious questions about hermeneutics, claiming, for example, that Gadamer overlooks social processes involved with language. Habermas also questions Gadamer's "rational character of understanding," but perhaps his strongest critique concerns the claim to "universality" by Gadamer and others in hermeneutics. Habermas criticizes validity claims for being "universalistic." Both rationality and universalism, of course, have been historical foundations for truth claims, as reason and universality have justified the dominant truths. Habermas associates truth claims with domination and force; Gadamer wants to see authority of the great work and of the teacher who explains it as a claim on us that is rooted in knowledge and in free recognition, never in force.

In retrospect, the concerns that Gadamer and Ricoeur have developed over the issue of truth claims, within their respective philosophic work, have resulted in what might be called a "discourse of truth." This philosophical-theoretical discourse of truth has had universalistic intentions and has not questioned the very nature of this discourse or the very possibility of making truth claims. To the contrary, Gadamer holds the hope that the spirit of dialogue and open communication—both important for this hermeneutics—can prevail in society. He argues for the inexhaustibility of truth that is handed down by tradition—by way of the works of predecessors. Gadamer agrees with post-structuralists such as Jacques Derrida and Roland Barthes that the text has no fixed meaning or truth, but, in the end, Gadamer distinguishes himself from the post-structuralists by returning to the idea of some meaning that the interpreter finds through the linguistic community and tradition. By means of these concepts, Gadamer has remained faithful to the tradition of the discourse of truth.

If truth claims have their roots in this philosophical-theoretical discourse of hermeneutics, issues of truth also have a venerable tradition in discussions of strictly literary texts. The Anglo-American New Critical tradition provided for the acceptance of the "poetic truths" that poets establish with the carefully delineated boundaries of the autonomous text. Under these rules, the poetic voice establishes a "truth" that has a meaning as "truth" because of the inherent unity and coherence of the text, a truth discovered by the reader. From these "poetic truths" internal to the text, "universal" truths were often extrapolated, or at least inferred.

Ricoeur's hermeneutics coincide in some ways with this idea of the "poetic truths," for Ricoeur is willing to accept the idea that truths can be created within the framework of an individual text. He affirms: "Even the imagination has its truth with which the novelist is very familiar as well as is the reader: a character is true when its internal coherence, its complete presence in the imagination, dominates its creator and convinces the reader".[15] Similarly, Ricoeur privileges the power of the individual novelist to evoke truths in texts:

On the contrary, he will create something
new, something which is socially and
politically valid, only if he is faithful
to the power of analysis which flows from
the authenticity of his sensitivity as well
as from the maturity of the means of expression
which he has inherited.[16]

For Ricoeur, writers establish orders of truth that are mutually contested and then reinstated in an endless "circle."

Many contemporary writers, including prominent Latin American novelists, have taken positions on the truth claims implied by these "poetic truths." Mario Vargas Llosa, however, calls these illusions lies, rather than the truths of fiction.[17] Vargas Llosa would agree with Ricoeur's proposition that truths somehow flow out of an unconscious level of the artist's creation. Ricoeur states: "True art, in conformity with its proper motivation, is engaged when it has not deliberately willed it, when it has agreed not to know the principle of its integration within the total setting of a civilization."[18] Gabriel García Márquez makes numerous statements about being a "realist" who attempts to describe the reality of Colombia as truthfully as possible, despite the insistence of many foreign readers on classifying him as a fantasy writer or an imaginative fabricator of the chimeras associated with the now defunct magic realist enterprise. For Carlos Fuentes, the historians of Latin America have so distorted or ignored truth that it is the responsibility of the Latin American novelist to tell the "other history," to find truth in the imagined past. In the 1960s, both Julio Cortázar and Carlos Fuentes questioned the Western philosophical search for universally valid truths, pointing out that this search has always been a Western, logocentric exercise.

The modern and postmodern novel in Latin America have given a different status to truth. Modernists such as Gabriel García Márquez and the young Chilean postmodern writer Diamela Eltit represent, in certain ways, these different approaches to truth. In the first chapter of García Márquez's *One Hundred Years of Solitude*, José Arcadio Buendía, after an apparently thorough search, announces proudly to his wife, Ursula: "The world is round, like an orange." In the next line, the narrator registers Ursula's reaction: "Ursula lost her patience."[19] This interchange is the first of many juxtapositions of writing versus oral culture, for Ursula consistently reacts, throughout the novel, as a person who belongs to a primary oral culture. As such, her truths are fundamentally contextual, and she responds to the most immediate circumstances.[20] The very idea of truth claims represents as much nonsense to her as the idea of her obviously flat town described as a piece of round fruit. Consequently, she consistently ridicules truth claims throughout the novel, as would any member of an oral culture.[21]

José Arcadio Buendía, unlike Ursula, both understands and believes in truth claims, as is evidenced in the sign that he places at the entrance of Macondo, "God exists." His claim is a repetition of traditional Catholic doctrine that has predominated in Latin America for five centuries. Nevertheless, the reader laughs at José Arcadio Buendía's truth claim because of the contextual error that José Arcadio Buendía commits, substituting the everyday instructions of traffic signs with a grandiose truth claim of biblical rather than bureaucratic language. By ridiculing the ultimate truth claim—the claim of the existence of God—this novel associates truth claims with the superannuated language of medieval disputes and, finally, with absurd propositions.

A third truth claim is written as an anecdote of a banana workers' strike. The subject of this part of the novel is truth. The event that occurs in it seems impossible: the workers of Macondo declare a strike and a rumor spreads that the government has massacred hundreds of workers, if not more. The passage is incredible, seemingly one of the most fantastic of the novel: a historic massacre is reduced to rumor and story. Nevertheless, historians and literary scholars have documented the fact that this chapter is one of the most historical, indeed, the most truthful, of the entire novel, for it refers to the massacre of striking banana workers in Ciénaga, Colombia, in 1928.[22] In this sense, *One Hundred Years of Solitude* is a novel that relates truths that, unlike those "poetic truths" consistent only with textual strategies, correspond to real historical issues.

For Gabriel García Márquez and Latin American writing, *One Hundred Years of Solitude* represented a culmination, in 1967, of a modernist project that still privileged issues of truth. A follower of William Faulkner and Franz Kafka since the beginning of his writing career, García Márquez began writing in the late 1940s and published his first novel, *Leafstorm*, in 1955. He continued his Colombian elaboration of Yoknopatawpha County, which he called the town of Macondo, with the publication of two novels and a volume of short stories; he then synthesized his entire project in *One Hundred Years of Solitude*. This literary production coincided with the growing complicity in First World academia between the formation and reproduction of the discipline of English (the dominant form of literary studies) and the very notion of modernism itself.[23] García Márquez's modernist project was relatively late in arriving on the First World modernist scene. It was written almost exactly, in fact, at the time when John Barth began his postmodernist reflections on the literature of exhaustion and when Leslie Fiedler, for better or for worse, popularized the term *postmodern*.

In this sense *One Hundred Years of Solitude* was one of the last significant confrontations with truth in Latin American modernist fiction. At the same time that the possibilities for universal truth claims are questioned in this book, there was a general sense among the contemporary Latin American novelists that they were among the most resonant voices of the few in such closed societies who could speak for historical truth. They shared with Habermas and the critical theorists in general (and with Gadamer, as well) their project of social emancipation, their defense of reason as an ideal, and the Enlightenment faith in social progress as possibly analogous to the progress of knowledge achieved in the sciences.

Modernist aesthetic theory, as practiced by many First World writers, functioned on the basis of a separation of the sphere of art from other cultural and political practices. This separation had little acceptance in Latin America, where two generations of modernists, from Miguel Angel Asturias and Alejo Carpentier to García Márquez and Fuentes, enthusiastically appropriated the narrative strategies of Western modernism. But they insisted on bringing to bear their own political agenda and their interest in historical truth, the same search for truth found in García Márquez's revelation about the 1928 strike and Asturias's denunciation of Latin America's historical dictatorships.

"Modernity is the transcient, the fleeting, the contingent; it is one half of art, the other being the eternal and the immutable," Charles Baudelaire stated in 1863 in his essay "The Painter in Modern Life." This is the modernity of García Márquez and his generation in Latin America, for their key works, *One Hundred Years of Solitude,* Fuentes's *The Death of Artemio Cruz,* and others, express the contingent at the same time that they reveal their desire for the eternal and the immutable.

The commonly accepted tenets of literary modernism, were developed by writers such as Marcel Proust, James Joyce, and T. S. Eliot, and further exploited by Kafka and Faulkner. These tenets involve formal innovation (fragmentation, the use of multiple points of view, the use of neologisms, and the like), a breakdown in the nineteenth-century insistence on causality, and an incessant search for order within an apparently chaotic world. The British scholar Raymond Williams criticizes the ideology of modernism because it gives preference to some writers "for their denaturalizing of language, their break with the allegedly prior view that language is either a clear, transparent glass or a mirror, and for making abruptly apparent in the very texture of their narratives the problematic status of the author and his authority."[24] Williams concludes that modernism is uncritical and has lost the "anti-bourgeois stance" of some previous literary expression. This is not necessarily the case with the Latin American modern novel.

Seen in retrospect, modernism as practiced in the North Atlantic nations has suffered harsh critique in general, even from its former supporters. Walter Benjamin, an admirer of some modern writers, nevertheless lamented after World War I the devaluation of "experience" in the modern novel.[25] Frank Kermode criticizes its "elitist" need for order and its revolutionary formal innovations.[26] David Daiches, one of the early champions of modernism, later questioned its anarchistic urge to destroy existing systems and its reactionary political vision of an ideal order.[27] Jean-François Lyotard is very critical of its melancholy regret for the loss of presence and its experimental energy and power of conception.[28] Some, but not all of these critiques, might be posed before the Latin American novel, particularly in the area of the politics of modernism in nations with a strong tradition of writing as social protest, as well as faith in certain utopian ideals and truths.

Jameson agrees with Benjamin's questioning of modernism and sees high modernism as a dead phenomenon: "This is the sense in which high modernism can be definitely certified as dead and a thing of the past: its Utopian ambitions unrealizable and its formal innovations exhausted."[29] Jameson views the modernist search for truth as exhausted and failed.

The Anglo-American modernist project also became associated with a subjectivist relativism, as critic Steven Conner points out.[30] Consequently, modernism had increasingly less to do with the world of "ideas or substances which may be objectively known in themselves" than with the fictionalization and understanding of the world that can be known and experienced through individual consciousness.[31] A first generation of modernists in Latin America, consisting of relatively ignored avant-garde novelists of the 1920s and 1930s— Jaime Torres Bodet, Vicente Huidobro, Martín Adán, and others—enthusiastically subscribed to this credo. Torres Bodet's *Primero de enero* ("First of January," 1934), for example, was just one prominent celebration of this subjectivist relativism. In these pioneer Latin American novels, truth became a subjectivized part of each individual's psychological experience. In *El Señor Presidente* (1946), Miguel Angel Asturias filters the image of a dictator through the individual consciousness of several characters, using a series of strategems well developed in First World modernism. Similarly, García Márquez uses Faulknerian strategies in *Leafstorm*, which is related by three narrators; he also privileges individual consciousness. His later work shares the modernist predisposition toward subjective relativity, where truth is mediated by individual consciousness, and universal truth comes into play inasmuch as one can argue for the supposed universality of the individual experience fictionalized in the modern novel.

The modernist novelistic tradition in Latin America spans from the 1920s to the present, but its most notable production was really from the 1940s (with the advent of Jorge Luis Borges, Miguel Angel Asturias, Agustín Yáñez, and Alejo Carpentier) to the 1960s, culminating in such complex exercises in elaborating individual consciousness as Juan Rulfo's *Pedro Páramo* ("Pedro Páramo," 1955), Salvador Garmendia's *Los pequeños seres* ("The Little Beings,"1962), Carlos Fuentes's *The Death of Artemio Cruz* (1962), Mario Vargas Llosa's *The Time of the Hero* (1963), Cortázar's *Hopscotch* (1963) and Juan Carlos Onetti's *Juntacadáveres* ("Gathering of cadavers," 1964). In First World modernism, this subjectivism was accommodated with a whole series of announcements of the end of individual subjectivity, such as Eliot's famous defense of impersonality in "Tradition and the Individual Talent" and Joyce's promotion of an aesthetic authorial detachment, in which the author of a literary work removes himself or herself from the work.[32] Fuentes makes a similar announcement in his *Death of Artemio Cruz*, balancing Cruz's subjective (first-person and second-person) passages with the detachment of third-person sections. During this Boom of the modernist project in Latin America, truth, whether a function of individual subjectivity or authorial detachment, was at its apotheosis. The culture industry of modernism was also an industry that developed and protected the truths of liberal humanists, including the Latin America of the Boom years of the 1960s.[33] Many of these writers, agreeing with Habermas and the critical theorists—above all Fuentes and Cortázar—were acutely aware of the social processes involved with language.

But modernism is an ideological expression of capitalism, Fredric Jameson argues boldly in *The Political Unconscious*.[34] An analogy for Jameson's polemical statement is that modernism is the truth of capitalism. These were the truths of liberal humanism. Indeed, those pioneer Latin American modernists of the 1920s (for example, Jaime Torres Bodet, Martín Adán, etcetera) were accused of being "false" to Latin American social and political reality: the *Contemporáneos* and *Florida* groups in Mexico and Argentina, respectively, were under attack for their interest in individual psychology at the expense of the truths embodied in nationalistic and social concerns. Later, in the 1940s, the truths of human suffering fictionalized in *The Edge of the Storm* (1947) by Agustín Yáñez were still strategies of containment that ignored the massive capitalization of the Mexican economy and social injustice in the Mexico of the late 1940s, which operated under the institutionalized banner of nationalism and the Revolution.

The culminating moment of Latin American modernism called the Boom, however, can hardly be viewed simply as a product of capitalism (as Jameson maintains in the case of First World modernism) that engages in the strategies of containment to deny the truth of history. In *The Death of Artemio Cruz* (dedicated to the Marxist economist C. Wright Mills), Fuentes does not engage in the strategies of containment that Jameson finds in certain modernists or that I have noted in the pioneer novelists of the 1920s in Latin America.[35] To the contrary, Fuentes's early fiction is a strong critique of Mexico's institutionalization of modern capitalism. Seen from various perspectives, then, the Latin American novelists of the modernist project, although adopting many of the narrative strategies pioneered by First World modernists, still believed in the possibilities of articulating truths through the 1960s. In this sense, they coincide with the totalization project proposed by Gadamer and Ricoeur. Given their understanding of literary language and the social processes involved with language, they did not engage in the strategies of containment that, according to Jameson, characterized much First World modernist narrative.

With respect to postmodernism, common concepts used in the context of the North Atlantic nations have been discontinuity, disruption, dislocation, decentering, indeterminacy, and antitotalization. As Hutcheon points out, the cultural phenomenon of postmodernism is contradictory, for it installs and then subverts the very concepts it challenges.[36] Postmodernism works to subvert dominant discourses. In *The Dismemberment of Orpheus*, Hassan was instrumental in developing a critical language and concepts for postmodernism, creating parallel columns that place characteristics of modernism and postmodernism side by side. As Hutcheon points out, however, this "either/or" thinking suggests a resolution of what should be seen as unresolvable contradictions within postmodernism.[37] These unresolved contradictions are just as common to postmodern Latin American fiction as they are to postmodern North Atlantic architecture.

Differing concepts of First World or North Atlantic postmodernity are articulated most prominently by Jean-François Lyotard, Jean Baudrillard, and Jameson. These three theorists are interested, primarily, in the analysis of culture and society in the postindustrial North Atlantic nations, and all three frequently equate "post-industrial" with "postmodern." Lyotard's oft-cited *The Postmodern Condition: A Report on Knowledge* (1979) is an essay on the state of knowledge in postindustrial society. In his foreword to the English edition of Lyotard's influential piece, Jameson makes reference to the crisis of representation which, in turn, points to a crisis in the categories of adequacy, accuracy, and "truth" itself.[38] Lyotard maintains that we are now living at the end of the "grand narrative" or master narrative, such as the master narratives of science, the nation state, the proletariat, the party, and the like, which have lost their viability. In postmodern culture, according to Lyotard, "The grand narrative has lost its credibility, regardless of what mode of unification it uses, regardless of whether it is a speculative narrative or a narrative of emancipation."[39]

The deligitimation of the old master narratives in post-industrial society has also delegitimated the old discourse of truth:

> Knowledge, then, is a question of competence that
> goes beyond the simple determination and application
> of truth, extending to the determination and
> application of criteria of efficiency (technical
> qualification), of justice and/or happiness
> (ethical wisdom), of the beauty of a sound or
> color (auditory and visual sensibility), etc.[40]

As Hutcheon points out, Lyotard and other theorists, including Habermas, question the bases of our Western modes of thinking, which we usually label liberal humanism.[41] (At the same time, it should be noted that many of the premises of this Western humanism were placed into question by Cortázar and Fuentes in the 1960s.) The works of Lyotard, Baudrillard, Jameson, and other theorists of the postmodern have been translated into Spanish and have become central to the debates over modernism and postmodernism in Latin America.[42]

Postmodern society as viewed by Baudrillard shares many of the proposals of Lyotard, including his statement on truth. In *Simulations*, Baudrillard proposes that the real is no longer real, but the order of the hyper-real and of simulation. Questioning the existence of any difference between the true and the false, Baudrillard rejects the discourses of truth of the hermeneutic tradition by making statements such as "We are in a logic of simulation which has nothing to do with a logic of facts and an order of reasons."[43] According to Baudrillard "this anticipation . . . is what each time allows for all the possible interpretations, even the most contradictory—all are true, in the sense that their truth is exchangeable, in the image of the models from which they proceed, in a generalised cycle."[44] Baudrillard's postmodern is a world in which everything is seemingly exchangeable and nothing holds intrinsic value. In contemporary Latin American fiction, Baudrillard is not the subject of parody, but of pastiche, in the hands of writers such as Diamela Eltit.

Jameson describes postindustrial society in terms of a loss of history, the dissolution of the centered self, and the fading of individual style. He characterizes postmodernity as a result of the capitalist dissolution of bourgeois hegemony and the development of mass culture. In general, Jameson is skeptical of the postmodern enterprise and is often critical of postmodern fiction. For example, one of the characteristics he attributes to postmodernism is pastiche, or the random cannibalization of all the styles of the past, the play of random stylistic allusion. For Jameson, pastiche is a negative, while Hutcheon and others view such phenomena as examples of the inherent contradictions that are essential to postmodernism. In Latin America, this pastiche need not necessarily be seen in a negative light.

For a reading of Latin American postmodern fiction, the politics of postmodernism are an extremely important issue. Hutcheon argues against the critical postures Jameson takes toward a postmodernism that he sees as politically suspicious for its lack of historicism. She argues in favor of a postmodern novel that is indeed historical and gives numerous examples of postmodern novels with strong historical components. Her answer to Jameson is that "The past as referent is not bracketed or effaced, but given new and different life and meaning."[45] For Hutcheon, then, the postmodern novel does not strive for the truth, as Jameson might wish, but deals with truths and questions the conditions under which truths are established.

As poststructuralist thinkers who have had enormous impact on postmodern literary culture in general, Michel Foucault and Jacques Derrida have also been quite influential in Latin America.[46] Foucault attempted to establish the location of power in literary texts and rethought the subject as a discursive construct. Derrida questioned the concept of center as well as the possibilities of history capturing a way to truth. Obviously playing off Foucault and Derrida on the matter of the subject, the Tel Quel group in Paris organized an attack on the founding subject or concept of author. The Cuban Severo Sarduy, a member of the Tel Quel group, questions the idea of subject and then proceeds to parody Derrida in his novel *Cobra* (1972). Sarduy is frequently cited by the Latin American postmodern writers, including Diamela Eltit and R. H. Moreno-Durán.

Writing about contemporary fiction in general, Hutcheon is interested in the contradictions of postmodernism. Citing Larry McCaffery, she begins her definition of postmodernism by referring to literature that is metafictionally self-reflective and yet speaks to us powerfully about real political and historical realities.[47] For Hutcheon, the key concepts for postmodernism are paradox, contradiction, and a movement toward anti-totalization, all of which appear throughout her books *A Poetics of Postmodernism* and *The Politics of Postmodernism*. The concepts of the multiple, the provisional, and the different are also important for Hutcheon.[48]

Hutcheon proposes that the term *postmodernism* in fiction be reserved for what she calls "historiographic metafiction."[49] This postmodern fiction, as she describes it, often enacts the problematic nature of writing history to narrativization, raising questions about the cognitive status of historical knowledge. It "refuses the view that only history has a truth claim, both by questioning the ground of that claim in historiography and by discourses, human constructs, signifying systems, and both derive their major claims to truth from that identity."[50] Historiographic metafiction suggests that truth and falsity may not be the right terms. Rather, we should be speaking of truths in the plural.[51]

Umberto Eco claims that the postmodern is born at the moment when we discover that the world has no fixed center, and that, as Foucault taught, power is not something unitary that exists outside of us. This moment occurred in Latin American literature with the rise of Borges, who became a seminal figure for both many European theorists and Latin American postmodern novelists in the 1960s and 1970s, even though the now-classic Borges fiction they were reading dated back to the 1940s. The two books that contained these groundbreaking stories were *The Garden of Forking Paths* (1941) and *Ficciones* (1944). One of the repeated images in Borges's fiction was the labyrinth as a centerless universe, a figure developed ·n stories such as "The Library of Babel," and "Garden of Forking Paths"; the concept of the labyrinth as a centerless universe is elaborated most directly in "The Library of Babel." In "The Circular Ruins," language has priority over empirical reality, as the protagonist, who has the power to dream a person into being, realizes at the end that he, too, is an illusion, that someone else was dreaming him. Consequently, the imagined reality of dreams, which are figments of the imagination, and language, which is the written product of the imagination, are both more powerful than empirical reality.

Borges's stories "The Library of Babel" and "Pierre Ménard, Author of the *Quixote*" are also foundational texts for postmodern fiction in Latin America. In them, the line between essay and fiction is blurred, opening the gates for the fictionalized theoretical prose of Piglia, Sarduy, Balza, Pacheco, and several others.

Some critics view Borges's writing as too autonomous and independent from sociopolitical reality and conservative as a literary project. Borges's fiction often functions on the basis of an abstract rather than Argentine or Latin American referent. Nevertheless, Borges's literary discourse functions in a way similar to what Hutcheon notes in Berger: the narrator's discourse is paradoxically postmodern, for it both inscribes a context and then contests its boundaries.

Some critics of postmodernism, such as Alex Callinicos, are confused or made impatient by its inherent contradictions, and view the contributions of poststructuralist theorists—in particular, Gilles Deleuze, Jacques Derrida, and Michel Foucault—as the source of an incoherent thrust to postmodernism. In reference to these three theorists, Callinicos states: "Despite their many disagreements, all three have stressed the fragmentary, heterogeneous, and plural character of reality, denied human thought the ability to arrive at any objective account of reality, and reduced the bearer of this thought, the subject, to an incoherent welter of sub-and trans-individual drives and desires."[52] Much postmodern writing, of course, gives human thought a considerably more privileged status than Callinicos would have us believe. Many Latin American writers discussed in this book, who have been enormously influenced by Deleuze, Derrida, and Foucault, suffer from none (or very little) of the "incoherence" that Callinicos attributes to postmodern culture in general.

A concept of what exactly constitutes the postmodern in Latin America is just as polemical among critics of Latin American culture. Despite the doubts of Joaquín Brunner, Adolfo Sánchez Vásquez, and others, Latin American society and culture have experienced the same crisis of truth that Lyotard, Baudrillard, and Jameson describe as existing in the North Atlantic nations. With the breakdown of the grand narratives of the nation-state, Latin America's traditional ruling classes now respond to the same multinational companies, corporate leaders, high-level administrators, and the like that Lyotard describes as the new rulers of the North Atlantic nations.[53]

The discourse and concepts of First World postmodernism are now circulating in Latin America—lo indeterminado (the indeterminate), la problematización del centro (the problematization of the center), la marginalidad (marginality) la descontinuidad (discontinuity), la simulación (simulation) and the like. One of Diamela Eltit's common terms, precariedad (precarious) is similar to "the provisional," which is emphasized by many of the North Atlantic postmoderns. Perhaps the word North and South share the most, however—with no translation necessary—is Borges. The same Borges who was cited by the European poststructuralist theorists Barthes, Foucault, Baudrillard, and Lyotard, also planted the seeds for a Latin American postmodern fiction with his stories of the 1940s.

After Borges, the most notable contribution to the later publication of a Latin American postmodern fiction was Julio Cortázar's Hopscotch (1963). Cortázar's novel in itself was not really a postmodern work, but its Morelli chapters at the end were a radical proposal for postmodern fiction (see chapter 4). In the late 1960s and early 1970s, the postmodern novel began to appear in Latin America, almost always inspired by either Borges or Cortázar, and it was constituted by such experimental fictions as Guillermo Cabrera Infante's Three Trapped Tigers (1967), Néstor Sánchez's Siberia Blues (1967), and Manuel Puig's Betrayed by Rita Hayworth (1968). As mentioned, another key novel for the formation of a Latin American postmodern was

Severo Sarduy's *Cobra* (1972). Interestingly enough, Charles Jencks proposes that 1972 was a turning point for modern and postmodern culture, for Jencks dates the end of modernism and the passage to the postmodern as July 15, 1972, when the Pruitt-Igoe housing development in St. Louis was dynamited. Soon several other radically experimental novelists appeared on the Latin American scene—most since Sarduy—including the Argentines Ricardo Piglia, Reina Roffé, and Héctor Libertella; the Mexicans Salvador Elizondo, Carmen Boullosa, and José Emilio Pacheco; the Colombians R. H. Moreno-Durán and Albalucía Angel; the Venezuelan José Balza; and Diamela Eltit of Chile. Eltit followed the linguistic innovations offered by Sarduy, except for parody, which she openly rejects. These writers offer radically different kinds of postmodernisms—perhaps a postmodern phenomenon in itself: if Culture (with a capital C and in the singular) becomes cultures in postmodernity, as Hutcheon has suggested, then the provisionality and heterogeneity of postmodern cultures in Latin America are even more extreme than in the North Atlantic nations. For the most part, these Latin American postmodern writers, like their First World counterparts, are interested in heterogeneous discourses of theory and literature. Sarduy's essays read like fiction and vice versa; Eltit's fiction appropriates the theoretical discourse of Derrida, Baudrillard, Deleuze, and others. Balza prefers not to distinguish between the essays and the fiction of his "exercises."

Some theorists, particularly those arguing from a neo-Marxist position, such as Christopher Norris and Alex Callinicos, find this fusion of theoretical and literary discourse potentially threatening. Norris and Callinicos, in fact, argue that to collapse the distance between theory and narrative is to "argue away the very grounds of rational critique.[54] In reality, much Latin American postmodern discourse uses rational methods to carry out its critique. Other highly critical writing questions the very foundations of Western "rational" methods. After all, both Adolph Hitler and Augusto Pinochet (characters in more than one postmodern Latin American novel) were most rational, as José Emilio Pacheco and Diamela Eltit have reminded us.

This Latin American postmodern shares many of the trends of First World postmodernism noted by Ihab Hassan, Brian McHale, Linda Hutcheon, and Steven Conner. A broad range of cultural critics share the consensus that the postmodern as a cultural phenomenon arose in the 1960s, an interesting parallel with Gadamer's *Truth and Method*, which was published in 1960 and which places emphasis on the truth, above all, of language. Gadamer states unequivocally that "All understanding is interpretation, and all interpretation takes place in the medium of a language that allows the object to come into words and yet is at the same time the interpreter's own language."[55] This privileging of language in itself became doctrine for postmodern writers. For Hutcheon, the 1960s "did provide the background, though not the definition, of the postmodern . . ."[56] In one sense, Gadamer's position is comparable to Cortázar's, for both are fundamentally totalizing moderns who help set the stage for the postmodern in the late 1960s.

Many Latin American women share with their First World counterparts what Hutcheon calls the postmodern valuing of the margins. The women postmodern novelists in Latin America frequently write with a self-conscious awareness of feminist and poststructuralist theory. This is the case with Albalucía Angel, whose recent novels incorporate the language of feminist theory, as do the writings of the Brazilian Helena Parente Cunha, Sylvia Molloy, Diamela Eltit, and others.

Numerous North Atlantic critics have observed the postmodern's bridging of the gap between elite and popular art. Since the 1960s, the Latin American writers who have been the object of intense academic study have, at the same time, frequently been best sellers, particularly García Márquez, Vargas Llosa, Isabel Allende, Luis Rafael Sánchez, and Manuel Puig. Three of the works that have sold particularly well to both the general public and to academe (and seemingly bridged the gap between elite and popular art) are Vargas Llosa's *Aunt Julia and the Script Writer*, Allende's *House of the Spirits*, and García Márquez's *Chronicle of a Death Foretold*—three novels that could arguably be called, for different reasons, postmodern. For Hutcheon, postmodernism's relationship with contemporary mass culture is not just one of implication, but also one of critique.[57] This critical position toward mass culture is particularly evident in Vargas Llosa's *Aunt Julia and the Script Writer* and Luis Rafael Sánchez's *Macho Camacho's Beat*. Jameson tends to categorize postmodern fiction in terms of mass culture, limiting the postmodern to what might be considered its "lighter" versions.[58]

In a recent study of postmodernism and popular culture, Angela McRobbie suggests that recent debates on postmodernism possess both a positive attraction and a usefulness to the analyst of popular culture.[59] Citing the work of Andreas Huyssen, McRobbie notes the "high" structuralist preference for the works of high modernism, especially the writing of James Joyce or Stephan Mallarmé. Postmodernism, in contrast, has been more interested in popular culture than the canonical works of literary modernism. McRobbie also draws parallels between Susan Sontag's perspective on a camp sensibility and what Jameson calls pastiche.

One major difference between North Atlantic postmodernism, as it is articulated in the First World, and Latin American postmodernism, centers on the issue of critique. Some critics, such as Jameson, consider North

Atlantic postmodernism politically neutral or uncritical. Latin American postmodernism is resolutely historical and inescapably political, as Hutcheon argues for the North American case.[60] This argument is perhaps stronger in the Latin American case because the historical and political have been consistently present in the entire tradition of the Latin American novel.

To cite the example of Diamela Eltit, her postmodern novelistic project was born in the 1980s, after she began participating in cultural and political practices of an underground resistance in Pinochet's Chile during the 1970s and early 1980s. Her first two novels can most obviously be associated with the postmodernism of First World writers and Latin Americans such as Sarduy and Piglia. The first of these, *Lumpérica* ("Lumperica," 1983), takes place in a public plaza in Santiago de Chile, has no real plot, and has as protagonist a character named L. Iluminada. This public plaza is a postmodern world of Baudrillard, where human beings have the same exchange value as merchandise (see chapter 4). Eltit's second novel, *Por la patria* ("For the country," 1986), is even more markedly experimental. She alludes to the political repression of the Pinochet regime, always returning to the historical origins of language, repression, and resistance. In this way, returning to Medieval epic wars, she inevitably associates these historical conflicts with the contemporary situation. Consequently, Eltit's postmodern is patently historical and political, and could be identified as an allegorical fiction of resistance (see chapter 4). Her third novel, *El cuarto mundo* ("The fourth world," 1988), deals with family relationships and is related by two narrators: the first half of the work is narrated by a young boy, María Chipia, the son of the family, and the second half is told by his twin sister. *El cuarto mundo* is not a work of the broad historical truths elaborated in *One Hundred Years of Solitude* or *The Death of Artemio Cruz*. The generation of García Márquez and Fuentes remained not only overtly historical, but engaged in a project of the truths of social emancipation. *El cuarto mundo*, however, is about other kinds of truths—the truths of private and public space, the truths of relationships, the truths of the body, and a questioning of the possibilities language holds for articulating truths.

El cuarto mundo and other selected Latin American postmodern novels question the truth industry of modernism. In the Latin American case, the novel has moved from utopia to what Foucault calls heterotopia—from the centered and historical universe of the utopian Alejo Carpentier and Gabriel García Márquez to a centerless universe of the postmoderns Severo Sarduy and Diamela Eltit. What is at stake for the Latin American postmoderns who have arisen since the late 1960s—Pacheco, Sarduy, Moreno-Durán, Eltit, and others—is not truth. Lyotard claims that the question is no longer "Is it true?" but "What use is it?" and "How much is it worth?"; the latter are questions are posed in *El cuarto mundo* and in much of what might be called postmodern cultural practice in Latin America. Juxtaposing of García Márquez's modern project of *One Hundred Years of Solitude* (and his other fiction published from 1955 to 1967) and Eltit's postmodern writing reveals the transitional state of truth in Latin American fiction and the particular conditions—difficult ones, to say the least—under which truth claims can be considered. *One Hundred Years of Solitude* plays on images of center, with the ultimate centers being the Buendía family and Macondo. In contrast, Eltit's figures represent marginality—the lumpen and women, just as the art of her generation in Chile, *la avanzada* ("avant-garde"), uses imagery of the marginalized.[61]

In his vigorous questioning of the cultural critics and theorists of postmodernism, Callinicos laments the "contradictory character" of postmodern art. He states:

> Postmodernism corresponds to a new historical
> stage of social development (Lyotard) or it
> doesn't (Lyotard again). Postmodern art is a
> continuation of (Lyotard) or a break from (Jencks)
> Modernism. Joyce is a Modernist (Jameson) or a
> Postmodernist (Lyotard). Postmodernism turns its
> back on social revolution, but then practitioners
> and advocates of a revolutionary art like Breton
> and Benjamin are claimed as precursors.[62]

These apparent contradictions, which seem to confuse and irritate Callinicos, can be explained. First, the inherently contradictory character of postmodern culture needs to be accepted and, as Hutcheon argues so convincingly, should be seen as a value in itself. On the other hand, only a minimal literary sophistication and intellectual flexibility will allow one to accept the proposition that postmodern art can be both a continuation of (Lyotard) *and* a slight break from (Jencks) modernism. It is also relatively obvious for readers well acquainted with contemporary fiction that some postmodern fictions represent more of a continuation of modernism, and others are more of a break from it. With respect to Joyce, he has been considered a modernist by most informed literary critics for decades; only recently have a few scholars, those generally less informed on matters strictly literary (such as Lyotard), attempted to make this pioneer and ground-breaking modernist a postmodern writer. With respect to social revolution, again, some postmodern writers are more progressive than others. Seen in a literary context, then, Callinicos's confusion and irritation are somewhat disingenuous and simplistic.

Viewed within the context of Latin American fiction, two seminal precursors were Joyce and Borges. Rather than considering them postmodern writers, they should be recognized as modernists who facilitated or opened the doors to postmodernism with their particular use of language, their attitudes about literary language, and Borges's conflation of essay, literary theory, and fiction.

"Truth is the significance of fact," Mies van der Rohe has stated, and David Harvey has cited van der Rohe to point out that a host of cultural producers, particularly those working in and around the Bauhaus movement of the 1920s, intended to impose a "rational order."[63] This rational order (rational defined by technological efficiency and machine production) was for socially useful goals, such as human emancipation, emancipation of the proletariat, and the like.

Postmodern culture, as seen from the North and the South, does not support cultural practices leading to the establishment of textual truths. One limitation is observed by Edward Said, who sees the history of the twentieth century as a progressive withdrawal from general questions and responsibility and an increasing collusion with a system that divides knowledge into specialisms to disallow in advance any radical or effective engagement with general issues.[64] Similarly, Lyotard maintains that since this century's second European war, grand narratives have been losing their power to provide a legitimating force in society. In the case of the Latin American novel, the "grand narrative" was the modern writing of Fuentes, García Márquez, Cortázar, and Vargas Llosa in the 1960s; the opposite of this grand narrative is the work of Eltit, Pacheco, Sarduy, and the other postmodern writers.

In response to the complex questions of truth claims, the conditions are vanishing in Latin America for any textual assertions to be evaluated in terms of truth claims. Latin American writers such as Eltit and Piglia share with North Atlantic postmoderns a generalized mistrust of the capacity of any language to render truths about the world. The discourse of truth has been reduced to exchange values. Consequently, the very exercise of considering the implications of hermeneutical philosophical discourse of truth claims becomes a suspicious activity in those cultural spaces of Latin America—spaces occupied by Severo Sarduy, Ricardo Piglia, José Emilio Pacheco, Diamela Eltit, and numerous others—where postmodernism organizes new discourses.

These new discourses—these new postmodernities—grow directly from modernist writing in Latin America—the writing of Borges, Asturias, Carpentier, García Márquez, and others. They are also cultural practices that represent a fundamental break from this past as recent as the 1940s, the 1950s, and the early 1960s. Callinicos asks why it is that in the past decade so large a portion of the Western intelligentsia became convinced that both the socioeconomic system and the cultural practice are undergoing a fundamental break from the recent past.[65] In the Latin American literary case, as will be demonstrated in the following chapters, the reason is that literary practices undergo radical changes beginning in the late 1960s.

2

Mexican Postmodernities

The Mexican postmodern scene from the mid-1960s to the early 1990s—from the group of young writers called the Onda to a novel by Carmen Boullosa titled *La milagrosa,* published in 1993—was one of the most active and vital in Latin America. It covers a period from the October 1968 massacre of students by the government at the plaza of Tlatelolcoto the uprising in the State of Chiapas in January of 1994; from the expanding economy of the early 1960s to an economy of inflation and devaluation in the 1980s; from the music of the Beatles and the Rolling Stones (with Mexican variants in Spanish) to Pearl Jam and rap music (with their inevitable Mexican replicas); from the peso valued at 12.5 to the dollar to the *nuevo peso* in 1993 after the old, exhausted peso had reached 3,000 to the dollar. In the early 1960s a record number of the Mexican middle class purchased its first television sets; in the 1990s, they followed the NBA and NFL on cable, and saw the United States's invasions of Panama and Iraq live on CNN. In the summer, they followed the Dodgers; in the winter, the Dallas Cowboys. All year round, they watched *Dallas* and MTV—intercalated with Mexican soap operas and Mexican music videos. Despite the relative gains of the video-watching Mexican middle class during the 1970s and early 1980s, the predominant theme of postmodern Mexico is a sense of exhaustion.

Jean Baudrillard has written that Disneyland is more real than Los Angeles. The Los Angeles of Latin America, postmodern Mexico City, is real—real history, real urban sprawl, and real pollution—and in constant transformation. Los Angeles is the postmodern city with no centers, but Mexico City is the metropolis with multiple centers, from the original *centro histórico* to the next center of the Zona Rosa, to the center of the Colonia Roma, to downtown San Angel, to another center in Coyoacán, and the like. The postmodern architecture of Mexico City, from the spectacle of the Marquis Hotel to the glitzy Plaza Inn shopping mall, sits in tense juxtaposition with the colonial, nineteenth-century, and modern architecture that surrounds it. Consequently, the visual imagery of the "D.F." (as Mexicans refer to their capital, the Distrito Federal), unlike that of Los Angeles, provides a compelling sense of history. If Los Angeles seems to have been invented yesterday, the D.F. is being reinvented daily, as it has been for centuries. Breathing the air of Los Angeles is difficult; Mexico City is the urban center where Argentine Ricardo Piglia could have found the title of his novel *Artificial Respiration*. With no apparent solution to its pollution and related urban problems, the D.F. has developed to the point of economic, political, and social exhaustion.

Much of Mexico's literary culture has been postmodernized, commercialized, and sometimes trivialized in Mexico from the 1960s to today. The Mexican middle class saw the names of Octavio Paz and Carlos Fuentes regularly, and the novelists of the Boom remained in vogue, above all, Gabriel García Márquez and Mario Vargas Llosa. They also read Stephen King, Irving Wallace, Michael Crichton, Tom Robbins, and James Michener in both Spanish and English. Bookstores were replete with their novels in both languages; the same bookstores were also filled with self-help paperbacks in both languages. Mexicans saw an Octavio Paz industry arrive before, during, and after the awarding of the Nobel Prize in literature to Mexico's major poet.[1] This industry produced slick, new editions of Paz's work in a variety of formats, including videotapes of the poet reading. The Paz industry successfully promoted the image of Paz as Universal Poet. He also spoke as the voice of free-market and laissez-faire economic policies in Latin America, what became known as *neo-liberalismo* in Latin America and neo-conservatism in the First World.

But Paz, Fuentes, and the writers of the Boom were not the only producers of literary culture to penetrate mass consciousness in postmodern Mexico. The 1980s and 1990s have witnessed the popularity of women writers, a phenomenon begun in Mexico with the mass marketing of the fiction of the Chilean Isabel Allende throughout Latin America by the Plaza y Janés publishing company, a Hispanic arm of the German multinational Bertlesman. Two Mexicans, Angeles Mastretta and Laura Esquivel, have followed in Allende's footsteps. Mastretta's *Mexican Bolero* (1988) was a best-seller in Mexico for a full two years in the late 1980s, followed by Esquivel's *Like Water for Chocolate* (1990). The latter was the most commercially successful novel in Mexico during the early 1990s, then became a movie distributed in Mexico, and soon thereafter became a commercially successful movie and novel in the United States. *Like Water for Chocolate* appeared on the *New York Times* best-seller list in 1993.

Many Mexican intellectuals found it difficult to take the popular newcomers Mastretta and Esquivel as seriously as they did more established and technically sophisticated women writers, such as Elena Poniatowska, Carmen Boullosa, and María Luisa Puga. Since the publication of testimonial, nonfiction work in the 1960s and 1970s, Poniatowska has been a strong voice for Mexico's marginalized, as well as the author of the novels La "Flor de Lis" ("The 'Flor de Lis'" 1989) and Tinísima ("Tinísima," 1992).[2] Carmen Boullosa published five novels, and received the Premio Villaurrutia (national novel prize) for Antes ("Before," 1989). More recently, she has published the postmodern novel La milagrosa ("The Miraculous One," 1993). One of Mexico's most accomplished writers, María Luisa Puga, has published five novels. Other women novelists writing in postmodern Mexico are Brianda Domecq, Angelina Muñíz-Huberman, Barbara Jacobs, Ethel Krauze, Aline Petterson, Silvia Molina, Margo Glantz, Luisa Josefina Hernández, and María Luisa Mendoza.

A variety of heterogeneous cultural configurations have shaped postmodern Mexico. Gay writers, such as Luis Zapata, José Rafael Calva, and Luis Arturo Ojeda, have established a cultural space previously unknown in Mexico. Lesbian writer Sara Levy occupies a parallel space, and the journal Debate feminista as well as the magazine Fem promote the new sexual politics of gay and lesbian writing in Mexico. Then there is the detective fiction of the old modernism; Mexico is one of the few Latin American countries— along with Argentina and Cuba—with a vital production and consumption of detective fiction, led by Paco Ignacio Taibo II and Rafael Ramírez Heredia.

The postmodern debate appeared in Mexican journals and magazines, particularly in the context of critiques set forth by social scientists, such as the Mexican scholars Adolfo Sánchez Vásquez and Roger Bartra.[3] Neo-Marxists, such as Sánchez Vásquez, who tended to equate the postmodern with late capitalism, also tended to equate postmodern culture—as did the critical theorists of the Frankfurt School—with mass culture and mass media. Octavio Paz (arguing from the political right in the 1980s and 1990s), was also critical of postmodernism. The cultural debate in postmodern Mexico, however, did not focus primarily on postmodernism. Rather, the politics, legitimacy, and authority of the major cultural voices in Mexico—Paz and Fuentes—were debated in fierce polemics appearing in the pages of Paz's magazine, Vuelta, and Héctor Aguilar Camín's Nexos. The latter supported Fuentes and the progressive political left. By the early 1990s, the tensions between these two cultural and political powers had been polarized. Several other journals and magazines occasionally published articles related to postmodernism.[4]

The principal spaces of postmodern literary culture—theory and fiction—have been two bookstore-cafés on the south side of Mexico City, the Librería Ghandi in the Colonia San Angel and the Librería Parnasso in the Colonia Coyoacán. There, Mexican, Latin American, and First World theory and fiction have been amply available: Mexican, Argentine and Spanish editions of Michel Foucault, Jacques Derrida, Roland Barthes, Jean Baudrillard, Jacques Lacan, Gilles Deleuze, Felix Guatarri, Jean-François Lyotard, and the like. William Gass, Robert Coover, Donald Barthelme, and a broad selection of postmodern fiction writers have also been circulating, usually in editions translated and published in Spain. Similarly, the Mexican publishing company Ediciones ERA, which distributes amply in Mexico, published Deleuze and Guattari's *Kafka: por una literatura menor* ("For a minor literature," 1993).

From the 1960s to the 1990s, the postmodernization of Mexico has always been intimately related to Mexico's most important cultural fact and political institution: the PRI (Institutional Revolutionary Party). A key turning point in the PRI's relationship with its citizenry took place in October of 1968 with the massacre of students and workers in the Plaza de Tlatelolco. After that act, truth was no longer a viable possibility for a generation of Mexicans. After the devaluations of 1976 and the 1980s, the crisis of truth was generalized in postmodern Mexico. In the 1980s, in fact, Mexicans referred regularly to the state of national affairs simply as La Crisis. Although the middle sectors tended to understand La Crisis as an economic crisis, it was much more: it was a crisis of authority, of legitimacy, and of truth.

An early literary manifestation of this crisis in Mexico was the fiction of the Onda. Postmodern fiction in Mexico was a viable cultural expression in Mexico by 1967, when José Emilio Pacheco published the transitional and early postmodern *You Will Die in a Distant Land* and Carlos Fuentes published *Holy Place* and *A Change of Skin*, followed in 1968 by José Agustín's *Inventando que sueño* ("Inventing that I'm dreaming") all works with some postmodern qualities. In addition to Pacheco, Fuentes, and Agustín, writers of Mexico's first wave of transitional postmodern fiction were Salvador Elizondo and Gustavo Sainz. After 1968, a second wave of more patently postmodern fiction included some of the work of Fuentes, Agustín, Elizondo and Sainz, as well as the postmodern work of Ignacio Solares, Carmen Boullosa, Luis Arturo Ramos, María Luisa Puga, Brianda Domecq, Sergio Pitol, Federico Patán, Daniel Leyva, and Héctor Manjarrez. With the publication of Carlos Fuentes's *Terra Nostra* in 1975, the Mexican postmodern was clearly a dominant cultural force. Brian McHale has appropriately described *Terra Nostra* as one of the "paradigmatic texts of postmodern writing, literally an anthology of postmodern themes and devices."[5]

THE TRANSITIONAL POSTMODERN (1964–1968)

The first wave of Mexican transitional postmodern writing emanated directly from Jorge Luis Borges and Julio Cortázar, writers whom Pacheco and Fuentes popularized among Mexican intellectuals in the early 1960s. Fuentes had dominated the literary scene with his modernist works *Where the Air is Clear* (1958) and *The Death of Artemio Cruz*.[6] They were totalizing novels that questioned the state project of modernizing Mexico, a project initiated in the 1940s and soon to be internationally known as the "Mexican miracle." In these two novels, major narrative works of the century, Fuentes used many of the narrative strategies of the First World modernists, as did the modernists Agustín Yáñez, Juan Rulfo, Vicente Leñero, Juan García Ponce, and Fernando del Paso. The early reaction against this modernism came in the form of the irreverent young writers of the Onda, Gustavo Sainz and José Agustín.

Leñero was also one of the novelists who helped set the stage for later postmodern fiction in Mexico. In his novel *Los albañiles* ("The bricklayers," 1964), Leñero questions the possibilities of truth, and his play with versions of truth affected the postmodern production that came later. The novel deals with the identification of a murderer, but it also questions the epistemological constraints that define truth in a social context.[7] *Los albañiles* is a novel of diverse topics, but as one critic has pointed out, "the diverse aspects of *Los albañiles* come to bear on the question of knowledge, especially knowledge produced by scientific method and the epistemological dilemma of verifying that which is reported to be known."[8] Different versions predominate over any kind of truth, as they do in Pacheco's *You Will Die in a Distant Land* and Fuentes's *A Change of Skin*. Elizondo, Sainz, and Agustín published an entire body of experimental fiction in the 1960s and 1970s; Elizondo's *Farabeuf* ("Farabeuf," 1965), Sainz's *Gazapo* ("Gazapo," 1965) and Agustín's *De perfil* ("In portrait," 1966) constitute significant early contributions to the Mexican postmodern. All three novels were transitional works between the modernity of *Pedro Páramo* (1955) and *The Death of Artemio Cruz* and the postmodernism of *Terra Nostra* (1975). *Farabeuf* is one of the most hermetic novels of the period, narrating over and over again a limited number of the same situations. Devoid of significant action and of characters with fixed identity, *Farabeuf* places the reader in a vague space, unwillingly involved in the novel's main image: someone sitting between mirrors and looking at someone else. In a postmodern fiction that discards action and also discounts characters and content as worthwhile elements, it privileges language itself to such an extent that, in a world in which only language remains, human cruelty is neither an issue of morality nor immorality, but simply an amoral, neutral act (as it is also treated in Argentina in the equally violent fiction of Alejandra Pizarnik and Enrique Medina). Consequently, the title character, Dr. Farabeuf, executes the specialized techniques of Chinese torture, techniques of no more and no less moral content than those highly specialized narrative gestures of Salvador Elizondo and José Emilio Pacheco (as well as those gestures of Jorge Enrique Adoum, José Balza, and Diamela Eltit in other regions) and the equally specialized roles the fictionalized reader must play in order to execute the reading of *Farabeuf*. These specialized techniques of writing, reading, and torture reach extremes in *Farabeuf* rarely found among the diverse postmodernities of recent Latin American fiction, although Elizondo has been a much-cited model for the Argentine Héctor Libertella (see chapter 4).

The fiction of Gustavo Sainz and José Agustín questioned the traditional boundaries between high and low culture, a common strategy of postmodern writers. Like *Farabeuf*, Sainz's *Gazapo* affords the reader a sense of fiction and empirical reality as versions and possibilities, but shares little else with Elizondo's fiction. An early and key text of the Onda, *Gazapo* was a notable innovation for the Mexican postmodern: it brought the young language of adolescents into the Mexican novel, as well as the new technologies of communicating by means of tape recorders and other media. Above all, the fiction of Sainz was an irreverent antidote to the dominant modernist practices in Mexico in the early 1960s. A story of adolescent relationships and trivial actions, it seems apparently distant from the more evidently historical and political fiction of Fuentes and Pacheco. The history of *Gazapo*, however, is the history of a continual present in which the narrative transpires, for *Gazapo* privileges social reality by transcribing, literally, the events as they occur in Mexico City. *Gazapo* also privileges memory: what human memory might forget is recorded in precise detail on tapes. *Gazapo*, like much postmodern fiction, insists that we, as readers, remember as active participants; forgetting is not one of our options.

By 1967, signs of this early postmodern were evident with the publication of three experimental and historical novels that year: Pacheco's *You Will Die in a Distant Land*, Fuentes's *Holy Place* and his *A Change of Skin*. The three works have some of the epistemological qualities of modernist fiction and some of the ontological qualities of postmodernist writing. Pacheco and Fuentes ask epistemological questions in these novels, such as: How can I interpret this world of which I am part? What is there to be known? Who knows it? How do they know it and with what degree of certainty? In particular, they explore what the limits of the knowable are. These three texts also pose postmodernist ontological questions: what happens when different kinds of worlds are placed in confrontation? When are boundaries between worlds violated?

What is the mode of existence of a text, and what is the mode of existence of the world (or worlds) it projects?[9]

In *You Will Die in a Distant Land,* as in Fuentes's *Holy Place* and *A Change of Skin,* Pacheco questions how we know the world and with what degree of certainty. *You Will Die in a Distant Land* has historical referents such as the experience of the Jews under attack by the Romans in Israel in the first century, A.D., and the Holocaust in Poland during the Second World War. Pacheco the modernist questions how we know this world of human atrocity by rewriting and reinventing Jewish history in a fragmented form that invites analysis. The degree of certainty with which the reader believes Pacheco's text varies as the novel progresses: all the narrative segments become questionable. In the end, very little certainty is possible.

You Will Die in a Distant Land consists of 101 narrative segments that develop, on one level, as a modernist novel that moves from chaos to unity. The apparent chaos lies in the fact that the narration jumps—from one narrative segment to another—in time and space across centuries and oceans, from the first century A.D. to the twentieth, from Israel and Poland to Mexico. Adding to this initial impression of chaos is the presence of a series of inherently ambiguous narrative segments ("Salónica") that systematically negate anything they affirm. These "Salónica" sections initially portray a character named Eme (Em in English) who, from the window in an apartment building in Mexico City, observes a character named Alguien (Someone) sitting on a park bench below, reading a newspaper. Once this situation is clarified, however, the narrator begins subverting all the operating premises about this situation. Consequently, the reader necessarily questions whether Eme really exists, whether Someone really exists, and whether any of the situation ever existed. Finally, the reader questions in the early stages of the novel what relationships might exist between the destruction of the Jews in Israel and this setting in Mexico City, between the Holocaust in Warsaw and this setting in Mexico City.

After this initial impression of the chaos and disorder so common in modernist texts, the reader begins to discover relationships between the anecdotes set in the Old World and those set in Mexico City. There are parallels, for example, between the *mirada* (gaze) that Eme directs and the *mirada* (gaze) from the Torre Antonia down to the Jerusalem that they are about to destroy. Later, the reader of this modernist text discovers yet another parallel: the *mirada* (gaze) that Eme directs down to the Jews when he is torturing and destroying the Jews of Warsaw.

The postmodern of *You Will Die in a Distant Land* betrays and subverts the unity suggested in reading this novel as an ultimately harmonious, modernist text. The subversion of the situation of Eme and Someone does much more

than undermine the reader's confidence in the existence of these two supposed characters. By questioning these narrative segments, *You Will Die in a
Distant Land* questions the very possibility of writing history, the uses of
history, and the legitimacy of historiography.

The boundaries between worlds are blurred and violated in *You Will Die in
a Distant Land.* Pacheco shares the ontological concerns of the postmodern when
he blurs the boundaries between the ancient and the modern worlds, as well
as between the fascist operations of the Nazis and the "democratic" operations
of more democratic states, such as Mexico. He also blurs the traditional
distinction between story and history. Pacheco's novel becomes an ontological
text questioning its own mode of existence. Does *You Will Die in a Distant Land*
exist as testimony, as historiography, or as fiction? Avoiding the either/or
thinking of the Western tradition, Pacheco's text is a testimonial that subverts
the testimonial itself, a historiography that questions historiography itself and
it is a metafiction that questions the mode of existence of fiction.

The postmodernist ontological text can ask or imply the question "What
is this world?" and *You Will Die in a Distant Land* enters frequently into this type
of questioning. The narrator asks near the end of the novel:

> but who is em?
> who am I?
> who is speaking to me?
> who is telling me this story?
> to whom am I telling it? (my translation)

To be posing such questions to himself and to the reader this late in the novel
is just one indicator of how *You Will Die in a Distant Land* continues to question
itself and all its suppositions until the end.

You Will Die in a Distant Land is a transitional postmodern work that bridges
the epistemological and the ontological as just one element of its incessant
double coding. According to these rules of double coding, this novel is
history and is not history; its characters are unified subjects and not unified
subjects; Eme exists and does not exist; Eme watches Someone and does not
watch Someone; the Holocaust happened and did not happen. *You Will Die
in a Distant Land* is also the postmodern historiographical metafiction par
excellence: its historical vision is broad; it is also self-conscious as a novel, as
a book that narrates a story that, at the same time, it constantly negates.

Pacheco's generation of Mexican intellectuals had read Cortázar's *Hopscotch* (1963) with considerable enthusiasm and curiosity, and *You Will Die in
a Distant Land* is one of the most challenging post-*Hopscotch* novels to effect

Morelli's proposal for a "lector macho" or (stated in less sexist terms) an "active reader." *You Will Die in a Distant Land* contains a series of strategies that oblige the postmodern reader to engage in a more active role than required by the modernist complexities of Juan Rulfo's *Pedro Páramo* and Carlos Fuentes's *The Death of Artemio Cruz*. At several points, Pacheco offers affirmative readings and invites the reader to choose his or her own reading. The difference between the active involvement of the reader of much modernist fiction and the choices the reader must make in *You Will Die in a Distant Land* is Pacheco's postmodern turn in Mexico.

But the reader's potential activity in *You Will Die in a Distant Land* has even more serious consequences than Cortázar's then revolutionary proposal for an activated reader in *Hopscotch*. Among the postmodern reader's multiple activities in *You Will Die in a Distant Land* (as decipherer of the modernist text, as reader of history, as "active reader," etcetera) lies the frequent possibility of playing the role of voyeur. At the outset, the distanced reader merely observes the voyeuristic activities of Eme observing Someone, of Tito observing Jerusalem. As the novel progresses, however, the reader has numerous opportunities to play Eme's role as sadistic voyeur of Nazi atrocities, intellectual voyeur of perverse wartime aggression, innocent and disgusted bystander to a distant war, and the like. The novel's construction, however, creates a constant invitation to participate in the very voyeurism of which the repressive regimes in *You Will Die in a Distant Land* are guilty. The active reader of this novel, consequently, can easily fall into the trap of also being the "aggressive reader" fictionalized in *You Will Die in a Distant Land*. The politics of postmodernism thus escape the simple dichotomies of liberal or conservative thought, either of which the reader could often accept or reject with relative ease in modernist fiction.

Fuentes's *Holy Place* and *A Change of Skin* share many postmodern qualities with *You Will Die in a Distant Land*. The title of Pacheco's novel refers to an "other" space: a woman in Leipzig reads Eme's palm and tells him "Morirás lejos" ("You will die in a distant land"). In this novel, as in the two works by Fuentes, the space of the novel is the territory of the other. The "zona sagrada" ("holy place") of *Holy Place* is a sacred and personal space that, initially, is "lejos del espacio de mi madre, en el otro extremo de la ciudad" (far from the space of my mother, in the other side of the city).[10] Later, the narrator/protagonist, who occupies various urban spaces from Mexico City to Rome and from Paris to Orvieto, asks "Is there another place?" (the postmodern question par excellence with respect to space); later he expresses the desire to be, as he says in English, "out of bounds." Space in *Holy Place*, like the characters, is in constant transformation—a constant rearranging of boundaries. The narrator states at one point "Nada se desarrolla. Todo se transfigura." ("Nothing develops. Everything is transfigured.")[11] Indeed, characters, like space, are in a constant state of transformation, emphasizing their indeterminate and unfixed quality. The protagonist himself, the twenty-nine- year-old Guillermo Nervo, suffers an identity crisis under the shadow of a dominant mother, a film celebrity. He finds no resolution to this crisis but, rather, speaks of his other, "el otro ser" ("the other being").[12] Fuentes cites his postmodern doctrine on the self from an unlikely source, F. Scott Fitzgerald's *The Great Gatsby*: " . . . personality is an unbroken series of successful gestures."[13] In the end, Guillermo reaches a state of exhaustion comparable to the exhausted states of the characters and implied reader in *You Will Die in a Distant Land*.

The four main characters of *A Change of Skin* are burned out, too. Like *You Will Die in a Distant Land*, *A Change of Skin* is a historiographical metafiction and a novel in which characters have no fixed identity. Set in Mexico in the 1960s, *A Change of Skin* relates the story of two couples who spend a weekend together in Cholula, although there are numerous digressions into past history and other continents, including the Nazi period of *You Will Die in a Distant Land*. Following the model of Borges in "The Garden of Forking Paths," Fuentes creates a labyrinth of time comparable to the infinite novel left by Ts'ui Pen in the Borges story. An opening section of the novel moves back and forth, from one paragraph to the next, between the twentieth-century travel of the four main characters and the sixteenth-century conquest of Mexico by Hernán Cortés. The past, the present, and the future exist here and now. In this lengthy and complex novel, Fuentes pursues another time and space.

A Change of Skin is one of Fuentes's early experiments with characters of multiple (rather than just double) identities, as well as with characters and spaces in constant transformation. When it is ultimately revealed that the text of *A Change of Skin* has been produced by the mad inmate of an insane asylum, it is apparent that Fuentes's fiction has moved from concerns over the episte-mological (*Where the Air Is Clear* and *The Death of Artemio Cruz*) to the ontological.

Despite its unresolved contradictions and metafictional qualities, *A Change of Skin*, like Fuentes's other postmodern fiction, is deeply historical and political. His postmodern work is a "transhistorical carnival" (as McHale calls it) in which characters in their projected worlds interact with those of empirical reality.[14] Simultaneously, Fuentes engages in multiple intertextual boundary violation, including fictional characters from other novels in his texts. Consequently, the reader of Fuentes's postmodern fiction experiences an even more complex confrontation with history than does the reader of Fuentes's overtly historical and political modern texts.

The transitional postmodern in Mexico closes with the massacre at Tlatelolco and two experimental novels of 1968, Agustín's *Inventando que sueño* and Elizondo's *El hipogeo secreto* ("The secret cave"). Both are so experimental, in fact, that many readers in the late 1960s were unsure if they should even be identified as "novels." *Inventando que sueño* consists of a set of stories that can be read as separate stories or as a novel. As one critic has pointed out, it functions like an album of rock music with several songs while, at the same time, rock music is one of the predominant notes of the book.[15] Like Fuentes's *Old Gringo*, *Inventando que sueño* is a metafiction but not a historiographical metafiction. In the cases of Agustín and Elizondo, history is now, the present moment. Like much postmodern fiction, the structure of *Inventando que sueño* is metonymic, developing on the basis of associations. It develops different versions of the world represented, and like Elizondo's *El hipogeo secreto*, its main interests are more ontological than epistemological. In Elizondo's experimental metafiction, creating a character does not imply creating a "real" character.

In addition to a national tragedy and political disaster, the massacre at Tlatelolco was a notable metaphor for a postmodern culture increasingly focussed on technique over content. The human cruelty of this national tragedy might have surprised individuals who had not seen the precedents in *Farabeuf*, *You Will Die in a Distant Land*, and *A Change of Skin*, three novels that suggested the amoral (as opposed to the moral or immoral) postmodern condition. The spectacle of technique in these three novels simultaneously precludes moral judgment on the part of the characters and the readers, just as the techniques and technology of human cruelty were replayed under Latin American dictatorships in the 1970s and in Iraq in the 1990s, regardless of moral issues or related matters.

This group of transitional postmodern novels in Mexico demonstrates epistemological as well as ontological concerns, and several of them are historiographic metafictions. The action or lack thereof in most of these novels often results in fictions connected not by plot, but by gestures, *miradas* (gazes) and mirrors that are metonymically associated.

After the exhaustion of the content of history and culture, all that remains is language. This was the situation of the Mexican postmodern by the late 1960s: in *Farabeuf*, *You Will Die in a Distant Land*, *A Change of Skin*, and *Inventando que sueño*, the only value remaining was, in the end, language itself.

THE LATER POSTMODERN (1969–1993)

After the hyper-experimentation of the late 1960s, culminating in the fiction of Pacheco, Fuentes, Agustín, and Elizondo, post-1968 postmodern fiction in Mexico became progressively less hermetic and more accessible. Nevertheless, postmodern attitudes of the 1960s became more acute, leading to a metafictional literature of exhaustion by the late 1980s. In addition to the work of such internationally recognized writers as Carlos Fuentes, the later postmodern in Mexico included novelists such as Luis Arturo Ramos, Carmen Boullosa, María Luisa Puga, Brianda Domecq, and Ignacio Solares, who were widely read in Mexico and relatively unknown beyond.

Fuentes has been at the avant-garde of the second wave of postmodern fiction in Mexico, publishing the postmodern works *Birthday* (1969), *Terra Nostra* (1975), *Distant Relations* (1980), *Old Gringo* (1985), and *Christopher Unborn* (1987). But the Mexican postmodern was ample in the 1970s and 1980s, with the work of Salvador Elizondo, Gustavo Sainz, José Agustín, Héctor Manjarrez, María Luisa Puga, Sergio Fernández, Federico Patán, Luis Arturo Ramos, Sergio Pitol, and Angelina Muñíz-Huberman. Ignacio Solares and Carmen Boullosa closed this period with noteworthy novels of 1993, *El gran elector* ("The great elector") and *La milagrosa,* respectively.

"Displacement is the action of the novel," Fuentes has stated in an essay, and his five postmodern novels of the period are examples of this concept of "action." Set in London, the story of *Birthday* deals with a multiple set of identities: George, his son Georgie, his wife, characters named Nuncia and Nino, and the thirteenth-century Averroist philosopher Siger of Brabant. Their constantly transforming identities and distant relations associate and overlap in the most enigmatic fashion of any of Fuentes's novels until *Terra Nostra.*

One of the most important elements in *Birthday* is space, a factor that is signaled initially by George's profession as architect, as well as is a reminder that, for Fuentes's postmodern diction, displacement is indeed the action of the novel. The point of departure is a room that George and his wife occupy with their son Georgie; but this novel lacks a space to be identified as a center, and space is in constant transformation throughout the novel. In *Birthday,* Fuentes effects with space what Juan Rulfo had done with time in *Pedro Páramo* (1955), and Cortázar had done with character in *62: A Model Kit* (1968): radical innovation. *Birthday* is a lengthy meditation on space; experience is not separated into the worlds of inside and outside.

Birthday was written during Fuentes's initial creative stages of *Terra Nostra,* and the two novels share common conceptions of space and other elements. The descriptions of hermetically closed spaces occasionally evoke the equally hermetic space of El Escorial in *Terra Nostra.* The architectural constructs in *Birthday,* like those of El Palacio in *Terra Nostra,* are quite severe and harsh.

The conceptions of architecture and space are the most important connections between *Birthday* and *Terra Nostra.* The transhistorical operation that allows Fuentes to synthesize the thirteenth-century Siger of Brabant and the twentieth-century George is also a notable precedent to the transhistorical carnival of *Terra Nostra. Birthday* is even more experimental with space than *Terra Nostra;* only in the former are there concepts such as "la casa está siendo" ("the house is in the process of being").[16] In addition, Siger de Brabant insists on the same multiplicity that undergirds *Terra Nostra.*

Terra Nostra is Fuentes's rewriting of the architecture of El Escorial, his major and culminating rereading of Latin American culture and history. In addition, it is the major project of the Mexican postmodern on identity, knowledge, and the novel itself. Mario Vargas Llosa had asked the historical question "At what moment did Perú mess up?" and, in an attempt to respond to this question, wrote a lengthy historical and political novel, *Conversation in The Cathedral.* Near the end of *Terra Nostra,* Fuentes poses a similar question, but in broader terms: "At what moment did Spanish America mess up?"[17] In addition to the particulars of Latin American history, Fuentes is concerned with how history, culture, and identity are constructed and then understood.[18] As a reader of José Ortega y Gasset and Foucault, Fuentes has understood history not as a compilation of immutable truths, but as a living world in transformation. Once again, displacement is one of the major actions of the novel.

Although *Terra Nostra* has some modernist, totalizing impulses, it shares closer proximity to the postmodern, justifying McHale's description of it as an anthology of postmodern themes and devices. As a postmodern text, *Terra Nostra* articulates the twelfth-century proclamation that "Nothing is true, everything is permitted." Attributed to Hasa i-Sabbah in the year 1164, this statement is particularly appropriate because Fuentes, too, frequently returns to the Middle Ages in his act of recovering history and knowledge.

Like much postmodern fiction, *Terra Nostra* is strongly historical and political. Fuentes's awareness of historical discourse and, above all, his questioning of the very assumptions of Western historiography align *Terra Nostra* with the postmodern described by Linda Hutcheon. In this sense, *Terra Nostra* is more deeply historical and political than many modernist novels, including such overtly historical and political Latin American novels as García Márquez's *One Hundred Years of Solitude* and Vargas Llosa's *Conversation in The Cathedral.*

As a postmodern text, *Terra Nostra* is Fuentes's rewriting of the medieval, renaissance, and neoclassical architecture of El Escorial. For Jencks, one common postmodern architectural design is the skyscraper with perfectly modern lines, but with classical Greek columns in open opposition to the modern design.[19] In this postmodern construct, no harmonic resolution of these blatantly contradictory lines is designed or desired. They remain in unresolved (postmodern) contradiction. The palace and other aspects of *Terra*

Nostra function in this fashion. In his use of a "painting from Orvieto" (a mural by Luca Signorelli actually located in Orvieto, Italy), Fuentes appropriates this erotic mural from Orvieto and places it into El Señor's severe and austere palace. Just as the postmodern architect leaves the Greek columns on the modern building with no resolution, Fuentes leaves the Signorelli mural in the palace in open contradiction—with no visible resolution.

In similar fashion, Fuentes appropriates the well-known novelistic ruse of the manuscript in the lost bottle and uses it anachronistically in a novel published in 1975. In the process, Fuentes juxtaposes his typically modern novelistic strategies with the anachronistically traditional. The result is comparable, once again, to the postmodern architectural image of the modern skyscraper with its Greek columns.

The double coding of the postmodern, as described by McHale (and as already observed in *You Will Die in a Distant Land*) can be seen in the music of "The Commitments," an imitation of Wilson Picket and Detroit soul music, sung by whites in Ireland, as well as Mexican *rancheras* of the Peruvian Tania Libertad, who imitates the *rancheras* of the Mexican José Alfredo Jiménez.[20] The double coding of *Terra Nostra* is present in some overt cases, such as the presence of characters of Spanish Golden Age literature of the seventeenth century who also appear in *Terra Nostra*. The double voice of Fuentes's pastiche is more subtle when the narrator intercalates the phrase "polvo enamorado" ("dust in love") in the novel, thus evoking the simultaneous double voice of Fuentes, author of the novel we are reading, and Quevedo, author of the sonnet that ends with the same words. Similarly, the reader of *Terra Nostra* hears the double voice of Fuentes and García Márquez when the omniscient narrator uses the phrase "Many years later . . ." twice (near the middle and near the end of the novel). This phrase is followed by a clause in the conditional tense, exactly as it appears in *One Hundred Years of Solitude*.

Fuentes's tendency toward double coding is also evident in his characters. Many of them are at the same time specific historical characters while they also are not these historical characters. In many cases, such as the authority figures, they are and are not several historical Spanish kings and queens. Most of the novel's major figures, in addition, have double codes rather than any fixed, singular identity. These multiple identities in constant transformation, which question the very concept of psychic unity and the individual subject, align *Terra Nostra* with the postmodern.

In *Terra Nostra*, postmodern architecture is imposed on a neoclassical model of the empirical world of sixteenth-century Spain. The narrator of Borges's "Pierre Menard, Author of the *Quixote*" states the following: "there is no intellectual exercise which is not ultimately useless. A philosophical doctrine is in the beginning a seemingly true description of the universe; as the years pass it becomes a mere chapter—if not a paragraph or noun—in the history of philosophy."[21] Such is the ultimate destiny of the apparent truths of *Terra Nostra*, a fundamentally Borgesian and postmodern text that has Pierre Menard as a character. *Terra Nostra* is not the ultimate repository of truth that some critics have attempted to make it.[22] Rather, it is a Borgesian and postmodern text that questions, undermines, and subverts Western historical truth. The ultimate communication of *Terra Nostra* is not philosophical or historical truth, but an awareness of the paragraphs and nouns that construct social systems and legitimate truths. The narrator in "Pierre Menard" suggests this postmodern attitude toward truth: "History, *mother* of truth; the idea is astounding. Menard, a contemporary of William James, does not define history as an investigation of reality, but as its origin. Historical truth, for him, is not what took place; it is what we think took place."[23] In this sense, *Terra Nostra* and postmodern fiction are deeply historical and political—as returns to origins of historical thinking rather than history and truth. Fuentes takes to its ultimate consequences Michel De Certeau's proposition that "L'écriture de l'histoire est l'étude de l'écriture comme practique historique" ("The writing of history is the study of writing as a historical practice").[24] Borges, de Certeau, and Fuentes share the postmodern assumption that historical discourse is, in the end, another discourse.

Terra Nostra is Fuentes's postmodern architectural construct imposed on a medieval, renaissance and neoclassical architectural model. His construct rediscovers the heterogeneity of Latin American culture and the heterogeneity of postmodern culture in the Americas. Fuentes's palace is one of several unresolved contradictions. Representation in *Terra Nostra* is not just imitation and repetition, as in El Escorial, the building in Spain on which the palace is modelled.[25] Rather, representation in *Terra Nostra* takes as its point of departure and then exploits the representation of *Don Quixote* and the fiction of Borges. *Terra Nostra* is neither just the modern work positing truth (as suggested by Roberto González Echevarría) nor the totally enigmatic and mysterious work with no meaning (as suggested by Lucille Kerr).[26]

One of Fuentes's most complex novels, *Distant Relations* deals with Latin American cultural heritage from France, as *Terra Nostra* had done with Spain. Nevertheless, *Distant Relations* suggests just as much about Fuentes as a postmodern writer and his interests in literature, for this is the book that promotes the idea that living, in the end, is predicated on the act of telling a story. It suggests that in a work of art "la solución del enigma sea un nuevo enigma" ("the solution to the enigma is another enigma").[27]

Written after *Terra Nostra, Distant Relations* can be read as an extension of the former in the sense that it continues Fuentes's lengthy meditation on European-Mexican relations. Near the end, it is revealed that the person listening to the Conte de Branley is a man named Fuentes who, instead of returning to his native Mexico from Buenos Aires in 1945, remained in Río de Plata until 1955, when he went to France. As in *Terra Nostra*, the New World is conceived as a lost opportunity to create a universal culture, as Branley explains to Fuentes.[28] Above all, *Distant Relations* is a complex elaboration of two concepts from *Terra Nostra*: that the self and the other are inextricably bound in distant relations and that human experience depends on the act of storytelling.

Another of Fuentes's postmodern works, *Old Gringo* is set during the Mexican Revolution, and is the story of two Americans in Mexico, Ambrose Bierce and Harriet Winslow. Much of the novel consists of the actions and adventures already associated with the Mexican Revolution by most readers, images of the sort that Mariano Azuela had related in his classic novel *The Underdogs* (1915). One of the first scenes in *Old Gringo*, in fact, evokes an early scene in *The Underdogs*, when the old *gringo* crosses the Río Grande and looks back at a burning bridge. (In *The Underdogs*, the protagonist looks back to his burning home in a key early passage.)

Like *Terra Nostra, Old Gringo* is really a novel about language and writing. The old *gringo* carries *Don Quixote* along with him to Mexico, claiming that he wants to read it before he dies. But all the characters are obsessed with texts, with dreams, and with stories. Throughout this novel, reality is portrayed not as it is observed in the empircal world around the characters, but as it is conceived within the bounds of their language, their imaginations, and their stories. As in *You Will Die in a Distant Land* and *Distant Relations*, in *Old Gringo* the power of storytelling predominates over empircal reality.

Like so many novels of the Mexican postmodern, *Old Gringo* is also a novel about frontiers, difference, and the other. Once the two Americans cross the Río Grande, these issues are evoked, generated as much by the history of the relations between the two nations as by actions of the characters. Harriet and Arroyo are fully aware of the baggage they carry as an American woman and a Mexican man in the discourse each represents on the other side of the border.

One of the most innovative fictions of the Mexican postmodern, *Christopher Unborn* is a lengthy and totalizing work, with obvious parentage in *A Change of Skin* and *Terra Nostra*. Here, a return to origins takes on a different meaning, for Cristóbal narrates on January 6, 1992, from the womb of his mother Angeles. In the novel, Fuentes imagines a Mexico of the future, a post-postmodern Mexico that has trivialized not only its national myths and its institutions, but also its very identity.

Christopher Unborn is Fuentes's most irreverent fictional critique of postmodern Mexico; the questioning of the nation's modernization to be found in *Where the Air Is Clear* and *The Death of Artemio Cruz* culminates in *Christopher Unborn* with images of a nation lost in the garbage and defecation that are the products of its own development. The *suave patria* ("gentle nation") of the (nationalistic) early twentieth-century poet Ramón López Velarde is now a mutilated land where the "external debt" has become an "eternal debt," where the jungle has been destroyed and the nation is covered with cement highways and excrement. Postmodern Mexico has reached a state of total exhaustion. Perhaps the most devastating critique, however, is the fact that Christopher, narrating from the womb, has no past at all, a postmodern condition unlike the Mexican characters of Fuentes's early fiction.

Even more than in *A Change of Skin,* and *Terra Nostra,* in *Christopher Unborn* Fuentes plays with language. This is a novel of postmodern play, a world of seemingly infinite substitutions. Humorous Joycean associations, such as the following, are common: "tu chere asada en mi boca hambrienta, tu cherezada tampiqueña con sus rajitas y sus frijolitos que estoy escarbando con mi dedo largo, tu cunto, tu cuento, tu ass chérie, tu cherry ass, Chere Sade, flagelada por mi látigo furioso. . . ."[29] *Christopher Unborn* is one of postmodern Mexico's most self-conscious metafictions; it plays off Fuentes' own words and other institutionalized languages in Mexico, both literary and political. In this sense, *Christopher Unborn* is the Bakhtinian text par excellence: a text of heteroglossia (or "other languages") with competing languages at play.

The characters in *Christopher Unborn* seem to be lost in time and space, possessing no past. This ahistoricism, however, does not represent the situation of Fuentes himself with regard to *Christopher Unborn.* To the contrary, he is well aware of the past in this book, parodying and subverting Mexican writers, such as the traditionalists Ramón López Velarde and Mariano Azuela, as well as some of the writers present in much of Fuentes's work—Miguel de Cervantes, Desiderius Erasmus and Nikolai Gogol.

Distant Relations, Old Gringo and *Christopher Unborn* continue the postmodern themes and strategies of *A Change of Skin, Birthday,* and *Terra Nostra.* Characters of multiple and transforming identities are evident in these three texts, and Fuentes flaunts the unresolved contradictions that are a sign of the postmodern. As frequently happens in postmodern texts, the reality of texts, of fiction, or of storytelling predominate over empirical reality and often subvert it. These are fictional worlds that inevitably revert back to language as their principal subject. Fuentes's postmodern fiction, despite its unresolved contradictions and metafictional qualities, is deeply historical and political. His postmodern work is indeed a transhistorical carnival in which characters in their projected worlds and empirical reality interact. Simultaneously, Fuentes engages in multiple intertextual boundary violation, including fictional characters from other novels in his texts. Consequently, the reader of Fuentes's postmodern fiction experiences an even more complex confrontation with history than in his overtly historical and political modernist texts, *Where the Air Is Clear* and *The Death of Artemio Cruz*.

Some postmodern fiction of the 1970s and 1980s, such as that of José Agustín, Salvador Elizondo, Héctor Manjarrez and Sergio Fernández, followed the experimental and hermetic model of the late 1960s *You Will Die in a Distant Land* and *Birthday*. Agustín's *Se está haciendo tarde (final en laguna)* ("It's getting late [ending in the pond]," 1973), Manjarrez's *Lapsus* (1971), and Fernández's *Segundo sueño* ("Second dream," 1976) are three novels of this sort. Agustín's novel has little plot, practically no psychological development of its characters, and a paucity of description of the setting. It deals with a group of young Mexicans' experiences in Acapulco. These disconnected and discontinuous experiences consist mostly of regular and self-indulgent consumption of drugs and American rock music from the late 1960s to early 1970s. Like a poster, the postmodern *Se está haciendo tarde* demonstrates neither the pretention nor the intention of becoming a modernist classic. As one art critic has pointed out, posters live in our horizontal and not in our vertical way of thinking, they represent the perfect elegance of the surface.[30] The poster and Agustín's text share common visual strategies. For example, the narrator intercalates visual signposts that interrupt and guide the reader through the narrative, just as a poster interrupts a linear "reading" of a wall or street. Unlike novels in which only the textual space with words has value, this work valorizes open space for specific effects just as the poster often does.[31] Elizondo's *El grafófago* ("The graph writer," 1972), Manjarrez's *Lapsus* and Fernández's *Segundo sueño* also live in our horizontal and not our vertical way of thinking, as does much experimental postmodern writing. After writing the self-conscious and anti-representational *El grafófago*, Elizondo spoke of his literary "dead end."[32] In *Lapsus*, Manjarrez invites the reader to invent an episode of the novel, and creates the unstable identities already noted in much postmodern fiction. Fernández's *Segundo sueño* has the hermetic and metafictional qualities of the most complex Mexican fiction of the period.

Some postmodern fiction in Mexico, while still more innovative than its modern predecessors, was far more accessible than the early postmodern production. Luis Arturo Ramos, Sergio Pitol, Federico Patán, María Luisa Puga, and Brianda Domecq are postmodern writers in this line. Ramos, Pitol, and Puga tell stories with clearly defined plots, but like the postmodern Fuentes of *Distant Relations* and *Old Gringo*, they engage the reader in subtle games and devices associated with the postmodern. Ramos's early writing, particularly his short fiction, had clear affinities with Cortázar, and his story "Cartas para Julia" contains the paranoia typical of some postmodern fiction (see chapter 4). His most accomplished and patently postmodern novel, *Este era un gato* ("This was a cat," 1987), tells the story of Roger Copeland, a retired American Marine captain who had participated in the 1914 invasion of Veracruz. Copeland returns to Mexico sixty years later, where he dies on exactly the same date he fought there in 1914: April 21. This novel deals with the otherness and the fragile identities that characterize Fuentes's fiction of the 1980s. Like much postmodern historiographic metafiction, *Este era un gato* does not fall into either "presentism" or nostalgia in its relation to the past that it represents. It does denaturalize that temporal relationship. The text offers three possible conclusions, but ends in unresolved contradiction.

In *El tañido de una flauta* ("A flute's music," 1972), *Juegos florales* ("Flower arrangements," 1982), *El desfile de amor* ("The parade of love," 1984), *Domar a la divina garza* ("Taming the divine heron," 1988) and *La vida conyugal* ("Conjugal life," 1991), Sergio Pitol constructs metafictions that are in dialogue with film and literary texts.[33] *El tañido de una flauta* is a dialogue with film and theory, but *Juegos florales* and *Domar a la divina garza* are Pitol's most innovative postmodern texts. The protagonist of *Juegos florales* travels to Italy to finish a novel on Billie Upward also titled *Juegos florales*. He goes back to Rome to rewrite stories he had started there some twenty years before. The reader observes the narrator still struggling with his old relationships and the numerous vicissitudes of writing fiction. *Juegos florales*, like the work he is writing, always seems to be in a Bakhtinian process of dialogue rather than a completed project. *Domar a la divina garza* is an even more self-conscious Bakhtinian project, with a narrator-protagonist who selects Bakhtin as the theorist he will use to write his novel. He also selects a character named Marietta Karapetiz as the antagonist with whom he will engage in an ongoing literary dialogue, particularly on Nikolai Gogol, the Russian writer about whom Karapetiz has considerable expertise. The constant digressions in their conversation, however, point to the discontinuity that characterizes this tale of parody and uncertainty. This is a postmodern text that breaks down the standard dichotomy between fiction and theory, and disrupts the decorous hierarchy of literary genres. Like *Terra Nostra*, it strives toward an encyclopedic condition, to allow a myriad of access points.

María Luisa Puga and Brianda Domecq have written a substantive body of postmodern fiction. Puga has published *Las posibilidades del odio* ("The possibilities of hatred," 1978), *Cuando el aire es azul* ("When the air is blue," 1980), *Pánico o peligro* ("Panic or danger," 1981), *La forma del silencio* ("The form of silence," 1987), and *Antonia* ("Antonia," 1989). *Las posibilidades del odio* and *Cuando el aire es azul* are fundamentally modern texts, but Puga's later works show more postmodern impulses. Like the novels of Pitol, Puga's fiction is often in the process of coming into being as it relates its story. *Pánico o peligro* is a metafiction which, like *Distant Relations*, suggests that narrating and living are basically the same activity, and in which characters suffer unstable identities. In *Pánico o peligro*, fictionalizing a story is a method for understanding the self. *La forma del silencio* is a more self-conscious meditation on the novel, suggesting that reality constructs the novel and the novel constructs reality. Puga's focus on words in particular contributes to this work's metafictional quality; the use of an enigmatic style once again blurs the boundaries between traditional genres. A historiographic metafiction, *Antonia* relates the story of a Mexican woman who goes to London in search of traces of Virginia Woolf, but confronts an identity crisis. Brianda Domecq has published two novels of interest within the context of the postmodern, the innovative works *La insólita historia de la Santa de la Cabora* ("The strange story of Saint Cabora," 1990) and *Once días . . . y algo más* ("Eleven days . . . and more," 1991).

Federico Patán, Daniel Leyva, and Angelina Muñiz-Huberman are more technically innovative than Ramos, Pitol, Puga, and Domecq, and figure among the most hermetic postmodern Mexican writers of the period. The protagonist of Patán's *Ultimo exilio* ("The last exile," 1986) lives between the margins of empirical reality and fictional reality, but never on a stable terrain. He lives in physical exile, but his interior exile into the world of fantasy and literature is more severe, and comparable to the situation of characters in the short fiction of Luis Arturo Ramos and Julio Cortázar. Leyva's *ABCDErio o ABeCeDamo?* ("ABCDE or ABeCeD?, 1980) and *Una piñata llena de memoria* ("A piñata full of memories," 1984) are two of the most experimental Mexican novels of the 1980s; like the writing of Ramos and Patán, this fiction reveals readings of Cortázar. *Una piñata llena de memoria* recalls *Hopscotch* in that it offers the reader the choice of several different readings. Muñiz-Huberman's *Dulcinea encantada* ("Enchanted Dulcinea," 1992), like the works of Ramos and Patán, blurs the boundaries between interior and exterior reality, between fantasy and empirical reality. It is a metafiction that offers the possibility of multiple levels of intertextual reading; the fragmented narrator-protagonist alludes to numerous writers, including Cervantes and other writers from the Spanish Middle Ages and Golden Age, as well as to Virginia's Woolf's Orlando, Santa Teresa, Emily Brontë, Elizabeth Browning, Rodrigo Díaz de Vivar, and Lord Jim.

Two novels published in 1993 that have been well received among Mexican readers provide a final insight into the Mexican postmodern, *El gran elector* by Ignacio Solares and *La milagrosa* by Carmen Boullosa. Solares had already established well-defined interests in both history and invention in his novels *Puerta al cielo* ("Door to the sky," 1976), *Anónimo* ("Anonymous," 1979), *El árbol del deseo* ("The tree of desire," 1980), *La fórmula de la inmortalidad* ("The formula for immortality," 1982), *Serafín* ("Seraphim," 1985), *Casas de encantamiento* ("Charmed houses,"1988) and *Madero, el otro* ("Madero, the other," 1989). *El gran elector* is a novel about a Mexican president who represents a composite of all the Mexican presidents of the PRI since 1930. (Speeches from numerous former presidents are the speeches of this fiction-alized character.) The most predominant sign of the postmodern in *El gran elector* is the fact that everything, in the end, is discourse—different levels of speech—including the nation.

La milagrosa is Boullosa's fourth novel in a body of work with several postmodern qualities. Her first novel, *Mejor desaparece* ("Better to disappear," 1987) contains the subjective *mirada* (gaze) of Fuentes's and Ramos's fiction. A historiographic metafiction set in the seventeenth century, Boullosa's *Son vacas, somos puercos* ("They are cows, we are pigs," 1991) espouses a postmodern ideology of plurality and recognition of difference. In *La milagrosa*, Boullosa tells the story of a religious faith healer; the novel seems to be symptomatic of a nation and of a fiction that is not truly irrational but, paradoxically, involves a search for understanding of things beyond the rational.

Both *El gran elector* and *La milagrosa* are critiques of politics in postmodern Mexico. They represent the crisis of authority in Mexican society, a crisis of a world with little transcendence and little truth. Both novels contain a multiplicity of differing discourses—popular, political, ecclesiastical—in unresolved contradiction. Their concerns are predominantly ontological in a world with characters suffering identity crises. After Solares and Boullosa, the newest figures to appear on the Mexican postmodern scene are Juan Villoro and Dante Medina.

Innovative and experimental fiction has been amply developed in Mexico since the rise of the modern in the 1940s, 1950s, and 1960s with Agustín Yáñez, Juan Rulfo, Carlos Fuentes, Vicente Leñero, Juan García Ponce and Fernando del Paso. They were the producers of the grand narrative, memo-rable characters, and their interests were fundamentally epistemological. These modernist writers were interested in history, as generations of Latin American writers have been, but they generally did not produce the histo-riographic metafiction of the postmodern novelists. The initial rupture with the basic tenets of Mexican modernist writing came in the rebellion of the Onda, which blurred the boundaries between popular and high culture, ridiculed many of the implicit assumptions of an already conventional modernist fiction, and generally revolutionized attitudes about fiction as it was being written in Mexico. After the Onda, Mexican writers have been regularly engaged in blurring multiple types of boundaries.

Following the initial inroads made by the Onda, and strongly influenced by Borges and Cortázar, Mexican postmodern fiction of the late 1960s and 1970s entered a period of hyper-experimentation, a tendency headed by the Fuentes of *Birthday* and *Terra Nostra*, the Pacheco of *You Will Die in a Distant Land* and the Elizondo of *Farabeuf* and *El hipogeo secreto*. The interests of these writers were generally more ontological than epistemological, with characters suffering from a lack of psychic unity, fragmentation, and unstable identity. The Mexican postmodern writers of the 1980s and 1990s have continued many of these tendencies, as well as other postmodern topics and devices, such as double coding, in fictions that are generally less technically experimental and more accessible.

More recent Mexican postmodernities have been less aggressively innovative in technique. Ramos, Solares, and Boullosa use narrative strategies associated with modernist fiction (fragmentation, multiple narrators, high levels of ambiguity, etcetera) but they also develop their narratives using some of the proposals of Cortázar in *Hopscotch*. Like Pacheco, nevertheless, they require the active reader proposed by Morelli in *Hopscotch*—a postmodern reader. Ramos has also written occasional short fictions, which one critic has defined as the "paranoiac tale" and which is present throughout Latin America among postmodern writers.[34]

To paraphrase Fuentes once again, displacement has indeed been the action of the Mexican postmodern novel. David Harvey has suggested that space is as much a concern with the postmodern writers as time had been with the modernists;[35] experimentation with space has been an important innovation in Mexican postmodernities since *Farabeuf* and *Birthday*.

Politics and ideology are as important for many of the postmodern writers as they had been for their predecessors in Mexico, where history and truth take on a new value. Truth and the construction of truth is questioned in many early postmodern works, such as *You Will Die in a Distant Land*. By the time *El gran elector* and *La milagrosa* were published in the 1990s, the writing of truth was no longer a viable category in Mexican postmodern fiction.

3

Andean Postmodernities

Cocaine is not only a new and transcendent economic fact; as one social scientist has correctly observed, it is, above all, a new cultural fact.[1] The postmodern condition of the Andean region has been considerably constructed, marked, and attenuated by the international drug industry centered in this area, but located primarily in Colombia, Perú, and Bolivia. The massive inflow of narco-dollars and petro-dollars to Bogotá and Caracas over the past three decades has created an enormous funnel of post-industrial and high-tech culture into these cities before the nations of the Andean region— Colombia, Venezuela, Ecuador, Perú, and Bolivia—have become fully industrialized or have fully modernized the other sectors of their respective economies and societies. Postmodern architecture is evident in Bogotá, Caracas, Quito, Lima, and La Paz. The first reliable electrical lines have only recently been laid in some of the most remote rural areas, yet, at the same time, in Bogotá, Lima, and Caracas the elite among intellectuals, the government, and the drug traffickers have had full access to cellular phones, CNN, computers, electronic communication networks, and MTV.

Some of Latin America's most prominent modernist writers, such as Gabriel García Márquez, Mario Vargas Llosa, Demetrio Aguilera Malta, Miguel Otero Silva, and Salvador Garmendia, write from the Andean region. Some of them have been occasionally afflicted by the postmodern, but the most radically innovative postmodern fiction of the Andean region is being produced by the Colombians R. H. Moreno-Durán, Albalucía Angel, and Darío Jaramillo Agudelo, the Venezuelan José Balza, the Ecuadorian Jorge Enrique Adoum, and the Bolivian Renato Prada Oropeza.

The vibrant center of the Andean postmodern is Colombia , and the turning point for postmodern Colombia was the early 1970s. The legitimacy of the nation's political institutions fell into severe crisis with the 1970 elections, which were fraudulent and resulted in the formation of the urban guerrilla group M-19; at the same time, drug trafficking became an increasingly significant part of Colombia's society and national economy (according to some experts, providing approximately one third of the nation's GNP in some years). Colombia's institutions, including its two traditional parties, have survived into the 1990s, but postmodern Colombia has suffered numerous, very severe crises, the worst being the 1984 massacre at the burning Supreme Court building in downtown Bogotá.

Colombia's postmodern cultural scene is not as exclusively centered on the capital as is Mexico's on Mexico City or the other nations of the Andean region on their capitals; the postmodern can be found on the north side of Bogotá and sectors of other large metropolitan areas of Medellín and Cali, as well as portions of small cities, such as Pereira.

In addition to the postmodern architecture of new structures in north Bogotá, such as the World Trade Center and the Century 100 Hotel, outlets such as the Oma Café/Bookstore provide Bogotá's elite with the latest postmodern fiction and theory from Europe and the United States, some in translation, some in the original French and English. Colombia's organs of the postmodern have included magazines such as *Quimera* (from Spain, with a Latin American edition temporarily published in Colombia) and the *Boletín Cultural y Bibliográfico*, and publishing houses such as Tercer Mundo Editores, Planeta, and Arango Editores.

George Yúdice has proposed that narcotics trafficking in its current transnational cartel form "is a grotesque (and fitting) parody of capitalist corporate culture."[2] This parody of multinational corporate culture of the 1980s and 1990s is just one postmodern characteristic of the Andean drug industry. Once drug-trafficker Carlos Lehder (currently serving a life sentence in the United States) organized his international communications system while García Márquez's *Chronicle of a Death Foretold* was being sold on street corners by the same vendors who previously hawked contraband packs of Marlboro's (in 1981), Colombia was participating in a multinational and postmodern economy and society. Lehder's genius was connecting Pablo Escobar and his Medellín Cartel with drug distributors in the United States; *Chronicle of a Death Foretold* was mass marketed throughout Latin America and Spain as no novel had ever been. Consequently, the phenomenon of García Márquez, beginning with his spectacular novel *One Hundred Years of Solitude*, followed by the mass marketing of his work, followed by the Nobel Prize and then more mass marketing, made the García Márquez phenomenon in Colombia almost as impressive as the rise of the multibillion dollar cartels of Medellín and Cali. During the 1970s, young writers in Colombia, including Gustavo Alvarez Gardeazábal, Fanny Buitrago, R. H. Moreno-Durán, and Marco Tulio Aguilera Garramuño, complained of the dismal situation of writing under the enormous "shadow" of García Márquez.

The uncomfortable juxtaposition of the premodern, the modern, and the postmodern in Colombia is particularly visible in towns such as Pereira, where it is possible to sit in the central plaza and observe, simultaneously, a traditional Catholic Church built in the early twentieth century, a modern sculpture of a nude Bolívar designed by Colombian sculptor Rodrigo Arenas Betancur, Hare Krishnas singing and dancing, and, in the distance, the postmodern architecture of luxurious apartment buildings in the neighborhood called Los Pinares. Sleek new buildings have been popping up in Los Pinares in the 1990s as narco-dollars and families from Medellín have been migrating to Pereira, a few hour's drive to the west of Medellín.[3]

Postmodern Venezuela is centered in Caracas, the Miami of Latin America. The streets are lined with neon lights advertising multinational products, and the city is in constant transformation, the capital of what Adriano González León has called the "portable country" in his novel *País portátil* ("Portable country," 1968). Unlike Bogotá, Lima, and Quito, Caracas has virtually no remnants from the Colonial period; the architecture of Caracas is predominantly modern and postmodern in a city that has been inundated in the past two decades with the apparatus of high tech and postindustrial economies.

The Bolivian social scientist Fernando Calderón has suggested that Latin America lives in incomplete and mixed times of premodernity, modernity, and postmodernity, and that each of these is linked historically in turn with corresponding cultures that are, or were, epicenters of power.[4] This is certainly the case for Ecuador, Perú, and Bolivia, which have been bound historically to indigenous cultures; their modernizations have come slower and with less progress than Colombia and Venezuela; and, consequently, the postmodern sectors of their respective societies have been negligible.[5] Colombian narco-dollars have funded the construction of postmodern buildings in Quito, and one sees some similar postmodern designs in the Miraflores sector of Lima and even in Bolivia. In the Bolivian case, as Yúdice has pointed out, given the attempt to modernize by "developing" extractive industries for export, under the aegis of "central economies," modernity takes "ghoulish" forms. Some of these forms are similar to the forms of the postmodern.

POSTMODERN FICTION IN COLOMBIA

Given his numerous contributions to the Colombian cultural scene and the enormous shadow he has cast on all fiction writers in Colombia since 1967, it is logical to assume that the pioneer of modernist fiction in Colombia was García Márquez. In reality, a group of novelists of the 1940s (when García

Márquez was still an adolescent reading Franz Kafka and William Faulkner) were the first to attempt to modernize Colombia's intensely traditional and conservative cultural scene, but these writers, including Jaime Ardila Casamitjana and Tomás Vargas Osorio, still remain relatively obscure, even in Colombia.[6] The cultural magazine *Mito*, which was published in the mid-1950s, brought the modern European writers of the 1940s and 1950s to the attention of Colombian intellectuals. With the publication of the overtly Faulknerian novels *Leafstorm* (1955) by Gabriel García Márquez, *La casa grande* (1962, appeared in English under the same title, *La casa grande*) by Alvaro Cepeda Samudio, and *Respirando el verano* ("Breathing the summer," 1962) by Héctor Rojas Herazo, Colombia had a better-known set of modern precedents to the excitingly modern novel that overwhelmed Colombia's provincial and backward literary elite, *One Hundred Years of Solitude* (1967).[7]

Colombian postmodern fiction has its roots in the 1960s, and can be most clearly identified in the novel *Mateo el flautista* ("Mateo the flute player," 1968) by Alberto Duque López. Innovative precedents to postmodern fiction, hardly noticed in Colombia's tradition-bound literary culture, were the still ignored novels *Después de la noche* ("After the night," 1963) by Eutiquio Leal, *Los días más felices del año* ("The most happy days of the year," 1966) by Humberto Navarro, and *El terremoto* ("The earthquake," 1966) by Germán Pinzón. After the freedom of imagination announced by the Argentines Jorge Luis Borges and Julio Cortázar (who were widely read by Colombia's young intellectuals in the 1960s) as well as García Márquez's *One Hundred Years of Solitude* and Duque López's *Mateo el flautista* in Colombia, the postmodern innovators to appear on the scene in the 1970s were Andrés Caicedo, Umberto Valverde, Albalucía Angel, Marco Tulio Aguilera Garramuño, Rodrigo Parra Sandoval, and R. H. Moreno-Durán. Moreno-Durán published a substantive body of innovative fiction in the 1980s and 1990s; other postmodern fiction writers who published their initial books in this period were Darío Jaramillo Agudelo, Boris Salazar, Hugo Chaparro Valderrama, Héctor Abad Faciolince, and Orietta Lozano.

R. H. Moreno-Durán published a hermetic trilogy titled *Fémina Suite* ("Feminine Suite") in the late 1970s and early 1980s, and then *Los felinos del Canciller* ("The felines of the chancellor," 1985) and *El caballero de la invicta* ("The undefeated gentleman," 1993). He considers himself an individual of international postmodern culture first, a Colombian second. His literary masters were Cervantes, the European moderns (particularly Robert Musil and Pierre Klossosky), Jorge Luis Borges, Julio Cortázar, and the Mexican Juan García Ponce. He also knows the American innovators well, from Ron Sukenick to William Gass and Robert Coover, all of whom he admires. The roots of

Moreno-Durán's *Fémina Suite* are found not in the empirical reality of Colombia but rather, as in the case of much postmodern fiction, in modernist literature. Moreno-Durán has explained how poems by T. S. Eliot and Paul Valéry generated the first novel of the trilogy, *Juego de damas* ("Lady's game," 1977).[8] The reader's most immediate literary association with *Juego de damas* is the work that announced the postmodern project in Latin America, Cortázar's *Hopscotch*: both the elements of the former (such as the split columns on the page) and the content (such as youths listening to jazz) recall Cortázar's proposal for a new, open novel, as articulated in *Hopscotch*.[9] *Juego de damas* deals with female intellectuals, beginning with their radicalized student life in the 1960s and passing through three stages of social climbing and power acquisition, stages in which the narrator identifies them as *Meninas* (young intellectuals), *Mandarinas* (middle-aged social climbers) and *Matriarcas* (elderly women in power). As in most of his fiction, Moreno-Durán develops elaborate relationships between language and power: he employs a series of strategies, including parody and euphemism, to subvert language. This subversive activity is supported in the text by Monsalve, a character who serves as an author figure. The two main characters of the second book of the trilogy, *Toque de Diana* (1981), Augusto Jota and Catalina Arévalo, are also intellectuals who engage in the linguistic and sexual exercises found in *Juego de damas*. Augusto is a military man who fails both in the military and in his sexual relationship with Catalina; in the lovemaking of these two devotees of Latin, she "conjugated" while he "declined." In the third and most hermetic novel of the trilogy, *Finale capriccioso con Madonna* ("Capriccioso finale with Madonna," 1983) Moreno-Durán exploits to the utmost both the eroticism of language and the language of eroticism. He poses the question, for example, of the relationship between "semantics" and "semen" and in the process creates a lengthy, playful, and dense passage of a menage a trois. From the introduction of Laura, the main character, who finds herself caught between two men, this novel develops a series of triangular relationships. It is a playful novel of erotic and linguistic excesses with intertextual allusions ranging from Marcel Proust to Salvador Elizondo. Several factors unify Moreno-Durán's trilogy as a single postmodern project, but, above all, the role of language itself is the main subject of all three books.

Moreno-Durán's *Los felinos del Canciller* lacks some of the hermetic qualities of his previous work and much postmodern fiction, and in this connection one might speak of an early postmodern attitude in the Andean region that produced relatively inaccessible works (the early Moreno-Durán, in this sense, corresponds to the early Severo Sarduy and the early Néstor Sánchez in Argentina) and a later, more accessible postmodern fiction. The difficulties and inaccessibility of many postmodern texts are replaced in *Los felinos del Canciller* by wit: Rather than functioning as a barrier, Moreno-Durán's subtle manipulation of language is frequently the material of humor.

An initial review of the novel's plot suggests another family romance—the modern Latin American family story—as seen in García Márquez, Carlos Fuentes, or Alejo Carpentier. *Los felinos del Canciller* chronicles three generations of the aristocratic Barahona family of diplomats, from the patriarch Gonzalo Barahona to his son Santiago and his grandson Félix Barahona. Félix is the principal focalizer through whom the Barahona clan is remembered in New York in 1949. Historical referents allow the reader to follow the elegant diplomatic family's story from the Colombian Regeneration (end of the nineteenth-century) through the various "grammarian presidents" and the rise of the Liberal party in the 1930s and, finally, the swan song of the old-fashioned diplomatic life in the 1940s.

Only a superficial reading of *Los felinos del Canciller*, however, would emphasize the family history; the most important referents and the main subject of this postmodern novel are language and writing. The verb that essentializes the novel's action is "to manipulate." Indeed, the art of diplomacy, as practiced by the Barahona family, is the art of manipulation. More significant to the experience of this novel, however, is the manipulation of language, for if diplomacy is Gonzalo's profession, philology is his passion.

The males of the family are always at least as obsessed with philology as with their respective careers. During the late nineteenth century, the years of the Regeneration, Gonzalo decides to study not medicine but philology and, as the ideal gentleman—scholar of the Regeneration, he finds access to politics and diplomacy by means of his philology. He first appears in the novel in this context: in the opening pages Félix remembers Gonzalo's philological tastes and, consequently, he mentions the Colombian term for the useless bureaucrat—*corbata*. At the end of this first chapter the narrator explains that the Barahona family, as philologists, "se limitaban a decir que el fulano era un *kalos kagathos*, expresión que los más ignaros les sonaba a grosería" [they limited themselves to saying that the guy was a *kalos kagathos*, an expression that sounded like a vulgarity to the most ignorant ones].[10] This sentence, combining the Barahonas's knowledge of Greek and the narrator's colloquial language, provides an entertaining introduction to the Barahonas's modus operandi. Félix Barahona studies Greek and tends to view the world within a philological context.

Los felinos del Canciller parodies Colombian institutions, above all, the institutionalized concept of Bogotá as the Athens of South America. Félix is characterized as the "perfect Attic gentleman." The novel also questions the cultural superiority claimed by Colombian intellectuals who were rooted in classical tradition. In order to carry out this parody of Bogotá as Athens, the narrator presents Colombia as a distant *ese país* (that country). On those rare occasions when the narrator admits identity with this nation, using the first-person plural, the vision is of a citizen abroad, observing this philological paradise with spatial and temporal distance.

The transgression of sexual norms is yet another level of parodic play in *Los felinos del Canciller*. As in *One Hundred Years of Solitude*, the sexual transgressions often consist of symbolic rather than direct physical acts. Félix Barahona is depicted from the novel's first paragraph as potentially incestuous. He feels that the day begins with the odor of his daughter. Diplomacy, as practiced by the Barahonas, is incestuous: international relations are a function of a family—an incestuous grouping of inward-looking individuals—rather than an outward-looking group of international mediators. Additional allusions to physical incest abound in the text, frequently relating to Félix Barahona's desire for his sister Angélica.

Significant parallels are drawn among several of the elements discussed above: the Barahona family, as diplomats, manipulate human beings and relationships; the Barahonas, as philologists, manipulate language; the narrator, as another Barahona, manipulates both individuals (characters in the novel) and language. As has been noted, moreover, the narrator engages in humorous and parodic language manipulation, quite similar in content and effect to the operations of the Barahonas. These lead to an initial equation: in *Los felinos del Canciller* diplomacy is equal to language. Similarly, the narrator cultivates equivalencies between language and diplomacy, key images for this equivalency being the use of diplomacy and language as art and as protocol.

The equivalencies between language and diplomacy lead to entertaining consequences. The postmodernity of this text is signaled by the fact that, in the end, not just diplomacy but everything becomes the art of language and writing. That is, unique equivalencies are created between language and sexuality, between language and politics, and, finally, between language and writing. The relationship between language and sexuality has already been suggested in the earlier passage relating Gonzalo's exercise in impotency with philological discourse. Other anecdotes from his life confuse his philological and sexual activity, until the narrator even concludes that Gonzalo "spoke the same way that he manipulated in the bedroom." The narrator, as just one more Barahona, uses the same type of equivalencies as the Barahonas.

Activity (all acts of manipulation) in *Los felinos del Canciller* refers to language and writing or is a metaphor for them, both for the characters and for the narrator. When Gonzalo initiates his love affair with Lesley-Anne, the two of them convert the relationship into a writing affair, exchanging love letters. The narrator transforms this affair into a literary relationship by stating that their letters crossing in the mail became "crossed soliloquies."

Los felinos del Canciller is a significant contribution to the Andean postmodern. For both the reader and the narrator, it is a novel of surfaces: All actions are superficial in the sense that the very act of manipulation is always more significant than any content or product of this act. Both language and diplomacy are devoid of content. In a narrative situation in which characters act as focalizers (mostly Félix), consequently sharing the revelation of the fictional world with the narrator, and in which this narrator ultimately only manipulates, the novel in the end possesses no final authority. Having language as its subject and only absences and indeterminacy as its constants, *Los felinos del Canciller* emerges as the postmodern text par excellence. Like the narrator and the Barahonas—all etymologists who seek truth in origins—Moreno-Durán investigates his own origins in the language of the Hispanic and Andean traditions synthesized in the phrase "Athens of South America."

Moreno-Durán continues his postmodern project with *El caballero de la invicta*, which contains many of the same strategies already observed in his fiction. It deals with a Bogotá in deterioration, which he satirizes with observations such as "a marriage ceremony without photographs is an unconsummated marriage." As in his previous work, he subverts any sense of truth, observing that "Palabras como *uneth*, que quiere decir verdad, alternaban con otras como *dreck*, que significa *mierda*" ("words such as *uneth*, which means truth, were alternated with others such as *dreck*, which means *shit*"). With this and his previous work, Moreno-Durán is assuming a role of the chronicler of postmodern Bogotá.

Other postmodern novelists in Colombia—Albalucía Angel, Marco Tulio Aguilera Garramuño, Darío Jaramillo Agudelo, Alberto Duque López, Rodrigo Parra Sandoval, and Andrés Caicedo—are generally as demanding of their readers as Moreno-Durán. Angel's recent novels, particularly *Misía Señora* ("Ms. Lady," 1982) and *Las andariegas* ("The travellers," 1984) are part of a feminist project that emanates directly from feminist theory and fiction. She had already published two early experimental novels, *Los girasoles en invierno* ("Sunflowers in the winter," 1970) and *Dos veces Alicia* ("Alicia twice," 1972), in addition to one on the historical period in Colombia called La Violencia, *Estaba la pájara pinta sentada en el verde limón* ("The colored bird was sitting on the green lemon tree," 1975). *Misiá señora* and *Las andariegas* are her most hermetic and feminist works. *Misiá señora* deals with different aspects of female sexuality and gender issues. The fictional world of this novel creates a tenuous line between empirical reality and pure imagination. An important aspect of this richly imaginative experience is the creation of a new, feminist discourse as part of Angel's feminist project. *Las andariegas* is a radical experiment that can be read as a double search: on the one hand, a search for a female language; on the other, an evocation of a feminine identity. As in the fiction of Moreno-Durán and many postmoderns of her generation, language is the principal subject in *Las andariegas*. Much of the narrative consists of brief phrases with unconventional punctuation often functioning as images. The use of verbal imagery in the novel is supported by visual images—a set of twelve drawings of a female body. Angel also experiments with the physical space of language in the text, often in a manner similar to concrete poetry. The four pages of this type offer a variety of circular and semicircular arrangements with the names of famous women. The total effect of this visual imagery is to associate the body of the text with the female body. *Las andariegas* ends with a type of epilogue—another quotation from Monique Wittig—consisting of four brief sentences calling precisely for the project that is the radical essence of these two novels: a new language, a new beginning, a new history for women.

The postmodern projects of Moreno-Durán and Angel are distant from the modernity of García Márquez and his novels set in Macondo. Marco Tulio Aguilera Garramuño, on the other hand, began his writing career with a self-conscious reaction to the Macondo fiction in his parodic *Breve historia de todas las cosas* ("Brief history of everything," 1975). The narrator, Mateo Albán, playfully narrates from prison the story of a small Costa Rican town. In addition to the town's development (similar in many ways to Macondo), Mateo Albán describes the problems he confronts as creator and as narrator. This metafictional mode reaches its most extreme situation in the sixth chapter when Albán discusses his problems with his fictional readers. Like Moreno-Durán and Angel, Aguilera Garramuño playfully subverts some of Colombia's most sacred institutions: in this case, the Catholic Church, *machismo*, and the fiction of García Márquez. In *Paraísos hostiles* ("Hostile paradises," 1985), a dialogue on fiction and philosophy, Aguilera Garramuño moves away from the context of Colombia and García Márquez, but he continues in the metafictional mode. He creates a perverse and hellish fictional world located in a sordid hotel. Several of his economically impoverished but intellectually rich inhabitants write novels, and one of them proposes a novelistic aesthetic that is quite similar—though not coincidentally—to the reader's experience in *Paraísos hostiles*.

Darío Jaramillo Agudelo's only novel, *La muerte de Alec* ("The death of Alec," 1983), is also a metafiction—in this case, a self-conscious meditation on the function of literature. It is an epistolary work directed to an unidentified "you," one of the characters implicated with Alec. This "you" and the letter writer are friends of Alec, who dies during an excursion. The characters are Colombian, but the novel is set in the United States; the letter writer is a novelist in the University of Iowa Writers' Program. Jaramillo Agudelo inverts the commonly accepted relationship between empirical reality and fiction: according to the narrator, it is not literature but life that is artificial, baroque, twisted. Similarly, the acts of storytelling (placing order to a story) and interpretation (giving meaning to a story) become the predominant forces, taking precedence over other forms of understanding reality. As in *Paraísos hostiles*, this novel also alludes to the very mechanisms used in telling the story.

Andrés Caicedo, Rodrigo Parra Sandoval, Alberto Duque López, and Umberto Valverde have conceived different kinds of postmodern projects. Caicedo's *Que viva la música!* ("Let music live," 1977) like the fiction of the first generation postmoderns in Mexico of the Onda, involves a fictional world of 1960s rock music and drugs. Beyond this superficial comparison, however, Caicedo has little in common with the young Mexican writers. *Que viva la música!* is an experimental confrontation with a particular generation's cultural crisis in 1960s Colombia. Caicedo deals with this crisis with sobriety rather than with the humor and playfulness of the Mexican postmoderns Gustavo Sainz and José Agustín. Rodrigo Parra Sandoval's *El album secreto del Sagrado Corazón* ("The secret album of the Sacred Heart," 1978) is a collage of texts—books, newspapers, letters, documents, voices—representing an assault on the novel as a genre. The implied author suggests that the genre suffers limitations similar to those experienced by the protagonist who lives in a very limiting and repressive religious seminary. Colombia's postmodern cultural crisis, as seen in Caicedo, is depicted in Parra Sandoval's novel as a questioning of the nation's official, institutional images. *El album secreto del Sagrado Corazón* contains two main characters so ambiguously portrayed that they could well be the same person; Alberto Duque López proceeds similarly in *Mateo el flautista* (1968), which in two parts offers two versions of the protagonist, Mateo. There is no authoritative voice in this narrative nor any authoritative version of Mateo's life. Consequently, *Mateo el flautista* is a quintessential postmodern text that clearly emanates from *Hopscotch*, as indicated by the novel's dedication to one of its characters, Rocamadour. An admirer of Guillermo Cabrera Infante and the entire tradition of modern music in the Caribbean, Umberto Valverde fictionalizes the popular culture of Caribbean music in *Bomba Camará* ("Bomba Camará," 1972) and *Celia Cruz* ("Celia Cruz," 1981).

The most recent postmodern fiction in Colombia has been produced by the young writers Héctor Abad Faciolince, Hugo Chaparro Valderrama,

Orietta Lozano, and Boris Salazar. Abad Faciolince's first novel, *Asuntos de un hidalgo disoluto* ("Matters of a dissolute gentleman," 1994) shares some of the attitudes of Moreno-Durán and Jaramillo Agudelo, while functioning on the same uncertain terrain of Balza and Ribeyro. Like Moreno-Durán and Severo Sarduy, Héctor Abad Faciolince cultivates the art of digression. *Asunto de un hidalgo disoluto* is a self-conscious and narcissistic story of a seventy-two-year-old man who narrates the vicissitudes of his life from his adolescence, using the model of the Spanish picaresque novel. Like several postmodern writers, such as Jaramillo Agudelo and the Mexican Luis Arturo Ramos, Abad Faciolince has a character who searches for signs and believes in a world of chance that is not limited by modern systems of rational thought.

The characters in Chaparro Valderrama's first novel, *El capítulo de Ferneli* ("Ferneli's chapter," 1992), also believe in *el azar*—reality as chance—but this metafictional work has origins in detective fiction, horror movies, newspapers, and the very act of creation. An outgrowth of Cortázar's *Hopscotch*, *El capítulo de Ferneli* also resonates with Sue Grafton, Alfred Kubin, Raymond Chandler, Rubem Fonseca, Luis Rafael Sánchez, and the Carlos Fuentes of *Hydra Head.* The protagonist is a writer who writes to understand, and the result is one of the most innovative fictions published in Colombia since Duque López's *Mateo el flautista.*

Known as a poet in Colombia, Orietta Lozano has produced a challenging novel of cultural resistance titled *Luminar* ("Luminar," 1994), which recalls the issues of Caicedo and relates to some directions of feminist fiction, particularly to the writing project of the Chilean Diamela Eltit. One of the most radically experimental texts to be published in Colombia since Duque López's *Mateo el flautista* and one of the most culturally provocative texts since *Que viva la música!, Luminar* is a metafiction about the postmodern urban condition of a group of youths. The young characters associate with a writer named Odette, who writes and reads texts; some of these characters also talk about *Luminar*, thus providing one aspect of the work's several metafictional qualities. Odette pushes the limits of living and writing and, like several characters in the fiction of Moreno-Durán, lives literature as a lifestyle. In this world of texts, alcohol and drugs, much is provisional and there is no empirical or textual authority. Like Eltit, Lozano tends to see reality as social construct; as in *Que viva la música!*, meaning is exhausted in the end, but in *Luminar* the exhaustion is not from drugs, but from language itself.

With a fundamentally conservative culture and society, Colombia has been radically transformed over the last three decades, probably more than any other society of the Andean region. Paradoxically, this conservative society that was still resisting modern culture in the 1950s and 1960s—when

García Márquez and his generation were considered marginal—has accommodated one of the most extensive and elaborate postmodern cultures in the Andean region. Even the story of Colombia's most canonical writer, José Eustasio Rivera, has been rewritten in the form of Boris Salazar's postmodern novel *La otra selva* ("The other jungle," 1991), a fictionalized biography of Rivera's last days in New York.

Colombian postmodernities follow two basic tendencies. The first consists of the hermetic fictions of Moreno-Durán and Angel, which connect with the type of international postmodern fiction originally defined and promoted by Ihab Hassan and which is represented in Mexico by writers such as Elizondo, José Emilio Pacheco, and the later writing of Fuentes. They require an active, postmodern reader. A more popular and accessible cultural reevaluation that implies a writing of resistence is effected by Caicedo, Valverde, and Lozano. This second tendency can be associated with postmodernities as diverse as the early fiction of Cabrera Infante and the postmodern project of resistence published by Diamela Eltit.

POSTMODERN FICTION IN VENEZUELA

Innovative fiction in Venezuela was pioneered by Julio Garmendia, a short story writer whose fiction of the 1930s and 1940s has been recovered and lauded by the younger generation writing in Venezuela today. Salvador Garmendia, Miguel Otero Silva, Adriano González León, Ramón Díaz Sánchez, Guillermo Meneses, and Oswaldo Trejo brought modernist fiction into Venezuela in the 1950s and 1960s, and several of them were involved with the literary magazine *Sardio* in the late 1950s and early 1960s, which also aspired to modernize the traditional cultural scene that still dominated. The function of *Sardio* in Venezuela was comparable to the role of the *Revista Mexicana de Literatura* in Mexico and *Mito* in Colombia.

A major modernist Venezuelan novel was Adriano González León's Faulknerian *País portátil*, but the most productive modernist writer in Venezuela has been Salvador Garmendia, who has published a series of novels in the modernist mode since the late 1950s, including *Los pequeños seres* ("The little beings," 1959), *Los habitantes* ("The inhabitants," 1961), *Día de ceniza* ("Day of ashes," 1964), *La mala vida* ("The bad life," 1968), and several other novels in the last two decades. Only recently has Garmendia's work taken a postmodern turn, notable in volumes such as *Crónicas sádicas*, a set of 29 brief *crónicas* which are light and entertaining anecdotes. Garmendia's play with language includes a piece written in praise of vulgar language, another written in praise of breaking wind, and yet another in praise of masturbation. The source of the humor in Garmendia's writing often is the juxtaposition of academic and colloquial language.

After the narrative irreverence of Guillermo Meneses, the pioneer innovator (and early postmodern fiction writer) in Venezuela has been Oswaldo Trejo, whose books of fiction *También los hombres son ciudades* ("Men are also cities," 1962), *Andén lejano* ("Distant platform," 1968), *Textos de un texto con Teresas* ("Texts of a text with Theresas," 1975) and *Metástasis del verbo* ("Prosthesis of the verb," 1990) represent the most wildly experimental and self-conscious body of fiction ever published by a single writer in Venezuela. Not only is Trejo uninterested in telling a linear story, but he rarely develops a plot at all. Some pages of his inventive prose read like concrete poetry, with words spread sporadically over the page. His roots are the Borges of "La Biblioteca de Babel," and his aesthetic kindred spirit is Morelli of in Cortázar's *Hopscotch*.

One of the most significant writers of the Venezuelan postmodern is José Balza, who has published numerous volumes of fiction in various forms, including several books of different variations and combinations that he, like Moreno-Durán, considers his "exercises." His novels are *Marzo anterior* ("Previous March," 1965) *Largo* ("Long," 1968), *Setecientas palmeras plantadas en el mismo lugar* ("Seven-hundred palm trees planted in the same place," 1974) *D* ("D," 1987), *Percusión* ("Percussion," 1982), and *Medianoche en video: 1/5* ("Midnight on video: 1/5," 1988). Balza, like Moreno-Durán, Ricardo Piglia, Severo Sarduy, and several other postmodern writers with whom he closely identifies, often blurs the line between fictional and essayistic discourses, writing fictions about literature and essays in a fictional mode. He sets forth a theory of the novel in a lengthy essay on *Don Quixote* titled *Este mar narrativo* ("This narrative sea") in which he refers to the usual literary father figures of the Latin American postmoderns: James Joyce, Cervantes, Borges, and Cortázar. He also pays homage to Guillermo Meneses, who had published a humorous metafiction in 1952, *El falso cuaderno de Narciso Espejo* ("The false notebook of Narciso Espejo"). In this essay, he privileges the unresolved contractions of the novel that are typical of postmodern fiction, and he often returns to the correlations between the body and writing. Balza's early novels of the 1960s and 1970s were fundamentally modernist works; *Marzo anterior* and *Largo* were influenced by the French *nouveau roman*. *Marzo anterior* is a fragmented novel of 19 narrative sequences that are the interior monologues of the narrator-protagonist. In *Largo*, the postmodern reader plays an active role and reads what is happening at the moment it is being written. With respect to narrative technique, *Setecientas palmeras* is more conventional than its predecessors.

Balza's postmodern fiction consists of the novels *D*, *Percusión*, and *Medianoche en video: 1/5*. He offers the subtitle of *ejercicio narrativo* to the novel *D*, which relates, in a most general sense, a history of the modernization of Venezuela as told through the development of radio and television. But this story evolves primarily through cassette tapes transcribed to form the major portion of the text. The cassette tape is preceded by two texts: the first text is one page of images of a prisoner incarcerated near the sea, and the second text consists of a twenty-page narration of a sixty-year-old retired discjockey, a former celebrity in Venezuela. After this narration, three cassette tapes relate the first half of the novel, and several more cassettes provide the anecdotal material for the second half. Two brief paragraphs appear before the second part, offering a set of images of prisoners escaping. These images at the beginning and end of the novel, the lack of an authorial voice, and the page that ends the novel are the factors that undermine any sense of traditional narrative in *D*. The last page, in fact, provides one of Balza's most significant postmodern turns: here he makes his most blatant metafictional statement, discussing the problems in reducing the narration of a text to one narrator, the problems of a unifying identity of this narrator, and his desire to write history as if it were the history of numerous people rather than of one individual. He also concludes with the Borgesian idea that provides the novel's title: that writing be absorbed by one letter.

Percusión and *Medianoche en video 1/5* are continuations of Balza's postmodern fictional projects that recall the title of González León's *País portátil*. *Percusión* relates the story of the narrator-protagonist's return to his hometown after years of absence, not typical material for a postmodern novel. But the transitory and provisional nature of all the settings and the protagonist's constant sense of metamorphosis, as well as his unstable identity are all factors that relate this novel to many other Latin American postmodernities. In addition, there is a frequent interaction between language and the body that modifies the conventional meanings of both. In the end, the protagonist faces not only exhaustion, but death. The fictional world of *Medianoche en video 1/5* is even more fluid and provisional, relating the stories of several characters as they float down the Orinoco River. Balza reproduces a nonverbal, postmodern world similar to Stanley Kubrick's film *2001*, and Kubrick is also cited in the text.

Postmodern fiction in Venezuela has also been produced by Alejandro Rossi, Francisco Massiani, Humberto Mata, Carlos Noguera, and Angel Gustavo Infante. A philospher by training, Rossi has published several volumes of self-reflective metafictions, often written in the philosophical tone of much of Borges fiction. His stories *El cielo de Sotero* ("The sky of Sotero,"

1987) evoke this tone and self-reflective quality. Massiani has written several entertaining and brief metafictions, beginning with the humorous *Piedra de mar* ("Sea stone," 1968), which deals with an individual's personal crisis and his writing. Mata, Noguera, and Infante, whose initial explorations into postmodern fiction, along with those of Balza, affirm a broad presence of postmodern culture in Venezuelan society.

POSTMODERN FICTION IN ECUADOR

Demetrio Aguilera Malta, Adalberto Ortiz, and Miguel Donoso Pareja were the primary writers responsible for modernizing Ecuadorian fiction, and they did so with superb fiction written during the 1930s and 1940s of which relatively few readers outside of Ecuador have been aware. Nevertheless, Aguilera Malta was a pioneer modernist writer not only in Ecuador, but all of Latin America, publishing the surprisingly modern novel *Don Goyo* in 1933, and thus anticipating most of the Latin American modern writers of "magic realism" by over a decade. The Afro-Ecuadorian Adalberto Ortiz also published an exceptional novel, *Juyungo*, in 1943.

After Aguilera Malta's continued work in the modernist vein with *Siete lunas, siete serpientes* ("Seven moons, serpents," 1970), and then *El secuestro del general* ("The kidnapping of the general," 1973), the central figures for a more experimental postmodern fiction have been Jorge Enrique Adoum, Iván Egüez, and Abdón Ubidia. One of the most radically experimental novels of the Andean region, and certainly one of the most innovative fictions ever published in Ecuador is Adoum's *Entre Marx y una mujer desnuda* ("Between Marx and a nude woman," 1976). A meditation on the novel and the nation of Ecuador, it is an encyclopedic work comparable in some ways to Fuentes's *Terra Nostra*. Both are anthologies of postmodern gestures, motifs, and narrative strategies. The similarities with *Terra Nostra* are not coincidences; Adoum shares with Fuentes direct roots in Joyce, Borges ("Garden of Forking Paths" and "The Library of Babel"), and Cortázar's *Hopscotch*.

Entre Marx y una mujer desnuda begins, in fact, with references to Joyce and *Hopscotch* on the very first page. The subject of the novel's opening pages is a self-reflexive metacommentary on how novels begin. The narrator questions the possibility of storytelling, and explains from the first paragraph that the traditional methods of ordering a story will not be used. Later in the novel, another metacommentary recalls Ihab Hassan's two-column description of the modern and postmodern novel, for it consists of two columns juxtaposing literary concepts such as "literary hermeneutics" versus "literary praxis," "verbal experimentation," versus "the creation of languages," and "the novel as object" versus "the novel as objective."

But perhaps the most telling feature of *Entre Marx y una mujer desnuda* is not the beginning, but the fact that the Prologue begins on page 233 of a 311 page novel. This five-page prologue is written in a standard linear prose and is Adoum's explanation of his generation's background and experience. His generation admired the writers of the "Grupo de Guayaquil" and was politically active. He concludes the prologue by expressing an attitude of exhaustion: this writing is testimony to the failure of Ecuador as a nation, to the failure of this novel, and to Adoum's personal failure.

Entre Marx y una mujer desnuda is an irreverent and fragmented novel full of footnotes (with more metacommentary as well as stories), Zen readings, and pieces from a plethora of texts. Adoum also plays with language, injecting neologisms and other linguistic experiments. No constant plot line is ever developed, and the fragmented anecdotes about the characters' past lovers and political commitment include variations on the plot that the reader has the choice of accepting or rejecting. Like Pacheco and Moreno-Durán, Adoum requires a postmodern reader. With Adoum's sense of exhaustion and sense of everything having been written already, *Entre Marx y una mujer desnuda* is one of the most radical outgrowths of Borges's fiction (particularly "Garden of Forking Paths" and "The Library of Babel") of the Andean region.

Despite the presence of Adoum, Ecuadorean fiction is generally traditionalist and minimally affected by the postmodern. Iván Egüez, who has published several volumes of fiction since the 1970s, has written two novels with postmodern tendencies, *La Linares* ("Ms Linares," 1976) and *Pájara de memoria* ("Stream of memory," 1984). *La Linares* is a satirical and parodic novel set in the Quito of the 1940s and 1950s, and told in a linear fashion. *Pájara de memoria* is a far more complex narrative adventure, and offers the possibility to the reader of beginning the reading on any page of the novel. The last word of the work, in fact, is "nin," which is completed with the first word on the first page "guna," thus producing the word "ninguna" (none), and suggesting that the reading of the novel is continual and circular. The protagonist's ongoing interior monologue in *Pájara de memoria* relates personal and national history from the Colonial period to the twentieth century. Disconnected chronological jumps are created, however, with the text of a diary that appears throughout the novel.

Abdón Ubidia, another of Ecuador's more accomplished contemporary fiction writers, has been relatively uninvolved with postmodern fictional exercises. After *Sueño de lobos* ("Dream of wolves," 1986), which is comparable to the genre of the detective fiction, Ubidia published a set of light entertainments titled *Divertimentos* (1989) with a notable opening piece titled "RM Waagen, Fabricante de Verdades" ("FM Waagen, truth maker"). In this piece, Ubidia satirizes the multinational postmodern truth industries of mass communication, such as radio, television, and the press.

Postmodern fiction represents a small sector of Ecuador's cultural production. Nevertheless, the historiographic metafiction of Adoum, who is one of the strongest postmodern voices of the Andean region, as well as the postmodern contributions of Egüez and Ubidia, make postmodern fiction an increasingly viable form of cultural expression in Ecuador.

POSTMODERN FICTION IN PERÚ

The grandfather of innovative fiction in Perú was an avant-garde poet of the 1920s and 1930s, Martín Adán, whose experimental novel *La casa de cartón* ("The house of cardboard," 1928) was an extraordinary fictional anomaly in its time. Although an inspiration to many young writers, *La casa de cartón* has remained relatively obscure to this day.[11] Peruvian fiction was effectively modernized in the 1950s and 1960s with the contributions of Mario Vargas Llosa, Julio Ramón Ribeyro, Luis Loayza, Sebastián Salazar Bondy, and Gustavo Valcárcel. More recently, Alfredo Bryce Echenique and Gregorio Martínez have produced a substantive body of fundamentally modernist fiction, and Miguel Gutiérrez has authored a massive (three volume) novel with modernist and Faulknerian overtones, *La violencia del tiempo* ("The violence of time," 1991).

Fundamentally a modernist writer who has written under the signs of Faulkner and Gustave Flaubert, Vargas Llosa has, nevertheless, participated in some postmodern practices since the 1970s. His most evidently modernist novels in terms of narrative strategies have been *The Time of the Hero* (1962), *The Green House* (1966) and *Conversation in The Cathedral* (1969). A Peruvian postmodernism came with the later work of Vargas Llosa, some of the later work of Ribeyro, and that of younger writers. Vargas Llosa has been affected by the postmodern in *Captain Pantoja and his Special Service* (1974), *Aunt Julia and the Script Writer* (1977), and in his work after his totalizing work of a more modernist impulse, *The War of the End of the World* (1981).[12] His recent postmodern fiction consists of *Who Killed Palomino Molero?* (1986) and *In Praise of the Stepmother* (1988).

With *Captain Pantoja and his Special Service* and *Aunt Julia and the Script Writer*, the serious and modernist Vargas Llosa turned away from his totalizing projects and discovered some of the playful and humorous possibilities of fiction. The humor in these two novels comes from their situations: *Captain Pantoja and the Special Service* is the author's satire of one of his most consistent targets of criticism, the military; the comic tone of *Aunt Julia and the Script Writer* arises from a variety of sources, but above all from his use of melodramatic soap operas and self-parody. The former tells the story of a military officer—Captain Pantoja—who organizes prostitution for the military in the jungle of Iquitos. The semi-autobiographical *Aunt Julia and the Script Writer* relates the double story of a young Mario marrying his older aunt and the ongoing stories of radio soap operas in 1950s Perú.

These Vargas Llosa fictions are neither radically innovative nor fundamentally postmodern, but they do share notable parallels with certain kinds of postmodern fiction. *Captain Pantoja* contains numerous narrative voices and, thus, like Pacheco's *You Will Die in a Distant Land* and much of the fiction of Puig, lacks an authorial discourse as it parodies a variety of other discourses.[13] These strategies imply the necessity of a postmodern reader. A critic who argues strongly in favor of the postmodernism of all of Vargas Llosa's fiction since 1974, Keith M. Booker, suggests that the explorations of individual psychology in *Captain Pantoja* function not as legitimate epistemological inquiries but as parodies questioning the efficacy of such inquiries in general.[14] Fredric Jameson characterizes *Aunt Julia and the Scriptwriter* as "the very prototype of what we may call the postmodern mode of totalizing."[15] (This light and insignificantly postmodern work serves Jameson's purposes well if it is, indeed, the "prototype" of postmodernism.) Nevertheless, Booker and other critics point out that *Aunt Julia* is one of the most striking examples, for them, of postmodernism: "so many postmodernist writers use the language and images of pop culture as the stuff of literature."[16] In reality, the most significant postmodern aspect of *Aunt Julia* is its metafictional meditation on the creative process and authorship.

In *Who Killed Palomino Molero?* (1986), Vargas Llosa returns to a fictional character from *The Green House*, Sergeant Lituma, who is accompanied by Lieutenant Silva in this parody of a spy thriller. These two characters spend the novel searching for clues to who killed Palomino Molero, a young soldier in love with a young girl named Alicia Mindrau. As they systematically interview people who knew the young couple, Lieutenant Silva dreams of a sexual adventure with a fat woman, *doña* Adriana. In resumé, *Who Killed Palomino Molero?* is a brief and light novel in which the reader slowly formulates an idea of who the author of the crime could be. In the sixth chapter Alicia Mindrau confesses to being the lover of Palomino Molero, and everything seems to point to her father, Colonel Mindrau, as the guilty one. Just as this happens the colonel commits suicide, apparently confirming his guilt. In the last chapter, nevertheless, nothing is resolved because the reader is offered no more legitimate information about Colonel Mandrau, and the local residents continue believing, as they have believed from the beginning, that the criminals are some "peces gordos," that is, some individuals who are never identified and always remain indefinite. The final surprise for the reader has absolutely nothing to do with the assassination, but with the sexual fantasies of Lieutenant Silva, whom *doña* Adriana humiliates and destroys at the end of the novel.

As a postmodern text, *Who Killed Palomino Molero?* is a search for fixed truths and a parodic play not only with the genre of the spy thriller, but also with Vargas Llosa's own work. Vargas Llosa's fiction style is present explicitly and implicitly, throughout this text. In addition, the irrational functions at various levels, but particularly in the attitude of the common people, who insist on returning constantly to the thesis of the "peces gordos," which is never founded nor justified. This rejection of modern reason and insistence on an almost mystical or superstitious belief is common in Latin American postmodern fiction, as has been noted in the Mexican postmodern fiction of Carmen Boullosa. This belief in irrational forces and the "peces gordos" also points to the crisis of authority in postmodern society, a phenomenon that has its parallel manifestation in the lack of authority in the postmodern text.

Vargas Llosa's more recent postmodern gesture is *In Praise of the Stepmother* (1988), a novel dealing with an incestuous relationship between a young boy and his stepmother. Like Moreno-Durán, Vargas Llosa creates certain parallels between sexuality and aesthetics. Booker points out that this novel continues Vargas Llosa's postmodernist interrogation of the boundary between official "high" culture and the "low" culture of popular genres by setting up a direct confrontation between "high" art and pornography. This art includes the work of classical painters in the text, such as that of Renaissance painters Titian and Fra Angelica, the later François Bouder, and the contemporaries Francis Bacon and Fernando de Szyszlo. *In Praise of the Stepmother* also breaks down conventional boundaries between literature and painting.

Julio Ramón Ribeyro, born in 1929, belongs to the generation of writers of the Boom and has published a set of novels and short fiction that are, like most of the work of that generation, modernist in impulse. Like them, he began writing in the 1950s with a pen in one hand, texts of Faulkner and Borges in the other. His novels *Crónica de San Gabriel* ("Chronicle of San Gabriel," 1960), *Los geniecillos dominicales* ("The Sunday hotshot," 1965) and *Cambio de guardia* ("Change of guard," 1975) were of the modernist mode. Somewhat of a traditionalist among those practicing modernist fiction, Ribeyro, nevertheless, has been affected by the postmodern in some of his recent short fiction. He has written some light and amusing "entertainments" that intersect with some postmodern modes, such as the story "Sólo para fumadores," with humorous and autobiographical overtones. In this story, the narrator-protagonist tells of his lengthy and intimate relationship with cigarettes, beginning with the first cigarette he smoked as an adolescent and ending with his useless efforts as an adult to quit smoking. He relates selling his books, as a student, to finance his vice, as well as other dramatic moments in his smoking career. Ribeyro's postmodern moments are those dedicated to digressions and to his characters' search for the destinies that they themselves invent. The empty play of "Sólo para fumadores" also associates Ribeyro with the postmodern. His fictional world tends to be one in which the only truth is the fragile truth of the elusive subject. In addition, he tends to use language itself to confirm his world.

Over the past three decades, Perú has not been a center of postmodern fiction in the Americas, although the later work of Vargas Llosa and Ribeyro exhibits some confluences with postmodern culture. Relatively talented but conventional younger writers, such as Alonso Cueto, Melvin Ledgard, and Daniel Rodríguez Risco relate stories depicting Perú's unstable postmodern condition of the 1980s and 1990s.

POSTMODERN FICTION IN BOLIVIA

Bolivian fiction remained a fundamentally traditional genre well into the 1950s and 1960s and has been, in this sense, a Latin American anomaly. The Bolivian innovators have been Renato Prada Oropeza and José W. Montes. Prada Oropeza has published several novels, and Montes was awarded the Casa de las Américas novel prize for *Jonah and the Pink Whale* in 1987. In the early 1970s Arturo Von Vacano published several novels, and more recently Ernesto Contreras Jiménez and Gonzalo Lema Vargas have won novel prizes in Bolivia.

Renato Prada Oropeza is a professor of literature in Xalapa, Mexico, and is known in Mexico primarily as a literary critic and theorist of literature. In addition to numerous publications of literary criticism and theory, Prada Oropeza has published the novels *Los fundadores del alba* ("The founders of the dawn," 1969), *Larga hora: la vigilia* ("Long hour: the vigil," 1979), *El último filo* ("The last line," 1979), *La ofrenda* ("The offering," 1981), *Mientras cae la noche* ("While the night falls," 1988), and *Poco después humo* ("A little after the smoke," 1989). Prada Oropeza's early work followed modernist schemes and dealt with moral problems in their social contexts in Bolivia. *Los fundadores del alba* is set in Bolivia during the end of Che Guevara's life as a guerrilla there. *Larga hora: la vigilia* portrays an individual who questions his role in a military government in Bolivia. *El último filo* begins with the informal *tú* and a tone reminiscent of Fuentes's *The Death of Artemio Cruz*, and tells the story of a man caught in the network of absolute power. In this, as in all of Prada Oropeza's early fiction, the protagonist faces the need for political commitment.

Mientras cae la noche is a historiographic metafiction with several other characteristics of postmodern fiction, and shows some affiliation with Cortázar's *Hopscotch*, beginning with a protagonist who is an intellectual named Horacio. More important, it offers alternative versions of the plot in the form of occasional footnotes that relate what else happened or what might have happened. These footnotes also consist of brief reflections on the novel, making *Mientras cae la noche* similar to Pacheco's *You Will Die in a Distant Land*, although Prada Oropeza does not demand the same level of reader participation as Pacheco. Throughout the novel, which recounts a coup d'etat in Bolivia in an atmosphere of political repression and random violence, Horacio writes a novel that develops along parallel lines with *Mientras cae la noche*, thus adding yet another level to the metafictional quality of the novel. Prada Oropeza's language itself is generally traditional, although he does include some ambiguous experiments with the narrator as a person. The novel's surprising denouement underlines a sense of impotence and exhaustion, evoking at the same time Roland Barthes's famous declaration of the death of the author, proclaiming the priority of texts over authors.

Bolivia, like Perú, is not central to the production of postmodern fiction in the Americas or even the Andean region. Most of the fiction published in Bolivia is commercial and very conventional. Besides the experimental metafictions of Prada Oropeza, the humorous and imaginative fiction of José Montes also demonstrates some postmodern tendencies.

The Andean postmodern writers are, for the most part, participants in a new international order who have tended to publish most of their work abroad first, and then in their native country. Their masters have been Cervantes, Joyce, Borges, and Cortázar, but now they like to associate their writing with the fiction of William Gass, Robert Coover, and other international postmodern writers. Their total work is often narcissistic, and the most intense narcissists of the Andean region are Moreno-Durán, Balza, and Adoum, writers whose essays and fiction, seen in their totality, are voluminous and international in vision, but still essentially narcissistic exercises.

Among the younger novelists, the Andean region has a new generation of writers who participate in international postmodernism. Moreno-Durán, Jaramillo Agudelo, and Balza, for example, consider themselves international writers first and citizens of their particular homelands second. They read First World postmodern fiction, theory, film, and they tend to publish in international venues, mostly in Spain, Mexico, and Colombia. The generation of even younger writers, such as Hugo Chaparro Valderrama and Orietta Lozano in Colombia, Humberto Mata and Angel Gustavo Infante in Venezuela, and Iván Egüez in Ecuador, are equally oriented toward the artifacts of First World postmodernism.

Despite arising as a new cultural phenomenon in the Andean region, cocaine, the drug industry, and their repercussions have relatively little to do with Andean fiction itself, although this condition is described by writers such as Andrés Caicedo and Orietta Lozano. As an art of digression and the indeterminate, perhaps postmodern fiction is not the appropriate cultural expression to deal with such a complex, immediate, and massive phenomenon as the drug industry.

In the Andean region, perhaps more than any other, the postmodern novel is an expression of an exhausted truth. Moreno-Durán subverts the etymologists who seek truth in linguistic origins; one of the characters claims at the end of *Mientras cae la noche* that novels never tell the truth; the exhaustion is generalized in Lozano's *Luminar*. In addition, no viable character in the postmodern fiction of Moreno-Durán, Balza, Adoum, or Vargas Llosa can be a convincing voice of any truth. Rather, an attitude of exhaustion pervades the respective novelistic worlds of these characters, and a writer such as Ubidia in Ecuador satirizes the truth industry itself in his story titled "RM Waagen, Truth Maker" about the "truth maker."

For Hans-Georg Gadamer, tradition grows out of the sense of historicity and the concept of horizon. At the same time, the renewed fusion of ever-changing horizons is crucial to the understanding of ourselves—as interpreters and as part of a tradition. In the Andean region, perhaps more than others, writers share a sense of tradition as described by Gadamer; a strong sense of tradition and of historicity has resulted in less radically experimental fiction than some regions, and a strong thread of historical fiction.[17] The Andean region, in fact, is generally one of the least experimental with fiction when compared to the postmodernities of Mexico, the Southern Cone, and the Caribbean region.

On the other hand, Andean writers have written much historiographic metafiction. Adoum, Balza, and Prada Oropeza, among other Andean writers who are essentially narcissistic, are not blinded historically by their fascination with the act of creating fiction. In this sense, the Andean postmodern writers do not break from their traditional and modernist predecessors, who have often been fundamentally historical in vision.

Several writers of the Andean region, like the Fuentes of *Terra Nostra* have been the central contributors of modern fiction in the region, and then, in the latter stages of their careers, have been afflicted by the postmodern. Such is the case of Vargas Llosa, Ribeyro, and Garmendia, all writers whose careers have been primarily a response to the modern impulse.

The most significant postmodern writing of the Andean region is not the light, later work of Vargas Llosa and Ribeyro (as Jameson would like us to believe, attempting to convince us with his own "strategies of containment"), but the cultural and political resistence implied in the postmodern fiction of Moreno-Durán, Angel, Caicedo, Lozano, Balza, Adoum, Egüez, and Prada Oropeza. The postmodern reader of Andean fiction discovers that postmodern fiction in this region is frequently as political as most of the other Latin American postmodernities of the 1980s and 1990s.

4

Postmodernities in the Southern Cone

Cultural critics in Chile, Argentina, and Uruguay often make references to their respective nation's status on the "periphery" of the West and even on the periphery of postmodernism. Nevertheless, these Southern Cone nations have each produced notable postmodern artifacts from their respective cultures and literatures, with the similarities and differences to be expected. All three nations lived through repressive military dictatorships in the 1970s or 1980s, and this experience has left a special mark on this region's postmodern condition. Many of their intellectuals worked as underground resisters or were in exile, and the cultures of the Southern Cone region, which were already the most European in the Americas, have been intensely internationalized in the past three decades, even more so than some other regions. Participating in the free-market economies promoted by Ronald Reagan and some economists located in Latin America, two of these nations (Argentina and Uruguay) now cooperate economically in Mercosur.

Some of the most accomplished Latin American modernist writers since the 1930s have written from the Southern Cone region, including the Argentines Jorge Luis Borges, Macedonio Fernández, Adolfo Bioy Casares, Leopoldo Marechal, David Viñas, and Julio Cortázar; the Uruguayans Mario Benedetti, Juan Carlos Onetti, and Carlos Martínez Moreno; and the Chileans María Luisa Bombal and José Donoso.

The Southern Cone region has also become one of the most intensely productive of a postmodern fiction, perhaps because of the conjunction of a strong, modernist European tradition and the rise of repressive military dictatorships. In any case, postmodern writers such as Ricardo Piglia, Diamela Eltit, Sylvia Molloy, Alejandra Pizarnik, Héctor Libertella, and Armonía Sommers make this "periphery," paradoxically, a vital center of postmodern fictional creation.

The turning point for postmodern Chile was September of 1973 when the military, headed by General Augusto Pinochet, overthrew the Unidad Popular government of Salvador Allende, thus terminating abruptly and violently the utopian project of the Chilean Left. As the Chilean intellectual Bernardo Subercaseaux has pointed out, the realities learned in Chile during the 1970s and 1980s were not found in the writings of Jean-François Lyotard or in the images of Andy Warhol, but in the realities of military violence and repression.[1] According to Subercaseaux, this violence created a new sensitivity, an exhaustion from the grieving process over the 1973 debacle and a loss of interest in politics as a method for forging one's destiny. Since the 1970s, the Chileans have also experienced rapid technological modernization and the omnipresence of mass culture. This political repression, exhaustion, and modernization have all been part of the Chilean legacy since 1973, and have resulted in a national crisis of truth.

The postmodern cultural scene in Chile is as heterogeneous as one would expect in a society that is both very European and very Latin American. Besides its fiction writers, the Chilean postmodern has its exponents in poetry (Juan Luis Martínez and Diego Maquieira), in theater (Jaime Vadell, Ramón Griffero and Marco Antonio de la Parra), and in other artistic expressions. A group of architects with the magazine *ARS*, including Humberto Eliash, Christian Boza, and Manuel A. Moreno, have carried out an ongoing critique of modern architecture. In 1988, a group of Chileans won the Gran Premio de Gráfica Utilitaria for a project called *Esa ciudad imaginaria*, defined by its authors as "an experience of postmodern and neo-conceptual language."[2] In the 1980s, young Chilean rock groups, such as Fulano, Los huasos caóticos, Los Ka-Ka, Los Prisioneros, and The Pinochet Boys sang rock in Spanish that combined a postmodern aesthetic of both counterculture and oppositional politics.

The cultural critic Nelly Richard has been the exponent and critic of postmodern art and literature in Chile during the 1980s and 1990s. In addition to editing the journal of postmodern dialogue *Revista de Crítica Cultural*, she has been the critical voice behind what she calls the "Escena de la Avanzada," the scene of avant-garde and oppositional visual arts, headed by Dittborn, Lepe and Díaz. They are a group of artists whose non-representational, postmodern art functions in opposition to establishment art, much of which played off either the patriotic mission of the dictatorial regime or foreign tastes for the magic or exotic Latin American. The *Revista de Crítica Cultural* has been an important organ for the theoretization of a *cultura alternativa* in Chile. It has published interviews with Jacques Derrida and Felix Guattari, for example, as well as articles on the postmodernity of Cuba, the democratization of Latin America in the context of postmodern culture, and Jean Baudrillard's theory of simulation. This seminal journal has also published the essays of cultural critics such as the Argentines Beatriz Sarlo and Nicolás Casullo, the North Americans Fredric Jameson and John Beverly, and the Chileans Diamela Eltit and Adriana Valdés.

The most important cultural fact in Argentina was the series of repressive military dictatorships that ruled that nation almost continuously from 1966 to 1983 (with the exception of the Juan Perón government from 1973-1976), and even more significant was the "dirty war" from 1976 to 1979, orchestrated under the banner of the "Process of National Reorganization." These authoritarian regimes mounted a program of institutionalized violence; the most intense period was from 1976 to 1979. It was a repression that made it impossible to affirm truth publicly within Argentina and created a crisis of authority and truth equivalent to 1968 Mexico and 1973 Chile. These dictatorships gave rise to an entire literature in exile and very special and particular literary responses among those who remained in Argentina, writing under censorship and often with the threat of violence and death for their publications. Julio Cortázar, Manuel Puig, David Viñas, Luisa Valenzuela, Griselda Gambaro, Oswaldo Soriano, and Mempo Giardinelli are just a few of the novelists who wrote in exile. On the other hand, Ricardo Piglia, Luis Gusmán, Enrique Medina, and Alejandra Pizarnik were among the most prominent writers to publish a literature of resistance—a *literatura contestataria*—within Argentina during the dictatorships, much of which was written under the sign of the postmodern.

The culture of opposition during the authoritarian regimes became a precarious form of opposition that was often marginal and forgotten. In a climate of censorship, the dictatorships also produced autocensorship in which writers censored themselves to avoid retaliation. They banned Enrique Medina's novel *El Duke* in January of 1977, just eight months after the military coup.

Argentina returned to democracy in 1983, and since then the process of "redemocratization" has brought many of the artifacts of postmodern culture to the forefront. The Argentine postmodern is centered in Buenos Aires, and is well attuned to cultural changes in Paris and New York. In probably no other nation has Lyotard's *La condición posmoderna* been a best seller, as it was in July of 1991 in Argentina. The postmodern culture of Argentina (and critique thereof) is to be found in magazines such as *Punto de Vista* and in bookstores such as the Librería Clásica y Moderna, which is only one of several to carry translations of Lyotard, Baudrillard, Gilles Deleuze, and the other principal theorists of the postmodern and poststructuralist theory.

"Argentina is not a nation, but a style and a language," Argentine writer Osvaldo Lamborghini wrote from Barcelona to an Argentine writer.[3] This postmodern attitude toward Argentina is more fully analyzed by Beatriz Sarlo in a book titled *Escenas de la vida posmoderna*. Using her own observations, as well as the work of Walter Benjamin, Fredric Jameson, Jean Baudrillard, Gianni Vattimo, Nelly Richard, Matei Calinescu, George Yúdice, and a host of others, Sarlo analyzes Argentina's postmodern condition. She comments on a society living with extreme abundance and in extreme poverty simultaneously, as well as a society of First World "zapping," of the operations of mass media, of television, of popular culture, of mass markets for popular culture, and of video culture in general. She also described a situation in which the intellectuals, who used to have a public presence in Argentina, are now the specialists and experts hidden in academia, as they are in the United States. She calls for a cultural criticism for which she provides a model in this narrative (rather than strictly "essayistic"), personal account of the postmodern scene in her native land.

The crisis of authority and legitimacy in Uruguay began in the 1960s and was placed before the nation's eyes when the Tupamaros guerrillas captured the city of Pando in 1969. In the late 1960s and early 1970s, the Tupamaros carried out a series of bold actions, openly challenging the power structure of the "Switzerland of Latin America." Their assassination of the American businessman Mitrione in 1970 polarized Uruguayan society. By 1973, a military regime terrorized the Tupamaros and much of the remainder of the population until 1985. During this dictatorship, the regime jailed Juan Carlos Onetti, eliminated many of its democratic institutions, and punished several writers, such as Hiber Conteris and Nelson Marra.

Modern Uruguay promoted its traditional national identity as the "Switzerland of Latin America," but its postmodern identity on the periphery of the Americas is as the exporter of software. Postmodern culture in postdictatorial Urugay is located in Montevideo; from there, cultural critic Hugo Achúgar and others have reflected on the postmodern condition of Uruguay, the Southern Cone nations, and Latin America in general in the 1980s and 1990s.[4] Citing Richard Rorty, however, Achúgar maintains that defining the place from which one speaks is not just a geo-cultural observation, but a determining of the subject and the mode of enunciation.[5] His postmodern reflections from the periphery reflect readings of Teresa de Lauretis, Nelly Richard, Jean Franco, Gayatri Spivak, Beatriz Sarlo, George Yúdice, Linda Hutcheon, Edward Said, Sylvia Molloy, and numerous others.

Uruguay has promoted modernist and postmodern writing throughout the Americas with the publication of the weekly journal *Marcha* since 1939. Dealing with a large range of social, political, and cultural issues, the literature section of *Marcha* has been directed by novelist Juan Carlos Onetti and critics Emir Rodríguez Monegal, Angel Rama, and Jorge Ruffinelli. *Marcha* promoted the writers of the Boom quite well, and until its recent demise had continued to do so with writers of the generations that have followed. Now Uruguay has no equivalent to the journals that theorize postmodern culture in Chile and Argentina, such as the *Revista de Crítica Cultural* and *Punto de Vista*. Rather, the more popular magazine *Graffiti*, published in Montevideo, provides general information about the Uruguayan cultural scene, from rock music to new books.

CHILEAN POSTMODERN FICTION

The first narrative attempts at a modern writing in Chile were the novelized experiments of the poets Pablo Neruda and Vicente Huidobro in the 1920s and 1930s. Neruda published his novel *El habitante y su esperanza* ("The inhabitant and his hope") in 1928 and Huidobro published several playful and modern experimental fictions, including *Cagliostro* ("Cagliostro," 1934) and *Mío Cid Campeador* ("Cid the champion," 1929). Chile's contemporary postmodern writers also identify with the avant-garde fiction of Juan Emar. As was the case throughout Latin America, these modern fictions remained relatively ignored by the predominant culture. The modern novel was not recognized as a viable literary expression until the 1950s and 1960s, with the rise of José Donoso, Jorge Edwards, Carlos Droguett, and Enrique Lafourcade and the publication of novels such as Donoso's *Coronación* ("Coronation," 1957), Lafourcade's *Para subir al cielo* ("To go to heaven," 1958), Edward's *El peso de la noche* ("The weight of the night," 1965), and Droguett's *Patas de perro* ("Dog's paws," 1965). Later, Isabel Allende became Chile's first mass-marketed modern writer, beginning with her initial imitations of Gabriel García Márquez's magic realism in *The House of the Spirits* (1981).

The first clear register of an imminent Chilean postmodern fiction appeared in 1968, the same year as in Argentina and much of Latin America. In the Chilean case, this narrative innovation was an experimental and relatively obscure novel titled *Job-Boj*, published in 1968 by Jorge Guzmán. This invitation to experiment with the postmodern, accompanied by the theory revolution, an international postmodern fiction, and Pinochet's repressive regime (among other factors), led to the publication of the radical fictions of Mauricio Wacquez and Enrique Lihn. Guzmán's *Job-Boj*, the early José Donoso of *The Obscene Bird of the Night* (1970), and the radical fictions of Mauricio Wacquez and Enrique Lihn represent the first wave of Chilean postmodern, followed by a second wave consisting of Diamela Eltit, Alberto

Fuguet, Antonio Ostornol, Ariel Dorfman, and the Donoso of *The Garden Next Door* (1981) and *Taratuta/Still Water with Pipe* (1990).

Guzmán tantalizes the reader with the structure of *Job-Boj*, a novel with two story lines (in two different countries), which appear in alternating chapters, with no ultimate explanation of the relationship between the two plots. The reader is tempted to speculate that they represent two periods in the life of one person, except that one character is always anxious and introverted, and the other is generally content and extroverted. As one critic has pointed out, the question is whether they are two different men, two facets of a single personality, or two periods in the life of one man.[6] Given the indeterminate character of things, the reader necessarily assumes the kind of active role that Cortázar's Morelli had suggested in *Hopscotch*.

With *The Obscene Bird of the Night*, one of the most complex novels ever published by a Chilean writer, Donoso made a far more visible statement for a Chilean postmodern than had been the case with Guzmán's relatively ignored *Job-Boj*. A book that demands multiple readings, *The Obscene Bird of the Night* is fundamentally unstructured and self-contradictory, never leading to the ultimate unity or harmony that is the outcome of most modernist texts. Like Carlos Fuentes's *Terra Nostra* and Jorge Enrique Adoum's *Entre Marx y una mujer desnuda*, it is an anthology of postmodern devices and motifs. The transformation of the main narrator, as well as the unified identity of other characters, also point to a postmodern idea of the unfixed identity. If the experimental use of space is particular to the postmodern, as David Harvey suggests, *The Obscene Bird of the Night* is one of the Latin American postmodern novels par excellence.

Internationally recognized as a poet, Enrique Lihn wrote radically experimental novels that went generally unnoticed outside of Chile, with the exception of postmodern writers of equally hermetic tendencies, such as the Argentine Héctor Libertella. Writing on Lihn's two novelistic type books, *La orquesta de cristal* ("The cristal orchestra," 1976) and *El arte de la palabra* ("The art of the word," 1980), Libertella proposes that Lihn's work with literary discourse is an attempt to critique the excessive rhetoric of the "dead" Spanish language by distancing his own discourse from it. Lihn finds he needs to write in hermetic codes to avoid the literal reproduction of the dominant discourses that become the object of parody and pastiche in his writing. Lihn thus identifies with the hermetic as a political strategy. The multiple footnotes of *La orquesta de cristal* and the metadiscourse of *El arte de la palabra* make language the main subject of these two novels. Mauricio Wacquez shows a similar fascination with language itself, and demands the active participation of the postmodern reader in his experimental fictions *Excesos* ("Excesses," 1971) and

Paréntesis ("Parenthesis," 1975). He also questions the idea of a referent or a connection to an identifiable empirical reality.

After these early experimentations of Donoso, Lihn, and Wacquez, the second wave of Chilean postmodern writers consisted of Diamela Eltit, the later Donoso, Alberto Fuguet, and Antonio Ostornol. Eltit's postmodern project consists of the four novels *Lumpérica* ("Lumperica," 1983), *Por la patria* ("For the country," 1986), *El cuarto mundo* ("The fourth world," 1988) and *Vaca sagrada* ("Sacred cow," 1991). Julio Ortega has described this work as part of "an ample re-appropriation of the discourse of the figurative that various Latin American women writers have proposed."[7] As her first three books were written under Pinochet's dictatorship, Eltit joined other young novelists in the creation of a writing of resistance. Along with the work of Piglia and Fuentes's *Terra Nostra*, her total writing represents one of the most ambitious, challenging, and profound searches of historical origins recently published in Latin America. *Lumpérica* takes place in a public plaza in Santiago de Chile, a plaza that Ortega considers a metaphor for the absent community.[8] This novel, which has no real plot, presents a protagonist named L. Iluminada. The characters' relationship to the physical space of the plaza and to language are a substitute for action. In one rainy scene on the plaza, the narrator states "No hay acciones posibles más que su propia lengua que aún, en lo propicio del ambiente, no surge" [There are no possible actions but one's own language that, with respect to the atmopshere, doesn't arise].[9] In addition to being a setting for a novel that never takes place, it is a setting for a film, for there is a constant presence of a camera that films this self-conscious fiction/film. It is a self-conscious fiction/film because the characters and situations are often discussed in the text as fictions. For example, the narrator states "Este lumperío escribe y borra lo imaginario, se reparte las palabras, los fragmentos de letras, borran sus supuestos errores, ensayan sus caligrafías, endilgan el pulso, acceden a la imprenta" [This lumpen writes and erases the imaginary, distributes the words, the fragments of letters, erases supposed errors, tries calligraphies, take the pulse, accedes to the letter].[10] More specifically, characters and situations in *Lumpérica* frequently appear as social constructs under the constant analysis of the narrator, or L. Iluminada. Each of the novel's ten chapters takes a radically different narrative strategy, with different types of language, organization, and even typography. The experimentation becomes progressively more intense as the novel develops, and chapters near the end of the novel become so experimental that their main subject is language itself. A minimal sense of coherence is created by the fact that the last chapter returns to the situation of the first, with L. Iluminada alone in the plaza, absorbed in contemplation.

The public plaza of Santiago de Chile in *Lumpérica* is a postmodern world of Baudrillard, where human beings have the same exchange value as merchandise, "como productos comerciales" [as commercial products] and "como mercancías de valor incierto" [as merchandise of uncertain value].[11] As the scenes in the novel are filmed and discussed, these discussions recall Baudrillard's admonition that "there is no longer any medium in the literal sense: it is now intangible, diffuse and diffracted in the real, and it can no longer even be said that the latter is distorted by it."[12] Hutcheon has pointed out that the different and the paradoxical fascinate the postmodern, and *Lumpérica* is populated by the urban lumpen of the public plaza who are identified as "lumpen" "los pálidos" [the pale ones] (most frequently), and occasionally as "desarropados" [the unclothed].

Lumpérica is a novel of *precarias verdades*—unstable, unsure, provisional truths. Even the anecdotes that are told in the novel are contingent and provisional for, as the narrator states, "ah, por una mirada, por un gesto, yo habría contado otra historia" [oh, with another look, another gesture, I would have told another story].[13] Similarly, the narrator describes the text as a revisable fiction: "la plaza será lo único no ficticio en este invento" [the plaza will be the only non-fiction of this invention].[14] Truth becomes the object of manipulation in the seventh chapter, which consists of an unidentified "interrogador" questioning an unidentified "interrogado" about a seemingly insignificant event that takes place on the public plaza when L. Iluminada apparently falls and the "interrogado" comes to her aid briefly. The "interrogador" repeatedly questions the "interrogado" about this until the latter finally changes his story, a replica of an interview of political prisoners under dictatorships such as Pinochet's.

Lumpérica is the first of Eltit's texts on the body. Sara Castro-Klarén has pointed out that this novel writes and explores the body under conditions of extreme pain.[15] L. Iluminada is the sum of a body that finds itself on the limits of death. Reduced to a minimal concept of "character," L. Iluminada is a fragment of a name with minimal contextual information. Given no past and no motives, the postmodern reader is forced to construct a story written in the margins of the female body.

A neo-epic novel, *Por la patria* is one of the most radical experiments of any of the postmodernities published in Latin America in recent decades. Ortega emphasizes that in this novel "the communitarian is the feminine subjective space of the subversive."[16] Eltit relates a story of contemporary Chile, alluding to the political repression of the Pinochet regime, but always returning to the historical origins of language, repression, and resistance. In this way, returning to medieval epic wars, she inevitably associates these historical conflicts with the contemporary situation. Consequently, Eltit's postmodern is patently historical and political. By exploring the origins of the "mother language" and incorporating numerous historical and colloquial languages into *Por la patria*, Eltit is concerned with the relationship originally explored by Michel Foucault between language and power and is the subject of much of Piglia's writing.

Eltit also explores the concept of linguistic incest in *Por la patria*. This problem relates to the fact that postmodern fiction poses new questions about reference. As Hutcheon points out, the issue is no longer "to what empirically real object in the past does the language of history refer?"; it is more "to which discursive context could this language belong? To which prior textualization must we refer?"[17] *Lumpérica* and *Por la patria* reveal a sense for origins in the Latin language, the "mother" language of the later Romance language family, a family present in both novels. The discursive contexts change in the different fragments of *Lumpérica*, evoking a connection with the past heritage in Latin and resonances of medieval Spanish and Italian. These historical languages coexist, in an unresolved contradiction, with a modern masculine discourse subverted by other contemporary discourses—colloquial Chilean Spanish and feminine discourse. The juxtaposition of these languages could be seen as the linguistic incest in the linguistic family inhabiting this novel as well as a questioning of the possibility of writing in the "mother tongue."

In *El cuarto mundo* the family is the private room that becomes foreign in the symbolic world of the body.[18] This novel deals with family relationships and is related by two narrators: the first half of the work is narrated by a young boy, María Chipia, the son of the family, and the second half is told by his twin sister. Both sections deal with the relations among the five members of the family: the twins, a young sister (María de Alava), and the two parents. The first part of the novel ends with a family crisis centered on the mother's adultery. In the second part, the family tensions center on the incestuous relationship between María Chipia and his twin sister. She becomes pregnant and continues her relationship with him as the crisis continues growing until near the end of the novel. Only in the last line is the pregnant twin sister identified by name: diamela eltit [*sic*].

El cuarto mundo is not a work of the broad historical truths elaborated in García Márquez's *One Hundred Years of Solitude* or Fuentes's *The Death of Artemio Cruz*. *El cuarto mundo*, however, is about other kinds of truths—the truths of private and public space, the truths of relationships, the truths of the body, and a questioning of the possibilities language holds for articulating truths. They are the relative truths of Baudrillard's postmodern. María Chipia begins the novel narrating as a fetus, and much of his narration consists of his attempt to understand the relationship between his own body, his mother's, and his sister's.

Consequently, it is a story of subtle spaces and of constantly changing personal distances. As a child in the cradle, he states that "Las miradas que nos acechaban a todas horas me llevaron a despreciar el espacio público" [looks that threatened us at all hours made me dislike public space].[19] As a one-year old, María Chipia sees a world of chaos around him and thinks that language will provide order: "Ingenuamente pensaba que el habla era un hecho misterioso y trascendente capaz de ordenar el caos que me atravesaba" [I innocently thought that speech was a mysterious and transcendent fact capable of ordering the chaos that shot through me].[20] The use of the word *ingenuamente* (innocently) suggests what will be evident later in the text: language will be the least viable vehicle for communicating orders and truths. By the time he is three, for example, María Chipia realizes that the idea of any transcendent meaning of language was a fantasy. Rather, his truths are found and then discarded within the different spaces in which he operates. For example, as a young adolescent he lives the desire for the space of a masculine paradise outside the home dominated by his mother, but he eventually realizes that such a space is yet another truth impossible for him to attain. Once he begins the incestuous relationship with his sister, he faces the novel's most complex truth: that he is a *sudaca*, a derogatory term for Latin American used by Spaniards. María Chipia constantly repeats "yo soy sudaca, soy un digno sudaca" [I am a *sudaca*, I am a dignified *sudaca*].[21] In the end, the most notable truths in *El cuarto mundo* are *verdades sudacas*, "sudaca truths," degraded truths. The narrator, "diamela eltit," observes her mother and her sister near the end of the novel and describes a postmodern condition of a "degradada humanidad sudaca" [degraded *sudaca* humanity].[22] As she nears birth and crisis at the end of the novel, she also describes her mother and sister as *perras sudacas—sudaca* dogs.

To speak of universal truth claims is clearly inappropriate with respect to the postmodern project of Diamela Eltit. The situation concerning truth reaches a conclusion on the last page. First, we note at the end that there is no authorial detachment-no pretension of knowing truth. To the contrary, the narrator identifies herself as "diamela eltit" with a "minúscula sudaca" [*sudaca* in small letters]. On this final page, it is evident also that the entire situation consists of degradation, commercialization, reification. The novel's last sentence states "La niña sudaca irá a la venta" [the *sudaca* girl will go up for sale].[23] The newly born child going up for sale belongs to the postmodern society of Jameson's late capitalism and Baudrillard's postmodern, one in which abstract qualities—such as goodness and knowledge—enter into the realm of exchange value. And we can include truth in these abstract values, which becomes degraded and meaningless in this *sudaca* world, as does language.

The "fourth world" of the novel's title can be postulated as a space consisting of a periphery of a periphery, for example, marginal space on the periphery of an already peripheral Third World nation. Written under the Pinochet regime, Eltit's work offers an allegorical level of reading. The four novels that make up Eltit's postmodern project can be approached by the postmodern reader as allegories of resistance. *Vaca sagrada*, like *Lumpérica* and *El cuatro mundo*, is a transgressive text written in the margins and on the body in an unstable space that frequently evokes the unspeakable.

Eltit has spoken about the "scene of power" as well as the ideology of the body in extratextual interviews and in her books of fiction. Her response to these "scenes of power" is a transgressive and irreverent fiction of cultural resistance. As Guillermo García Corales has observed, Eltit offers no solutions to power relations in Chile or elsewhere.[24] Rather, she forces the often uncomfortable postmodern reader of her texts to question the cultural and political constructs that legitimate power. Her writing on the female body is one of her several mechanisms for questioning authoritative discourses.

After Eltit, the young practitioners of Chilean postmodern are Antonio Ostornol (born in 1954) and Alberto Fuguet (born in 1964). In his third novel, *Los años de la serpiente* ("The years of the serpent," 1991), Ostornol challenges the postmodern reader with a variety of languages and texts that only vaguely constitute something like a "novel." Fuguet's *Mala onda* ("Bad wave," 1991) is a fictionalized testimonial of postmodern Chile under Pinochet's regime, written in the hip, young language of Chile's alienated youth of the dictatorship.

ARGENTINE POSTMODERN FICTION

Twentieth-century Argentina has always been at the avant garde of literary innovation, and Argentine writers have been a major influence on the modernization of literature and literary tastes since the 1920s. Two competing literary groups of the 1920s brought new literary and aesthetic ideas into the realm of Argentine and Latin American writing during this period. Borges and the poet Olivero Girondo headed an avant-garde aesthetic revolution of the literary group called Florida, which promoted the use of unusual metaphors and believed that a new expressive language could transform society. The Boedo group was aligned with a more overtly social and political literature and included the writers Elías Castelnuovo, Leónidas Barletta, Alvaro Yunque, Roberto Mariani, and Max Dickmann. The fiction writer and playwright Roberto Arlt, who later became a hero figure for Cortázar and

Piglia, associated himself with both Florida and Boedo. In the 1930s and 1940s, the magazine *Sur*, directed by Victoria Ocampo, also contributed to the modernization of Argentine literature; it published translations of numerous modern writers from Europe and the United States.

The rise of modernist fiction in Argentina was signaled by the publication of the short stories of Borges in the 1940s, and his friends and collaborators Adolfo Bioy Casares and Macedonio Fernández played quite important roles. Bioy Casares's *The Invention of Morel* (1940) is an imaginative type of science fiction in which a condemned man invents a machine that mechanically reproduces people. Macedonio Fernández wrote from the 1920s to the 1940s, but became a hero figure (similar to Arlt, in this sense) for the young intellectuals of the 1960s, such as Ricardo Piglia. Fernández died in 1952, and many of his poems and short stories were republished in the 1960s, along with his novel *Museo de la Eterna* ("Museum of the eternal one") which was published posthumously in 1967. Fernández's fiction was wildly experimental, beginning with *Papeles de recienvenido* ("Papers of a recent arrival," 1929), a fifty-page set of observations and philosophical musings of a narrator-protagonist who has recently arrived in Buenos Aires.

Leopoldo Marechal, David Viñas, Ernesto Sábato, Manuel Mújica Láinez, and Julio Cortázar were the most prominent of later contributors to modernist fiction in Argentina. Marechal's *Adán Buenosayres* (1948), Viñas's *Cayó sobre su rostro* ("He fell on his face," 1955), Sábato's *Sobre héroes y tumbas* ("On heroes and tombs," 1962), several novels of Mújica Láinez, and Cortázar's *Hopscotch* were all significant works in the rise of the modern novel in Argentina, and most of these writers published an entire body of modernist fiction. Since these writers, later generations of essentially modernist writers have continued the modernist tradition in Argentina, including novelists such as Abel Posse, Juan José Saer, César Aira, and Mempo Giardinelli. Posse and Giardinelli have been awarded Latin America's prestigious Rómulo Gallegos Novel Prize for impressive works of a fundamentally modernist impulse, *Los perros del paraíso* ("the dogs of paradise," 1987) and *Santo Oficio de memoria* ("Sacred office of memory," 1991), respectively.

Latin American postmodern fiction was born in Argentina; the Latin American postmodern writers of the 1970s and 1980s are the grandchildren of Borges (and their father figures were the writers of the Boom). In Borges's *Ficciones* (also titled *Ficciones* in English) originally published in 1941, are the self-conscious metafiction, indeterminacy, and unresolved contradiction, as well as other elements that became so important for the Latin American postmodern decades later. Fiction such as Borges's "The Library of Babel" and "Pierre Menard, Author of the Quijote"—short stories that were really more meditations on literature than a story with a plot—has been the model for many postmodern writers in Argentina, particularly Piglia and Libertella. After *Ficciones*, the key moment for the Argentine postmodern was the 1963 publication of Julio Cortázar's *Hopscotch*, a novel that was a late modernist experiment, but a novel that opened the doors to many subsequent postmodern exercises. The radical innovations proposed by Morelli in *Hopscotch* were, in effect, a call for a postmodern novel in Latin America.

In *Hopscotch*, Morelli questioned not only the assumptions of the realist novel, but many of the operations of modernist fiction, as well. He invited writers to undermine Western concepts of representation and time and, similarly, the very idea of linearity and plot. But one of his most radical proposals was for an entirely new role for the reader, for the active (*macho*) reader. The postmodern reader of much of the innovative fiction that has been published in Latin American since *Hopscotch* is fundamentally this active reader of Morelli.

The first wave to write radically experimental and self-conscious works in Argentina included the young writer Néstor Sánchez, whose novel *Siberia Blues* (1968) has intrigued many critics. With *Siberia Blues*, Cortázar's *62: a Model Kit* (1968), Héctor Libertella's *El camino de los hiperbóreos* ("The road of southern nations," 1968) and the fiction of Manuel Puig, in addition to Humberto Costantini's *Háblenme de Funes* ("Speak to me of Funes," 1970), it was evident that Argentine fiction was undergoing a revolution, clearly a break from the modernist tradition that had dominated in Argentina since the 1940s. One of the most technically experimental works published in postmodern Argentina, Sánchez's *Siberia Blues* focusses on language itself for its structure and theme and on the making of a sentence, which could well be the work's major event.[25]

After the publication of *Hopscotch*, several writers of the next generation of Argentine and Latin American postmodern accepted Morelli's invitation to create a novel more by the principles of chance than by reasoned logic. In chapter 62 of *Hopscotch*, Morelli suggests the possibility of creating a novel on the basis of random notes and observations. Cortázar himself pursued this idea in *62: A Model Kit*, a work in which even the very concepts of character and plot are placed into doubt, and where the "entities" (who often appear more as abstractions than characters who represent human beings) are caught up in a pattern of events that seem to occur at random in four places: London, Paris, Vienna, and the City. Libertella does create a protagonist in *El camino de los hiperbóreos*, but there is no traditional sense of plot, other than this protagonist's vague search for something undefined. In addition, Libertella subverts any concept of individual identity by creating a multiple identity in this character. In *Háblenme de Funes*, Costantini constructs a three-part structure consisting of three vaguely related stories, the third of which is a metafiction dealing with a writer's creative process. This writer's protagonist, in turn, invents even more characters. Costantini uses entirely different styles in the three parts of this book, which are related in a variety of ways.[26]

The postmodern fiction of Manuel Puig, which he initiated with the (then) daringly experimental *Betrayed by Rita Hayworth* (1968), consists of eight novels that had a major impact on the multiple directions of Argentine and Latin American postmodern fiction since the 1970s and 1980s. *Betrayed by Rita Hayworth* established a postmodern reader who necessarily had an active and unstable role to play, for there is no controlling narrator to organize the anecdotal material that is related by a multiplicity of voices that appear in the text as monologues or dialogues. The novel chronicles the life of a boy named Toto and his family and friends around him in Argentina of the 1930s and 1940s. Toto's principal referent, however, is not Argentina, but Hollywood film. This narrative about how imported popular culture can construct identity is a typically postmodern text, according to Lucille Kerr, for there is no privileged narrator upon whom the reader can rely for complete information, nor is there an authoritative discourse or figure to whom we can turn for something like an objective, final truth regarding its fiction.[27]

Puig's total oeuvre contains narrative structures, fictionalized postmodern readers, and themes similar to those in *Betrayed in Rita Hayworth*. His later work critiques gender-bound behavior and genre-bound thinking, particularly *Heartbreak Tango* (1969), *The Buenos Aires Affair* (1973), and *Kiss of the Spider Woman* (1976).[28] They also all deal with questions of authority and power. Truth, however, remains ever elusive in Puig, as Kerr explains: "The truth that is sought out by the reader is but the creation of the powerful object who gives the illusion of its presence, only to reveal it as a fiction at the end.[29]

A second wave of postmodern fiction in Argentina has been produced by writers well aware of their debts to Borges, Cortázar, and North Atlantic postmodern culture in general. They also tend to draw from their idols, Roberto Arlt and Macedonio Fernández. Among the most prominent of this second wave of postmodern writers in Argentina are Ricardo Piglia, Héctor Libertella, Sylvia Molloy, and Alejandra Pizarnik. As a group, these Argentine postmodern creators are generally politically progressive and among the most experimental fiction writers in Latin America.

The fiction of Piglia is one of the most aesthetically innovative and politically significant since the writings of Cortázar, and it certainly posits a forceful response to Jameson's categorization of the postmodern as politically conservative. Piglia's four books of fiction consist of *Nombre falso* ("False name," 1975), *Artificial Respiration* (1979), *Prisión perpetua* ("Perpetual prison," 1988) and *La ciudad ausente* ("The absent city," 1992), books that are most appropriately read as one body of fiction, just as Moreno-Durán's trilogy *Fémina Suite* should be read as one set of "exercises in style," and Balza's entire narrative can be read as one "narrative exercise." Piglia's four books can, in addition, be seen as an outgrowth of Borges's "The Library of Babel" and "Pierre Ménard, Author of the Quixote," for they are fictional meditations that can also be read as essays and, to a certain extent, must be read as literary and political essays. Piglia's fiction is a major rewriting of Argentine history and literature in a fictional world of the provisional truths of Diamela Eltit's *Lumpérica* and *El cuarto mundo.*

Piglia has joined Fuentes and Eltit in the search for the historical origins of the language and culture of the Americas. Consequently, Eltit's investigation into the "mother language" in *Por la patria* has as its equivalent in Piglia a questioning of the "father language" in *Artificial respiration.* In the fiction of Eltit, the reader is invited to move beyond the question "to what empirically real object in the past does the language of history refer?" and to ask, rather, "to which discursive context could this language belong? To which prior textualization must we refer?"[30]

Artificial Respiration opens with the question "Is there a story?" and then keeps the reader intrigued for the remainder of the novel, even though the action (in the traditional sense of *histoire*) is minimal. In the original Spanish, this question "¿Hay una historia?" carries the double meaning of "Is there a story?" and "Is there a history?", thus suggesting one of the major issues of this novel—the relationship between literature and history. *Artificial Respiration* emerges as a two-hundred-page meditation on Argentine cultural and political history. It consists of two parts, the first of which is narrated primarily by an aspiring writer named Emilio Renzi; the second is narrated by a Pole named Vladimir Tardewski living in Argentina. Part 1 deals with Enrique Ossorio, a private secretary of the nineteenth-century dictator Juan Manuel Rosas. Renzi collaborates with his uncle Marcelo Maggi to reconstruct the life of Enrique Ossorio. In part 2 the focus changes to a lengthy conversation (from 10:00 A.M. until the following dawn) between Maggi's friend Tardewski and Renzi. Their dialogue on literature includes a supposed encounter between Hitler and Kafka in Prague in 1909-1910.

For Seymour Menton, *Artificial Respiration* fits the label of "New Historical Novel" because of "the almost total absence of the recreation of historical time and space."[31] Menton also observes correctly that no attempt is made to re-create the flavor of these periods, and "the novel is much more concerned with projecting Borges's philosophical views on history in general."[32] In reality, Piglia's approaches to storytelling and history are typical of many of the postmodern attitudes observed in Piglia's generation throughout Latin America. Piglia is interested not only in Borges's philosophical views on history, but in rewriting the Argentine cultural history that holds Borges as an icon. *Artificial Respiration* is a pastiche (rather than a parody) of the philosophical style of Borges, Cortázar, and Macedonio Fernández.

Rather than re-creating historical space and time, Piglia delves into the question of how national histories are constructed and institutionalized. Like Eltit, Piglia is thus concerned with the concept of *patria* and its origins. *Artificial Respiration* returns to the roots of Argentine nationhood in the nineteenth century, as national history and family history are fused in this novel. The novel is an ongoing dialogue about the *patria*'s cultural and political history. Tardewski himself is a cultural statement, for he is the Argentine intellectual par excellence: a European who is situated on the periphery (in the province of Entre Ríos) speculating about European culture as it interacts with Argentine literature.

Piglia proposes a mediated version of historical truth, according to Daniel Balderson.[33] Actually, all understanding, historical and other, is considerably mediated in this novel. The narrative situation is such that a multiplicity of voices narrate, and there is no narrative authority. In part 1, the primary narrator, Renzi, is only a provisional narrator at best, for a substantial portion of part 2 consists of letters from other characters, such as his friends Marcelo Maggi, Juan Cruz Baigorria, and Echevarne Angélica Inés. The mediation takes more subtle technical forms, too, when Renzi narrates what others have written or told him. For example, a common rhetorical twist is the following: "under the present rules, he [Tardewski] tells me, Maggi writes. . . ."[34] In part 2, Tardewski narrates, but most of his narration is actually a quotation of another character, or a quotation of a quotation. This constant mediation in part 2 forces the reader to engage in an ongoing and intense process of evaluation of the sources of possible truths in the story. Further complicating this issue of mediation is the fact that both of the principal narrators are intellectuals who prove to be fundamentally unreliable narrators.

Tardewski paraphrases Ludwig Wittgenstein near the end of the novel and poses a question central to *Artificial Respiration*: "How to speak of the unspeakable?" The multiple mediated narratives of this novel constantly evoke this question, always avoiding speaking the unspeakable, which would be the contestatory language against the military dictatorship in Argentina when *Artificial Respiration* was written and published. The following key passage poses this problem as follows:

> What we cannot speak about we must pass over in
> silence, Wittgenstein said. How to speak of the
> unspeakable? That is the question that Kafka's
> work tries over and over again to answer. Or
> better still, he said, his work is the only one
> that in a refined and subtle manner dares to speak
> of the unspeakable, of that which cannot be
> named. What would we say is the unspeakable today?
> the world of Auschwitz.[35]

The reader is invited, of course, to answer differently, responding that the unspeakable "today" is the Argentine military tyranny.

Truth and its multiple manifestations are central issues in *Artificial Respiration*. The novel is dedicated to two friends of Piglia and evokes the issue of truth: "To Elías and Rubén who helped me to come to know the truth of history." Interestingly enough, both narrators frequently use verbal ticks in their speaking, such as "in truth," or "to tell the truth" that raise the question of truth and usually invite the reader to question the very truths that the narrators are asserting at that moment. Balderson makes several pertinent points with respect to truth, beginning with the fact that access to truth is always partial and frustrating.[36] The three main characters are engaged in a constant search for truth and an effort to assert truths, but their respective gift for speech is matched by their incapacity to develop fully their ideas in print. Consequently, their assertions are always tentative and the truth is never fully revealed.

The suspicious Arocena, a government worker, engages in a search for truth that recalls the predicament of several characters in postmodern novels, attempting to decipher false signs for truths. He fails in his attempt to find hidden, subversive truths in these letters, thus suffering the same fate as the protagonist in the Mexican Luis Arturo Ramos's story "Cartas para Julia" and other postmodern fictions where characters seek to find truth in signs that point to false destinies.

In the end, the dedication to friends who helped Piglia "come to know the truth of history" resonates with multiple meanings. After the experience of *Artificial Respiration*, it is difficult to imagine knowing any significant truths about Argentine history. The real truths are, in the end, unspeakable. On the other hand, the reader can speculate that "coming to know the truth of history" could well mean coming to know that the truth of history is impossible to know in nations such as Argentina. More than discovering Argentina's true past, the reader observes how truths are constructed in the Argentine cultural and political environment.

Artificial Respiration, like Eltit's *Lumpérica* and *Por la patria*, also sets forth the issue of *patria* and language. The lengthy discussions on Argentine literature (particularly in the second half of the book) bring to bear Piglia's position on the notions of patria and language. On the one hand, the characters are highly critical of the turn-of-the-century poet Leopoldo Lugones, a literary icon who has been institutionalized in Argentina. Lugones is criticized as the National Poet with the most "pure language" and thus can be associated, implicitly, with the "sanitization" process of the Proceso de Re-Organización Nacional. Arlt, on the other hand, is much admired by the characters in *Artificial Respiration* (as he is extra-textually by Piglia) and represents the opposite of Lugones, for Arlt's language can be characterized as often crude, clumsy, even vulgar. By criticizing Lugones and praising Arlt, Piglia critiques the very foundations of the traditional Argentine concept of patria.

The key modern characters in *Artificial Respiration*, tellingly enough, feel very limited and imprisoned by their "mother tongue" or unable to communicate in it. Senator Luciano Ossorio explains that a son inherits a future and a "mother tongue whose verbs one must learn to conjugate or, better still, a *father* tongue whose verbs one must learn to conjugate."[37] The principal narrator of part 2, Tardewski, speaks of the difficulties of narrating without his "mother tongue," which is Polish. He comments on the difficulty of searching for truth in a language other than his mother tongue. Tardewski also describes himself as a "writer without language."[38] As such, Tardewski seems to represent the situation of writers such as Piglia who, under the yoke of censorship and repression, find themselves without a language—with no possible form of expression.

Several other situations in *Artificial Respiration* lead the reader to conclude that these situations are metaphors for the writer's circumstance under a repressive regime, such as the Argentine military dictatorship of the 1970s. In this sense, *Artificial Respiration* can be read as an allegory of the work of art produced during the repression. Tardewski observes: "Joyce set himself a single problem: how to narrate real events."[39] An observation such as this, seemingly innocent enough, becomes a political statement in the context of this allegorical reading of *Artificial Respiration*, for "how to narrate real events" is both an aesthetic *and* a political problem under the dictatorship. The ongoing admiration for Kafka and Arlt also invites the reader to compare these two writers with the author of *Artificial Respiration*. All three face the problem of speaking the unspeakable.

Artificial Respiration is a critique of the military regime in Argentina, but it is a subtle critique that also places into question how language and writing can function and survive under such regimes. This subtle text places numerous demands on the reader who necessarily assumes the role of the active postmodern reader of this post-*Hopscotch* text. The reader of *Artificial Respiration*, however, is involved in subtle games of complicity that recall the reader's experience in *You Will Die in a Distant Land*. The reader joins Renzi and Maggi in their constant attempts to decipher the literary, cultural, and political reality of Argentina. But, again, things are not as simple and clear as they might appear, for there is another decipherer: the shadowy Arocena who works for the dictatorship, intercepts letters, and attempts to decipher them. Consequently, the readers must also think self-consciously about their role in the hermeneutic process, for even the act of interpreting, under these conditions, has political implications. As in *You Will Die in a Distant Land*, the reader is caught up in a horrific network of characters and situations that escape the simple dichotomies of liberal and conservative thought or radical and reactionary political positions.

Piglia's two other books of fiction, *Prisión perpetua* and *La ciudad ausente*, develop many of the same issues introduced in *Artificial Respiration*. *Prisión perpetua* is less a novel than a set of ten fictions that are related but that escape the classification of "short stories" for most readers, and some of which had appeared previously in the volume titled *Nombre falso*.[40] *Prisión perpetua* is divided into three parts. Part 1, titled "Prisión perpetua," contains the pieces "En otro país" and "El fluir de la vida." Part 2, "Las actas del juicio," contains six pieces that are the most comparable to modern short stories. Part 3 offers an "Homenaje to Roberto Arlt" and an "Apéndice: Luba." The two pieces in part 1 grow out of a certain type of Piglia's autobiographical writing: "En otro país" is what Piglia describes as a "relato" about himself that he presented as a lecture in 1987 in New York in a cycle of lectures titled "Writers Talk about Themselves." This supposedly autobiographical piece appears to be more and more like fiction, however, as it develops. This "false" autobiography, nevertheless, might be more "true" than the facts of a traditional autobiography; it is a demonstration of how Piglia's life has been a constant interaction between living and writing. In this autobiography, Piglia tells of his friend Steve Ratliff, an American, and the second piece is the story "El fluir de la vida," which Piglia explains was written the way Steve told stories and in the same tone. In these two pieces, the question of the real language or "mother tongue" surfaces once again: the first text is in Spanish, even though it was supposedly prepared for delivery in English (again, not the mother tongue); the second represents not the mother tongue of Piglia, but of Steve, which is also English.[41]

As has been seen in the readings of José Emilio Pacheco (chapter 2), Moreno-Durán (chapter 3), and Eltit, the post-*Hopscotch* active reader is required to play a variety of roles. As Ellen McCracken has demonstrated, Piglia pushes the concept of the active reader to its extreme in *Prisión perpetua*. McCracken has revealed how part 3 of the book consists of a double-coded metaplagiarism. In his "Homenaje a Roberto Arlt" in part 3, Piglia claims that he is publishing an unpublished text of Arlt. In reality, the text that follows "Luba" is a slightly altered version of a Russian short story titled "The Dark" by Leonid Andreyen (obviously not reproduced in the mother tongue in *Prisión perpetua*). McCracken shows how the active postmodern reader is urged to become a detective to find the textual clues to Piglia's metaplagiarism. McCracken concludes that "By performing the work of detectives and police, readers can arrive at the truth behind the literary puzzle of the story."[42] As in *You Will Die in a Distant Land*, the reader is invited to be "aggressive" (to use McCracken's term, not mine), but without exactly the same potential ideological consequences as seen in Pacheco's novel.

In *La ciudad ausente* (1992) Piglia reaffirms his invitation to the postmodern reader to decipher the unspeakable, written in a language always at least once removed from the mother tongue. It is Piglia's rewriting of Macedonio Fernández (whom he names constantly in the text) and his story of a "machine" that is located in a museum and which narrates stories. Emilio Renzi appears once again, relating stories to the principal narrator, who serves as mediator for Renzi's stories. But the machine's stories are transcribed directly from cassettes into the text and appear sporadically throughout it—evoking Macedonio Fernández, Bioy Casares, Borges, and other Argentine writers. Argentine literary and cultural history, then, is constantly emanating from this machine. As Sandra Garabano has observed, however, not only Argentine literature, but a plethora of European writers, from James Joyce to Albert Camus, appear or are evoked in the text.[43]

Two important elements in *La ciudad ausente* connect to Piglia's fiction and to the postmodern fiction of writers such as Pacheco, Luis Arturo Ramos, and Eltit. On the one hand, the machine "narrates in a foreign language," thus underlining the tendency of Piglia always to narrate in a language other than the mother tongue. On the other, *La ciudad ausente* is what one critic has called a "relato de paranoia" (paranoiac tale).[44] Characters in such stories interpret the world as a complex series of intrigues, plots, and arbitrary signs that always hide a play with power. If knowledge is used to guarantee access to truth, now the excess of information distances us from truth and places us in the paranoia of deciphering signs.[45] In *La ciudad ausente*, several characters are obsessed with deciphering the signs, putting order to the stories, and finding truth in this Baudrillard world of the superproduction of empty signs.

The fiction of Piglia does share the interests of the modernists in the epistemological and some of the ontological qualities of postmodernist writing. One of Piglia's central and most constant interests in all his writing, however, is truth. When asked in an interview what the specificity of fiction is, Piglia responded: "su relación con la verdad y lo que más me interesa es trabajar en esa zona indeterminada donde se cruzan la ficción y la verdad" [its relationship with truth and that which most interests me is that indeterminate zone where fiction and truth intersect].[46] All his writing deals with the truth of history, but more than fleshing out historical truths, Piglia's fiction questions how we get access to historical truth, how the true and false are constructed, and the multiple layers of written and spoken discourse that not only hide the truth, but can also question the possibility of speaking of truth.

Like Piglia and José Balza, Héctor Libertella's postmodern writing often blurs traditional boundaries between essay and fiction; two recent volumes that read more like essayistic than fictional exercises are his most significant postmodern contributions. In his theory of fiction (and fiction of theory) titled *Las sagradas escrituras* ("The sacred writings," 1993), Libertella posits what he identifies as a "lyrical criticism," and the two figures to whom he returns obsessively are the postmodern writers Enrique Lihn and Salvador Elizondo. Besides the Chilean Lihn and the Mexican Elizondo, Libertella is interested in other postmodern hermetic writers, such as the Cuban Severo Sarduy, and the Venezuelan Oswaldo Trejo, as well as postmodern authors of books he calls "novelas de lenguaje" (novels of language): Sarduy, Puig, Reynaldo Arenas, Néstor Sánchez, and Guillermo Cabrera Infante. As concerned as Piglia and Eltit are about the possibilities of still writing in the "mother language,"[47] Libertella poses the question in one essay ("Más acá de la interpretación"), in which Spanish the Argentine writer should write: an international Spanish or perhaps a translated Spanish?[48] In a postmodern turn, Libertella suggests that perhaps the Americas are nothing more than a geographical, political, and literary network, in accordance with how and why other disciplines want to appropriate them. The heterodox and provocative essays in *Las sagradas escrituras* lead Libertella and the reader to question the ontological status of Spanish and nationhood in Argentina.

Libertella questions the viability of both the Spanish language and writing in a subtle and subversive fashion in *El paseo internacinal del perverso* ("The international trip of the perverse one," 1990), a short novel that attempts to avert its status as a novel and as any fixed language. It also attempts to avoid any fixed subject, for the main character, an itinerant entity who travels around the world, never takes on any fixed identity. It is a book of constant transformation in which everything, in the end, is written *sous rassure.*

Sylvia Molloy, Alejandra Pizarnik, and Luis Gusmán are the authors of subtle fictions that are testimony to the heterogeneity of postmodern writing in Argentina and the different ways postmodern writers of the Southern Cone can be political. Molloy's *Certificate of Absence* (1981) returns to the postmodern origins of Borges, the Borges who offers reflections on the text, questioning the stability of the text itself. It is a self-conscious feminist text that defends its marginality and refuses to comply with many of the expectations traditional readers may have of masculine texts. Pizarnik's *The Bloody Countess* (1971) is a revisiting of the Dracula story in a postmodern world in which neither the truth of the moral or the immoral are factors, for it recreates a fictional world in which morality is not an issue. *En el corazón de junio* ("In the heart of June, 1983), Luis Gusmán's fourth novel, is a highly fragmented work that is a series of enigmas. Nevertheless, Balderson has shown how this novel, like *Artificial Respiration*, attempts to speak the unspeakable.[49]

URUGUAYAN POSTMODERN FICTION

Modernist fiction arose in Uruguay in the 1940s and 1950s with the fiction of Felisberto Hernández and Juan Carlos Onetti, and later with the writing of Mario Benedetti and Carlos Martínez Moreno. Hernández was Uruguay's inventive writer of an imaginative fiction comparable in some ways to the fiction of Bioy Casares and Borges. His comic and satirical writing, which was generally ignored when published, included *Nadie encendía las lámparas* ("No one turned on the lights," 1947) and *La casa inundada* ("The flooded house," 1960), and has served as a model for many young writers in Uruguay over the past two decades. Onetti was Uruguay's cornerstone modernist writer and published several morose works of fiction, frequently in the existentialist mode. His pioneer modernist novels are *El pozo* ("The well," 1939), *Tierra de nadie* ("Land of no one," 1941), and *The Brief Life* (1950).

Among Uruguay's modernist writers, Benedetti was the most forcefully committed to social change, a position evident in novels such as *La tregua* ("The truce," 1960) and *Gracias por el fuego* ("Thanks for the fire," 1965). He was joined in his social program by slightly younger writers who were equally committed, such as Jorge Onetti, Híber Conteris, Fernando Aínsa, and Eduardo Galeano. Writers and critics such as Benedetti, Martínez Moreno, and Emir Rodríguez Monegal, known as the Generation of 1945 in Uruguay, promoted modern literature in Uruguay in their journal *Número* during the 1950s.

The postmodern writers of Uruguay who have followed paths suggested by Felisberto Hernández, Borges, and Cortázar include Híber Conteris,

Armonía Sommers, Cristina Peri Rossi, Teresa Porzekanski, Napoleón Baccino Ponce de León, Silva Vila, José Pedro Díaz, Mercedes Rein, Amir Hamed, and Gley Eyherabide. As was the case throughout Latin America, this innovative and experimental fiction began to appear in the late 1960s. Author of five novels, Conteris has not been a technical innovator as much as writers such as Piglia, Libertella, or Eltit, but he has written under the sign of Cortázar and considers himself one of the most avid readers of Cortázar of his generation of writers in Uruguay.[50] He wrote his novel *Ten Percent of Life* (1986) in Spanish while in jail as a political prisoner from 1976 to 1983, during the military dictatorship. On a surface level, *Ten Percent of Life* can be read as a detective novel written under the influence of Raymond Chandler; it even has Marlowe and other Chandler characters in it, including Chandler himself. This novel is neither a parody nor an imitation of the American's texts, however, but a pastiche. Like Piglia and other postmodern writers from the Southern Cone, Conteris writes in a neutral language that evokes the style of translations, thus inviting the reader to question the possibility of writing in Spanish.

Like the fiction of Piglia and Eltit, *Ten Percent of Life* is a postmodern allegory of resistance. As Santiago Colas has pointed out, this novel needs to be read with an awareness of the context of the discourses in which it was written: the predominant discourse of the military dictatorship and the discourse of detective fiction.[51] In the classic detective novel, the detective's conclusions should become irrevocable truths and avoid the fact that truths are mere constructs. Conteris, however, subverts the very idea of definitive truths in his metafiction, thus subverting classic detective fiction. As the novel develops on two levels, and the postmodern reader finds political clues hidden in this detective novel, the work becomes an allegorical fiction of resistance. At some level, the reader never knows what happens, making this yet another novel of the Southern Cone region addressing the unspeakable.

The fiction of Sommers, Peri Rossi, Baccino Ponce de León, and Porcekanski demonstrates both modernist and postmodern tendencies. Sommers's modernist fiction dates back to her first novella, *La mujer desnuda* ("The nude woman," 1951), but her more postmodern writing includes the three short stories *Tríptico darwiniano* ("Darwinian tryptic," 1982) and her technically experimental and complex novel *Sólo los elefantes encuentran mandrágora* ("Only elephants find mandrágora," 1983). The feminist writing of Peri Rossi has consisted mostly of short fiction, but she has also published the novels *El libro de mis primos* ("The book of my cousins," 1969) and *Ship of Fools* (1984). Peri Rossi's postmodern fiction blurs generic boundaries, is often discontinuous, and is an art of proliferation and digression. *Ship of fools* is a metafiction that questions the boundaries between painting and fiction. An historiographical metafiction, Baccino Ponce de León's *Maluco* ("Maluco," 1990) also subverts multiple boundaries. Porzekanski has published several books of postmodern fiction, including the recent novel *Perfumes de Cartago* ("Perfumes from Cartago," 1994), a novel that questions the concept of truth and project the ideas of nation, gender, and self as social constructs.

Postmodern writers of the Southern Cone, such as Diamela Eltit, Ricardo Piglia, and Armonía Sommers, write from the periphery of a periphery. This postmodern fiction works to subvert dominant discourses and, in this sense, these writers' postmodernities of the Southern Cone are the most profoundly political response, among Latin American postmodernities, to the accusations of Jameson and others about the politics of the postmodern. Paraphrasing Kafka and Arlt, Piglia's fiction poses the question of how to speak the unspeakable in a repressive military dictatorship, while the fiction of Eltit, Libertella, Conteris, and Sommers represents a postmodern voicing of the unspeakable.

The fiction of Diamela Eltit, Ricardo Piglia, Híber Conteris, Armonía Sommers, and other selected Latin American postmodern novelists question the truth industry of First World modernism. In the Latin American case, the novel has moved from utopia to heterotopia—from the centered and historical universe of the Alejo Carpentier and García Márquez utopias to the centerless universe—Foucault's heterotopia—of Eltit, Piglia, and Sarduy. Obviously, what is at stake for many Latin American postmodern writers who have arisen since the late 1960s, and these postmodern writers of the Southern Cone who have arisen since the 1980s, is not truth. Lyotard claims that the question is no longer "Is it true?" but "What use is it?" and "How much is it worth?" and these approaches to truth in postmodern society are novelized in the postmodern cultural practices of Diamela Eltit and Ricardo Piglia. Postmodern society, in the fiction of these two writers, substitutes truth with images of degradation.

One specificity of postmodern fiction in the Southern Cone is the production of fiction that is a particular kind of writing between the lines— fictions that are complex allegories of resistance. Their hermeticism is not an exercise in being esoteric, but of a self-conscious hermeticism that results in these allegories of resistance. Piglia, Eltit, Lihn, and Libertella, who published during the military dictatorships, turned to this allegorical mode that was their method of speaking the unspeakable.

By returning to the icons of Argentina's national literature and by subverting figures as revered as Lugones, Piglia is carrying out an operation similar to Moreno-Durán's subversion of the concept of the "Athens of South America." Both Lugones and Bogotá had become national icons. The idea of Lugones as National Poet (comparable to Bogotá as the Athens of South America and Uruguay as the Switzerland of Latin America) was essential to the maintenance of traditional ideas of nationhood. As has been observed, Mexican and Andean postmodern fiction inevitably leads to images of exhaustion. The equivalent recurring image in the Southern Cone is of the loss of the mother tongue or the death of language, an image evoked, suggested, or elaborated by Eltit, Piglia, Lihn, Conteris, and Libertella. Consequently, their fiction pushes the limits of the Spanish language and often projects Spanish not as the original tongue, but as a "translation" or "another language."

In several cases, the language used in postmodern fiction of the Southern Cone comes from the expression of pain, thus inviting the reader to think of torture. Elaine Scarry has noted that "physical pain does not simply resist language but actively destroys it, bringing about an immediate reversion to a state anterior to language. . . ."[52] In *Terra Nostra*, Fuentes returns to a prediscursive logos, and in the Southern Cone novels such as *Lumpérica* by Diamela Eltit and *Ten Percent of Life* by Híber Conteris take the postmodern reader back to this prediscursive state.

5

Caribbean Postmodernities

The Caribbean region has multiple identities, depending on the cultural and political interests of those defining it, a fact that is evident in its various names: "the Caribbean," "el Caribe," "the West Indies," "les Antilles," and the like. The cultural unity of the region has always been more an ideal of its progressive writers and political thinkers than the realpolitik of the colonial powers—primarily the United States, Great Britain, France, and Holland—that have maintained long-standing economic interests in the region. Its heterogeneity and transformations led one eighteenth-century priest living in the Dominican Republic to write: "Yesterday I was born Spanish / by noon I was French, / at night I was an Ethiope, / I'm English today, they say: / What indeed will become of me!"[1]

Seen across the spectrum of the languages (Spanish, French, English, Dutch, Portuguese) and cultures in the region, the Caribbean has produced many contemporary novelists, and they have practiced their art throughout the world in different stages of permanent or transitory residence in the Caribbean. Much of their work has been written in exile. The names of these novelists are many, but the most productive since the 1970s have been Severo Sarduy (Cuba), George Lamming (Barbados), Alejo Carpentier (Cuba), V. S. Naipaul (Trinidad), Luis Rafael Sánchez (Puerto Rico), Maryse Condé (Guadeloupe), Wilson Harris (Guyana), Rosario Ferré (Puerto Rico), Merle Hodge (Trinidad), Lisandro Otero (Cuba), René Depestre (Haiti) Guillermo Cabrera Infante (Cuba), Pedro Juan Soto (Puerto Rico), Simone Schwarz-Bart (Guadeloupe), Emilio Díaz Valcárcel (Puerto Rico), Andrew Salkey (Jamaica), Marcio Veloz Maggiolo (Dominican Republic), Roy A. K. Heath (Guyana), Earl Lovelace (Trinidad), Stephen Alexis (Haiti), Pedro Verges (Dominican Republic), Reinaldo Arenas (Cuba), Daniel Maximin (Guadeloupe), Edgardo Rodríguez Juliá (Puerto Rico), and Antonio Benítez Rojo (Cuba).

The Caribbean's African heritage has been an important factor in the region's cultural unity. Cultural expression reached a full awareness of these African roots in the 1920s and 1930s, and the literary manifestation of this awareness was the rise of an Afro-Antillean poetry during this period. The Cuban poets Nicolás Guillén and Emilio Ballagas led the Afro-Antillean poetic movement, followed by the Puerto Rican Luis Palés Matos and others. For these poets, Caribbean culture as a whole was a mestizo culture and the product of the synthesis of European and African cultural elements on the islands of the region.[2]

The most significant political fact of the Caribbean region of the past three decades has been the Cuban Revolution of 1959, both for its declaration of economic independence from its former colonial powers and for the key role Havana has played as a cultural center of the Caribbean region and Latin America, particularly in the 1980s. A revolutionary model for many writers, especially in the 1960s, Cuba has defined much of the cultural discourse in the Caribbean since the revolution. During the Batista dictatorship, the leading cultural magazine of the 1950s was *Orígenes*, which promoted modernist writing and published Cuban poets often associated with a "creationist" or "pure" poetry, often seen as alienated from social reality. José Lezama Lima, Cintio Vitier, and Eliseo Diego were some of the poets associated with this group who, after the revolution, were under attack by writers who published in the newspaper *Revolución* and its cultural organ *Lunes de la Revolución*, directed by Guillermo Cabrera Infante. Fidel Castro closed down *Lunes de la Revolución* in 1961 and in 1971 imprisoned the poet Heberto Padilla, an act that produced a political division between the Latin American writers who supported and those opposed to Castro, over the issues of human rights and freedom of expression.

Since its takeover by the United States in 1898, Puerto Rico has lived the multicultural experience of a de facto binational and bicultural island. As an associated state ("Free Associated State") of the United States, Puerto Rico has lived on the margins of the United States, of the Caribbean, and the rest of Latin America. In his influential essay *El país de cuatro pisos* ("The country of four floors," 1980), the contemporary Puerto Rican writer José Luis González divides the development of Puerto Rican society and culture into four stories. The first of these four stories is the rise of a Creole identity in the eighteenth century under the Spanish government of Charles III. The second, beginning in the middle of the nineteenth century, consists of the creation of an elite, Hispanicized "new" Creole culture that dominated until the end of the century. The third "story" involves a cultural revalorization begun by the Generation of 1930 as a result of the United States' presence after 1898; this period lasted until the 1950s. The fourth period is the new Puerto Rican industrial society; it is currently under question by the intellectuals of the Generation of 1930.[3] Since the late 1960s, modern and postmodern cultures have coexisted in Puerto Rico.

Since its independence in the nineteenth century, the Dominican Republic has also suffered an ambivalent relationship with the United States, and an even more conflictive one than Puerto Rico, for U.S. troops invaded the Dominican Republic in 1916 (installing a puppet government) and once again in 1965 (installing the neo-Trujillist Balaguer regime). Dominican cultural production in this century has followed a pattern similar to Cuba and Puerto Rico, and the Creole poet Tomás Hernández Franco celebrated cultural hybridism as quintessentially Caribbean literature.

The Cuban writer and cultural critic Antonio Benítez Rojo has used the metaphor of water to describe the Caribbean's fluctuating, aquatic quality: "But the culture of the Caribbean, at least in its most distinctive aspect, is not terrestrial but aquatic, a sinuous culture where time unfolds irregularly and resists being captured by the cycles of clock and calendar.[4] This aquatic quality of the Caribbean is part of its inherent postmodernity.

The argument that Latin American postmodernism precedes the North Atlantic phenomenon can be most convincingly argued in the case of the Caribbean, for the Caribbean is defined by the same heterogeneity that has become a key word for the postmodern. In addition, social scientists have described cultural constants of the Caribbean as fragmentation, instability, isolation, uprootedness, cultural complexity, disperse historiography, contingency, and impermanence.[5] Obviously, several of these cultural constants are also closely related to concepts typically used to describe postmodern culture. The Caribbean text, according to Benítez Rojo, shows characteristics of the syncretic culture from which it emerges.[6] It is the consummate "performer" "with recourse to the most daring improvisations to keep from being trapped within its own textuality."[7]

Postmodern culture in the Caribbean region, like that of Mexico, has been considerably impacted by both mass culture and high culture of the United States, and generally more so than is the case in the Andean and Southern Cone regions. The Puerto Ricans, like the Mexicans, have been watching American television since the 1950s, and numerous bookstores in San Juan cater to readers of both Spanish and English; nowadays, the volumes in bookstores are being replaced, as they are in Mexico, by videos.

The leading figures of postmodern fiction written in the Spanish-speaking Caribbean are Cuba's Guillermo Cabrera Infante and Severo Sarduy (both of whom left Cuba in the 1960s to write in exile), Puerto Rico's Luis Rafael Sánchez and Edgardo Rodríguez Juliá, and several less productive and even less postmodern writers from the Dominican Republic.

POSTMODERN FICTION IN CUBA

Avant-garde and modernist fiction in Cuba has its origins in the 1930s, led by the experimental novelist Enrique Labrador Ruiz, and followed by the modernist writing of Alejo Carpentier, Lino Novás Calvo, and Lydia Cabrera. Labrador Ruiz's *El laberinto de sí mismo* ("The labyrinth of itself," 1933) is comparable to the experimental and avant-garde writing of the Contemporáneos in Mexico, the Florida group in Argentina, Vicente Huidobro's fiction in Chile, and Martín Adán's prose fiction in Perú. It is a playful and introspective novel that is a writer's fictional autobiography. Carpentier's first novel, *Ecue-Yamba-O!* ("Ecue-Yamba-O," 1933), is a fragmented work that tells the story of the black protagonist's cultural experience and conflicts in a racist society. Novás Calvo wrote short fiction and a historical novel, *El negrero* (1933), and this fiction made a valuable contribution to the modernization of Cuban literature, as did his translations of William Faulkner and other moderns.[8] Lydia Cabrera's short fiction, such as her Afro-Cuban narratives *Cuentos negros de Cuba* ("Black stories from Cuba," 1940) also made a valuable contribution to modernist fiction in Cuba.

Cuban modernist fiction continued its development throughout the 1940s, 1950s, and 1960s with the writing of Carpentier, Lisandro Otero, and Pablo Armando Fernández. A friend of Latin American modern writers—including Miguel Angel Asturias and Arturo Uslar Pietri—since his days in Paris in the 1920s, Carpentier's contributions to modernist fiction were substantive after the publication of *Ecue-Yamba-O*. In *The Kingdom of this World* (1949) and *The Lost Steps* (1953), Carpentier uses the techniques of modernism to fictionalize the history and culture of Cuba. In the latter, faced with the dilemma of history, he reconsidered the question of origin and of a beginning.[9] *Explosion in a Cathedral* (1962) is his historical novel set in the Caribbean and is one of the most in-depth treatments of the transition from the Enlightenment to the Romantic Age in Latin America.[10] Carpentier published later modernist novels, as did Otero and Fernández.

The most important precedent to postmodern fiction in Cuba was the publication of the poet José Lezama Lima's *Paradiso* in 1966. The most hermetic novel ever to be published in Cuba, *Paradiso* is a labyrinthine and complex story of a boy's maturation process and his growing awareness of the act of writing. The novel projects a sense of wholeness that associates it more with the modern tradition than the postmodern, but its emphasis on language as its overarching theme helps set the stage for the Cuban postmodern.

Early postmodern fiction in Cuba was signaled by one seminal book of the Caribbean postmodern, *Three Trapped Tigers* (1967) by Guillermo Cabrera

Infante. An initial indicator that Cabrera Infante belongs to the postmodern is his obvious affiliation with James Joyce, primarily because of his attention to language itself as a subject of the novel. As one critic has pointed out, however, Cabrera Infante's tone is of skeptical nostalgia, and this has nothing to do with Joyce.[11]

Three Trapped Tigers is a fragmented, open novel in constant postmodern movement and transformation. Set in the 1958 Cuba that was still living the music of Benny Moré and the acting of Veronica Lake, this novel communicates a sense of the end of an era and of finality. The novel's oft-cited opening takes place in a Havana nightclub, with the voice of an emcee. A variety of other voices—often unidentified—fill the novel, as ordinary people tell of their empty lives and often frenetic activity. The principal characters are a photographer named Códac, a television actor named Cué, and a writer, Silvestre. The author also interweaves narrations of a woman's sessions with a psychiatrist and the story of a singer, La Estrella.

Like many postmodern novels, the main subject of *Three Trapped Tigers* is language itself. The character La Estrella (The Star) represents the essence of sound, and other characters place emphasis on language as well. A character named Bustrófedon is an incarnation of language who is constantly engaged in linguistic play. Speaking of the ongoing process of inventing language, one critic has even suggested that the maximum experience of the novel is to reduce reality to nothing and then start over again.[12]

Three Trapped Tigers is a postmodern novel that emanates from Julio Cortázar's *Hopscotch* even though, on the surface, they appear to be quite different kinds of books. A series of literary parodies in *Three Trapped Tigers* imitating different Cuban writers recall some of the more playful Expendable Chapters of *Hopscotch*, and the active postmodern reader of this Cuban novel can exercise options in reading similar to those available in Cortázar's novel. The character Silvestre also makes some radical proposals for a novel similar to the most "open" aspects of *Three Trapped Tigers* and *Hopscotch*, and which emphasize the role of chance.

With this novel, Cabrera Infante was one of the Caribbean pioneers in blurring the boundary between popular and high culture, for in *Three Trapped Tigers* a multiplicity of popular and high cultures from within and beyond the Caribbean region coexist; these contradictions remain unresolved to the end of the novel. Popular music, American films, and Cuban writing of previous generations vibrate throughout this novel. This powerful breaking of boundaries undermined hierarchies of the literary tradition of the Spanish-speaking Caribbean so profoundly that movement toward postmodernism was seemingly inevitable after *Three Trapped Tigers*.

Three Trapped Tigers also marks a transition from epistemological to onto-logical concerns in Cuban fiction.[13] After the broad epistemological questions of Labrador Ruiz, Novás Calvo, and Carpentier, Cabrera Infante inquires what happens when different kinds of worlds are placed in confrontation. Numerous characters lack psychic unity in this novel, but the most notable case of fragmentation and unstable identity is the woman who attends psychiatric sessions throughout the novel; of nameless and vague identity, she is the work's postmodern figure par excellence. Cabrera Infante's leap to the ontological, as well as the series of other postmodern gestures in this novel, make *Three Trapped Tigers* an encyclopedia of postmodern motifs and devices comparable to Carlos Fuentes's *Terra Nostra* and Jorge Enrque Adoum's *Entre Marx y una mujer desnuda*. All three novels readily display their postmodernism, often with flashy narrative strategies.

The writing of Severo Sarduy differs radically from Cabrera Infante's, but it is the most significant contribution to the Caribbean postmodern and one of the bodies of postmodern work to have the greatest impact on the Latin American postmodern in general. Of Sarduy's numerous books, the novel with the most important influence in the context of the postmodern is the novel *Cobra* (1972). Citing John Barth and Jean François Lyotard, Roberto González Echevarría was among the first critics to recognize Sarduy's place among the postmoderns. According to Barth, postmodern fiction emphasizes self-consciousness, and it also expresses a spirit of subversion and cultural anarchy—characteristics that González Echevarría associates with Sarduy.

For González Echevarría, Sarduy's postmodern writing has four characteristics.[14] First, Sarduy's fiction (beginning with *Matreya* ("Matreya," 1978) and *Colibrí* ("Hummingbird," 1983), represents an apotheosis of storytelling. This does not mean a return to traditional storytelling, but the use of plot narrated by a variety of narrators. A second characteristic of Sarduy's postmodern writing, according to González Echevarría, is the absence of metadiscourse. A variety of cultural and political metadiscourses were present in the novels of the Boom, but Sarduy's postmodern novels reject metadiscourses of the larger systems in favor of the discourses of more local religious and cultural systems. For example, Sarduy closes *Colibrí* with references to James Jones's religious fiasco in Guyana. A third postmodern characteristic of Sarduy's writing is the lack of an authorial presence typical of modernist novels of the Boom. In Sarduy's novels, the author figure is often a ridiculous writer, rather than a weak one attempting to control the narration.

Despite González Echevarría's insightful introduction to Sarduy's postmodern writing, he minimizes the postmodern of *Cobra*. This novel consists of two interwoven narratives, the first of which, the Teatro Lírico de Muñecas

(Lyrical Theater of Dolls), takes place in a burlesque house. The protagonist is Cobra, who is a transsexual star at the theater. Cobra and the owner of the theater, La Señora, are involved in a process to reduce the size of Cobra's feet, but the drug they take reduces the pair to dwarfs, now named Pup and La Señorita. Then Cobra goes to India in search of the proper oriental paints and colors for the theater. In the other narrative, Cobra goes to Tangiers in search of a doctor famous for sex-change operations, Dr. Ktazob. In Tangiers, some drug pushers from Amsterdam direct Cobra to Dr. Ktazob. The novel concludes in the snow at the Chinese border of Tibet, where Cobra has gone with a motorcycle gang.

Written more under the hermetic sign of Lezama Lima than the playful chaos of Cabrera Infante, *Cobra* is Sarduy's novelistic reflection on language and writing. In this novel, language is not just a means of communication, but a way of demonstrating the function of language.[15] The novel's title refers to a poem by Octavio Paz from *Conjunciones y disyunciones* that dramatizes the generation of language. The association of words in this poem creates more words, a process parallel to much of *Cobra*.

The characters in *Cobra*, rather than attempting to portray "real" characters of fiction, represent only representation. The characters Cobra and Cadillac also project the artificial sexuality of their respective genders, and Cadillac represents excessive machismo. The characters' speech is artificial, obviously consisting of a variety of discourses that show the distance of the language from its origins.[16] Consequently, the postmodern characters in *Cobra* question the representation of the subject in traditional and modern fiction.

Cobra was one of the early texts of Caribbean and Latin American postmodern fiction to blur the line between "fictional" and "theoretical" discourse. The two stages of the journal *Tel Quel* reflect the changing interests of Sarduy, and the second stage of the journal (1964-1970), dominated by Jacques Derrida and Jacques Lacan, relate most directly to this novel. These two theorists place into question the concept of the subject as unifying element; the play of infinite substitutions, according to Derrida, frees language from the need for "unity" or "meaning." In *Cobra*, Sarduy uses such playful substitutions to carry out his parody of Derrida. The confluence of theory and practice in *Cobra* produces not an essence, but a lack of essence, thus pointing to the privileging of artificiality and superficiality in the novel.

If space is seen to be as much as a concern of the postmodern as time was with modernist writing, then *Cobra* is a premier example of the postmodern function of space in the novel. The unexplained and often irrational leap from one space to another in *Cobra*, often leaving the reader in doubt as to the setting, makes displacement a considerable portion of the "action" of the novel, thus fulfilling Fuentes's once-stated ideal for the genre (see chapter 2).

Cobra is also a work of ongoing double coding, with subjects who are and are not "real" characters, which tells stories that it then proceeds to negate. In the process of constant transmutation, Cobra is male, female, and transvestite, a castrato and, inexplicably, a square root itself. This novel also contains the double coding of parody as well as the double coding of fictional and theoretical discourse. These double codings challenge the literary hierarchies of modernist practices and challenge the active postmodern reader to confront the gaps produced by this ontological inquiry.

Sarduy's novels Maitreya (1978) and Colibrí (1983) represent a continuation of the author's postmodern project. Like Cobra, the protagonists in these two novels are subjects-in-progress. La Tremenda in Maitreya is also identified as la Expansiva, la Divina, La Colonial, la Masiva, la Toda-Mena, and la Delirium. Maitreya opens in the mountains of Tibet with the death of the "maestro"—a Tibetan lama—the Chinese invasion of Tibet, and the monk's abandonment of the monasteries. The characters travel through India to Ceylon. From there, the novel's various characters go to Sagua la Grande in Cuba. The twins who are born there spend time in New York, and later travel to Iran (where they open a massage parlor) and Algeria, but end up in Afghanistan. Maitreya is a violent novel in which characters are raped and mutilated. It is a novel replete with seemingly trivial details and actions. The question of finding the "meaning" of these individual details within the larger context of the novel, as González Echevarría has pointed out, is one of the themes of the novel, as well as an element that connects it with the hermeticism of Lezama Lima.[17] In addition, Maitreya offers some of the hermetic qualities of the postmodern fiction of Ricardo Piglia, Diamela Eltit and Fuentes, all of whom have been affected by Sarduy's postmodern fiction of the 1970s.

The ontological processes of Cobra and Maitreya pose the question of how violence and death can generate fecundity from decay.[18] The mutilation and decay pervasive in these two novels suggest a type of postmodern exhaustion. This process, nevertheless, is also one of transformation and, consequently, of production. One critic has also pointed out that mutilation in these novels functions as a confirmation of the heterogeneous nature of this narrative subject always portrayed in a complex verbal system.[19]

Colibrí begins with a group of youths wrestling in view of the wealthy and the military. It is the world of luxury and drugs where La Regenta (whose original sex is unknown) rules over her homosexual brothel. An athletic, blond boy, Colibrí arrives at this setting and becomes an admired wrestler. After travels through the jungles, which include love affairs and other adventures, Colibrí returns to La Regenta's establishment and eventually takes it over. The uncertain and unstable identities of the narrator and the protagonist are the most clearly postmodern aspects of *Colibrí*. The novel opens with the image of the protagonist dancing between the mirrors, nude, behind a bar, and these two mirrors multiply Colibrí's image ad infinitum. This multiplicity is played out in the remainder of the novel, from Colibrí's unknown origins to his amorphous character. The narrator, who seems to be an author figure, assumes both masculine and feminine guises.

Like Diamela Eltit, Ricardo Piglia, and the Carlos Fuentes of *Terra Nostra*, Sarduy returns to the very roots of Latin American culture, deconstructing its most basic elements, beginning with language. As González Echevarría has pointed out, Sarduy also reconsiders sex and being in *Colibrí*, as well as the social activities of this culture.[20] In *Colibrí*, Sarduy returns to one of the best-known topoi of the Latin American novel—the jungle. In his later novel *Cocuyo* (1990), Sarduy continues his postmodern project, novelizing many of the concerns already seen in *Maitreya* and *Colibrí*.

The foremost exponents of postmodern fiction from Cuba are Cabrera Infante and Sarduy. Nevertheless, a culture as inherently postmodern as Cuba's has produced several other writers with postmodern tendencies. Reinaldo Arenas, author of several outstanding novels, is one such writer, and more recent fabricators of fiction to be associated with the postmodern are Senel Paz and René Vásquez Díaz.

POSTMODERN FICTION IN PUERTO RICO

The first significant group of Puerto Rican writers this century were the Creolists and intellectuals of the Generation of 1930. For their immediate precursors, as Aníbal González has pointed out, Puerto Rican culture needed to be linked to the Hispanic past but also rooted in the insular landscape.[21] These intellectuals, such as Luis Lloréns Torres and Virgilio Dávila, used the figure of the *jíbaro* (peasant) as their emblem. Their archetypal Puerto Rican was the peasant from the mountains, with deep roots in the land, and connected by his language and culture to his Iberian past. The intellectuals of the Generation of 1930, which included the cultural critic Antonio S. Pedreira, the literary critic Concha Meléndez, and the novelists Enrique Laguerre, Emilio S. Belaval, and Abelardo Díaz Alfaro, affirmed Puerto Rican culture as an Hispanic, white, and Catholic variant of Western culture.[22] This generation was strongly influenced by José Ortega y Gasset and Oswald Spengler.

Modernist fiction came to Puerto Rico with the writings of the generation that wrote immediately after the Second World War, a group of writers identified by some as the generation of 1945 and by others as the Desperate Generation. These writers, including José Luis González, René Marqués, Pedro Juan Soto, José Luis Vivas Maldonado, and Emilio Díaz Valcárcel, brought the typical narrative strategies of modernist fiction and urban thematics to Puerto Rican narrative. González spearheaded the modernist movement in fiction with his book of short stories, *El hombre en la calle* ("The man in the street," 1948), and Marqués followed with *La víspera del hombre* ("Man's eve," 1959). More recently, Rosario Ferré has been a leading exponent of modernist fiction in Puerto Rico.

Luis Rafael Sánchez brought postmodern fiction to the forefront of Puerto Rican culture with the publication of *Macho Camacho's Beat* in 1976, after having previously published short fiction and plays. He proceeded with his postmodern project with a second novel, *La importancia de llamarse Daniel Santos* ("The importance of calling oneself Daniel Santos," 1988). After the breakdown of the frontiers between popular and high culture already effected by Cabrera Infante and Sarduy in Cuba (as well as Puig in Argentina), Sánchez's novelization of the popular culture of Caribbean music and American television in *Macho Camacho's Beat* was a logical step in the Caribbean postmodern. As Carlos J. Alonso has indicated, *Macho Camacho's Beat* was, indeed, a turning point for Puerto Rican cultural production.[23] This novel represents a postmodern turn from earlier canonical works, such as Antonio S. Pedreira's *Insularismo*, Luis Palés Matos's statements on Afro-Antillean culture, René Marqués's seminal essays, and the entire gamut of solemn pronouncements on Puerto Rican cultural specificity.

The title of Sánchez's novel in the original Spanish, *La guaracha del Macho Camacho*, refers to the Puerto Rican music that permeates the text, the *guaracha*. After the title page, the author's epigraph is a refrain from the song "La guaracha del Macho Camacho," which states "Life is a phenomenal thing, frontwards or backwards, however you swing." In his one-paragraph preface to the reader, he states that this novel is about the success of this song as well as the miserable and splendid extremes of life. At the end of the novel, Sánchez includes an appendix with the words to the song "La guaracha del Macho Camacho." The pages between these musical referents present a heterogeneous and fragmented text with multiple narrators who offer the popular music, mass culture, and the heterogeneous cultural reality of everyday life in Puerto Rico, highlighted by an enormous traffic jam and the presence of Puerto Rican television star Iris Chacón.

Sánchez appropriates a multiplicity of discourses in this novel, including the voices of a radio announcer (who appears in 19 segments), television and radio commercials, popular singers, and many other voices of the mass media. Sánchez also parodies writers associated with high culture, reproducing the African rhythm and sounds of poets such as Palés Matos. Latin American writers such as José Donoso and Severo Sarduy are also suggested in the text. The author makes allusions to a broad range of cultural figures and objects, including Frankenstein, Mohammed Ali, "From the Halls of Montezuma," Eugenio María de Hostos, George Wallace, Fidel Castro, Mao, "Over the Hills," John Wayne, the Green Berets, Marcel Schwob, García Lorca's *Romancero gitano*, Charlie Chaplin, and Cantinflas.

Macho Camacho's Beat is a double-coded novel whose parodic humor—on the surface, at least—seems to celebrate popular culture and such popular figures as television star Iris Chacón. Indeed, it can be read as a burlesque celebration of humor and music—as an upbeat experience that moves constantly to the rhythm of Macho Camacho. The other side of Sánchez's double-coded book, however, invites the postmodern reader to interpret it as a critique of Puerto Rico's colonial status and the function of American mass media in such a society. Similarly, it is an indictment of the language of American advertising in Third World countries. The active postmodern reader observes a variety of passive receivers of radio and television messages in this novel.

As in Sarduy, space and characters are conceived in a fashion radically opposed to typical modernist modes. In novels such as John Dos Passos's *Manhattan Transfer* and Fuentes's *Where the Air Is Clear*, the modernist author provides a broad, panoramic, and totalizing spatial field. The central event and spatial image of *Macho Camacho's Beat* is a *tapón*—en enormous traffic jam that immobilizes the characters and spatial field of the novel. The passage that describes this *tapón* stylistically blocks or marginalizes transitive action just as the *tapón* it describes physically blocks transit.[24] The *tapón* seems to deny the possibility of transitive action, and it negates the kind of mobility narrators and characters share in many classic modernist texts. The well rounded and psychologically profound characters are also denied this "human" dimension in Sánchez (as in Sarduy), functioning as surface (and superficial) subjects who articulate clichés and formulas, and are as much fictional constructs as are Frankenstein and Mohammed Ali in the text.

The status of truth in *Macho Camacho's Beat* is complex and ambiguous. The characters themselves do not seem to be fully conscious of the sources of the clichéd and formulaic language they speak and the questionable claims to truth of what they say. The postmodern reader, however, questions these truths and understands their subversive potential. The total novel questions the possibility that either mass culture or Puerto Rican literature can speak truthfully about the concerns of Puerto Rican culture and society. The multiple discourses in *Macho Camacho's Beat* share one obvious element with the heterogeneous discourse of the Mexican postmodern—their exhaustion.

Sánchez's *La importancia de llamarse Daniel Santos* is a more overtly postmodern text dealing with an author's search for the story of the popular singer of the 1940s and 1950s, the Puerto Rican Daniel Santos. The author figure, who is identified in the text as a gay writer named Luis Rafael Sánchez, travels from Puerto Rico to such places as Guayaquil, Caracas, Cali, Quito, Barranquilla, Managua, and Bogotá in search of the complete story of Santos, who had sung in those cities himself. Sánchez's search escapes generic definitions, as his book blurs the boundaries between fiction, biography, and testimonial writing. The author describes his text in the early stages as "una narración híbrida y fronteriza, mestiza, exenta de las regulaciones genéricas" [a hybrid, frontier and mestiza narration, exempt from generic regulations].[25] Near the end of the text he also overtly recognizes his debts to his modernist predecessor Alejo Carpentier and his postmodern predecessor Severo Sarduy.

This novel is a self-conscious analysis of myths. Many of Sánchez's traditional and modernist predecessors in Latin America created myths, and some of his modernist predecessors debunked myths. In *La importancia de llamarse Daniel Santos*, Sánchez neither creates nor debunks the myths surrounding the figure of Daniel Santos, but questions how popular figures such as he are mythified and demythified. For example, in one section of the novel, the narrator questions how Santos was mythified along with the popular bolero; in another, the narrator questions why he himself became so engrossed in Santos and his music. In other sections of the novel, the narrator speculates on how the image of the *macho* singer is promoted in Latin America.

Rich in a variety of colloquial languages—an open celebration of Caribbean Spanish—this novel subverts the monologic aims of official language. It self-consciously questions the monopolizing hegemonic space of the single truth, using language as its point of departure and penetrating a broad spectrum of the languages and cultures of Latin America. In this sense, *La importancia de llamarse Daniel Santos* can be read as an anthropological study as well as a fictive biography or a diary of Sánchez's own search for an understanding of Latin American culture.

The work of Edgardo Rodríguez Juliá also escapes traditional genre definition. His first heterogeneous text, *Las tribulaciones de Jonás* ("The tribulations of Jonah," 1981), is a testimonial account of the renowned Puerto Rican political figure Luis Muñoz Marín. *El entierro de Cortijo* ("Cortijo's burial," 1983) deals with the wake for a popular band leader, an experience that was especially significant for Puerto Rico's African-Americans. Alonso has pointed out that Rodríguez Juliá does not attempt to impose coherence on the conflicting and contradictory gestures in these two texts; there is no overarching interpretive scheme.[26] Rodríguez Juliá's postmodern attitude— leaving the interpretation open to the reader—is a rejection of the self-assured stances taken by his traditional and modernist predecessors in the Caribbean. *La noche oscura del Niño Avilés* ("The dark night of the Avilés boy," 1984) is also a text for the active postmodern reader, offering this reader a series of historical and fictional documents to decipher. Like *Terra Nostra*, this lengthy novel returns to the Spanish foundation of the Colonial period as part of its investigation into origins. Rodríguez Juliá shares with Fuentes the belief that truth is to be found in historical understanding. In a later work, the short novel *Una noche con Iris Chacón* ("A night with Iris Chacón," 1986), Rodríguez Juliá relates three stories about popular culture in Puerto Rico.

Postmodern fiction in Puerto Rico, like that of Cabrera Infante and some Mexican writers, often straddles the unstable and indeterminate cultural boundaries between the United States and Latin America. The Puerto Rican writers' leap to the ontological is often based on an awareness of the epistemological limits of writing in a society dominated by American culture.

POSTMODERN FICTION IN THE DOMINICAN REPUBLIC

After the rise of a Creole poetry and the modern poetry called "Independent" in the Dominican Republic, poets associated with La Poesía Sorprendida (surprised poetry) contributed to the modernization of literature. In 1943, the Chilean Alberto Baez Flores, Franklin Mieses Burgos, Aída Cartagena Portolatín, and Freddy Gatón Arce began publishing a literary magazine named *La Poesía Sorprendida*, which promoted the reading of European modernist and avant-garde literature. They published the following declaration of intentions: "We aim to promote a national poetry nourished by international currents as the only way to be authentic. We declare ourselves allied to the classics of yesterday, today, and tomorrow, with a limitless creativity blind to permanent frontiers and alive to man's mysterious world, always secret, solitary, intimate and creative."[27]

The modernist fiction writers in the Dominican Republic have been Aída Cartagena Portolatín, Marcio Veloz Maggiolo, Pedro Mir, and Pedro Verges. Cartagena Portolatín's *Escalera para Electra* ("Stair for Electra," 1969) is a modern version of the Electra story as well as a political allegory. Veloz Maggiolo exhibits some postmodern tendencies in his experimental novel *De abril en adelante* ("From April forward," 1975), a book which, according to one informed critic "intentionally fails to constitute itself as the narrative of the Revolt of April 1965."[28] In *Cuando amaban las tierras comuneras* ("When they loved the communal land," 1978), Pedro Mir evokes the United States's invasion of 1916. Verges's *Sólo cenizas hallarás* ("You will only find ashes," 1980) deals with the oppressiveness of the Trujillo dictatorship.

The Dominican Republic certainly is not a center of postmodern fictional production in the Americas. Nevertheless, Marcio Veloz Maggiolo, Efraím Castillo, Andrés L. Mateo, and Manuel García Cartagena do show some affinities with postmodernism. Veloz Maggiolo demonstrated interests in the postmodern with experiments such as *Florbella* ("Florbella," 1986, subtitled *arquenovela; "*archnovel" in English) and *Materia Prima* ("Raw material," 1988, subtitled *protonovela*). Neither of these novels is as experimental as their daring subtitles suggest, but they reveal Veloz Maggiolo's postmodern attitudes. In his novels *Curriculum (el síndrome de la visa)* ("Curriculum, the syndrome of the visa," 1982) and *Intihuaman o Eva Again* ("Intihuaman or Eva again," 1983), Efraím Castillo novelizes issues of American and Dominican culture, questioning dominant U.S. values. Andrés L. Mateo attempts experiments with language and chapter structure in *Pisar los dedos de Dios* ("Stepping on the fingers of God," 1979) and *La otra Penélope* ("The other Penelope," 1982), both of which deal with the subjective state of the characters in an urban setting. The young writer Manuel García Cartegena's first novel, *Aquiles Vargas, fantasma* ("Aquiles Vargas, phantom," 1989) is a self-conscious metafiction that questions the political future of the Dominican Republic as well as the status of his book as a novel.

The Caribbean postmodern is one of the most heterogeneous of Latin America, perhaps because of the multiple language and culture groups that coexist in close geographic proximity. In addition, the acutely hierarchical class structure in much of the Caribbean and the proximity to the United States contribute to the special heterogeneity of the Caribbean.

Benítez Rojo has described the Caribbean as a culture of "performers," and the postmodern fictions of Cabrera Infante, Sarduy, and Sánchez are indeed performances. *Three Trapped Tigers* is a virtuoso linguistic performance, *Cobra* is an exceptional performance with theory and narrative, and *Macho Camacho's Beat* is a magnificent multicultural performance. Benítez Rojo's reference to the "aquatic" quality of Caribbean culture also recalls the aquatic quality of these always-transforming texts. The heterogeneous, aquatic, and double-coded nature of these unresolved contradictions places them among the premier examples of postmodern fiction in Latin America.

The postmodern novelists of the Caribbean write with a full awareness of the provisional and precarious status of a Caribbean culture in close interaction with American culture, and often dominated by it. Truth is as unstable, provisional, and aquatic in the texts of these Caribbean postmodern writers as are many other features of this writing. Truth is as ambiguous as many of the characters themselves, who tend to speak in the formulaic patterns imposed on them by foreign and national mass media and popular culture.

6

In the Margins

The mainline and most amply distributed literature of Latin America today is primarily that of the modernist writers of the Boom and the modernist writers of the magic-realist vein. Recently, women writers, such as Isabel Allende and Laura Esquivel, have benefitted from the commercial interests in magic realism and the Latin American Boom. However, the most broadly recognized writings of the Boom and of magic realism are neither the most technically innovative nor the most experimental fictions being written in Latin America today.

Many Latin American women and men writers share with their First World counterparts what Linda Hutcheon calls the postmodern valuing of the margins.[1] Some of these writers in the margins often are not mainline enough to fit into standard literary histories, nor technically innovative enough to fit logically into a discussion such as this of Latin American postmodernities. Other writers and literary traditions have been marginalized for a variety of academic and institutional reasons. In the present chapter, several types of writing in the margins are taken into account. Although not all are as innovative and experimental as the type of postmodern writers discussed previously, some of them might be considered postmodern in accordance with other understandings of the term *postmodern*. Some of these writers—such as women writers and those dealing with gay and lesbian themes—do not fit easily into any academic categories. In other cases, the marginalization is geographical: Paraguay, Central America, and Brazil are frequently ignored in the history of Latin American literature. In some cases, the marginalized are similar to the innovative postmodern writers, as is the case of many feminist postmoderns.

From a North Atlantic perspective, the history of Latin American literature, in fact, is a continuum of marginality. Excluded for generations from
the canon of Western literature, all Latin American writers, from the two
centuries since the independence, have been, technically speaking, writing
in the margins. The concept of world literature, until the multicultural
debates began in the last decade in First World academia, had been limited
to specific kinds of writing from Western Europe and the United States.

The most prominent writers of Latin America, from its most accomplished
turn-of-the-century poets, such as Rubén Darío (who was recognized
throughout the Hispanic world as a renovator of literary language), to its first
generation of modernist writers—Miguel Angel Asturias, Alejo Carpentier,
Agustín Yáñez, Juan Rulfo, Leopoldo Marechal, and others—wrote in the
margins of the West. Only with the rise of Jorge Luis Borges, then the Boom,
the institutionalization of magic realism, and the more recent rise of multi-
culturalism has it been possible for Latin American writers to be considered
a part of the Western canon.

In the meantime, the cultural centers of Latin America—Buenos Aires,
Mexico City, Santiago, Bogotá, Havana—began creating a national and
Latin American canon that, for the most part, went unrecognized beyond the
national borders of Argentina, Mexico, Chile, Colombia, Cuba, and the
remaining Latin American nations. Nevertheless, the construction of national
literatures, a program initiated in the 1920s and 1930s with the first wide-
spread publication of national literary histories in Latin America, resulted in
the canonization of *criollista* (creolist) novels which, by the 1940s, were
broadly recognized in Latin America as "classic" national expression.[2]

The marginal writers in these marginalized nations were, for the most
part, those innovative writers who were the forerunners of the postmodern
writers in Latin America. Consequently, the fiction of the avant-garde
poets—Jaime Torres Bodet, Martín Adán, Vicente Huidobro, and others—
was virtually excluded from most discussions of national literature and a
national literary canon. Several other modern writers of later generations,
including Juan Carlos Onetti, Salvador Garmendia, and Julio Ramón Ribeyro,
have spent their lives writing in the margins of not only "Western Literature,"
but on the edges of their respective societies.

The phenomenon of marginality has continued into the current juncture
of modern and postmodern writing in Latin America, and the new writers in
this category are Elizabeth Burgos of Venezuela, Elena Poniatowska of
Mexico, and Miguel Barnet of Cuba, among numerous others. For the most
part, gay and lesbian writers as well as novelists in countries distant from the
cultural power centers of Latin America write in the margins.

FEMINIST POSTMODERNITIES

The recent popularity of the commercial writers Isabel Allende and Laura Esquivel, in conjunction with the general international interest in both Latin American writing and women's writing, has placed women writers in Latin America in the spotlight for the first time in the history of the region. Women have been writing in Latin America since the Colonial period, of course, Sor Juana Inés de la Cruz being the most prominent example. She had several nineteenth-century heirs, including figures such as the Colombian Soledad Acosta de Samper, who was one of the most productive writers of either gender in nineteenth-century Latin America. She was followed in this century by numerous important women writers who have written in the modernist vein, such as the Chileans María Luisa Bombal and Marta Brunet; the Costa Rican Yolanda Oreamuno; the Argentines María Mercedes Levinson, Beatriz Guido, and Silvina Bullrich; the Mexican Rosario Castellanos; and the Colombians Elisa Mújica and Fanny Buitrago.

Several women writers are producing an innovative postmodern fiction in Latin America, and some of these writers—such as Carmen Boullosa, Albalucía Angel, Diamela Eltit, Cristina Peri Rossi, Alejandra Pizarnik, Reina Roffé, Orietta Lozano—have already been mentioned in this book. In addition to these writers, novelists such as the Argentines Susana Torres Molina and Sylvia Molloy, the Brazilians Clarice Lispector and Helena Parente Cunha, and the Venezuelans Milagros Mata Gil and Ana Teresa Torres are making noteworthy contributions to a modern and sometimes postmodern fiction in Latin America.

For the critic Jean Franco, a well-informed British scholar practicing in U.S. academia, feminist theory fails as a theory if it does not change the study of literature substantially.[3] Latin American feminist theory, according to Franco, must use as a point of departure a critique of institutions and, above all, the literary system itself. This feminist theory need not begin from zero because its interests touch those of other intellectual tendencies, particularly those of deconstruction, semiotics, and Marxist theories of ideology. Deconstructionist criticism, as Franco points out, contributes to feminist analysis because it shows how rooted binary thinking is in Western thought, and the oppositions that it produces. Franco also points out that we are entering into a (postmodern) period of the end of the master narratives—the global and totalizing theories that were always based on the exclusion of the heterogeneous. Today, it is relatively easy to deconstruct binary systems of colonial or nationalist thought. But Franco concludes that pluralism also has its risks: if everything is valid, then nothing is of value.

The new feminist fiction of Latin America is characterized by daring attitudes toward literary discourse and a direct questioning of dominant ideologies. Many of the women writers of the 1980s, Torres Molina, Angel, Eltit, and Parente Cunha included, are not only aware of their roles as women writers in Latin America, but also are fully conscious of feminist theory. For the first time in Latin American fiction, the unmasking of ideology and an analysis of the social construction of gender are carried out with a self-conscious and overt understanding of ideology and feminist theory. For example, many of these women writers seek to understand the social and cultural practices that clarify how gender relations are constituted, repro-duced, and contested. Most of these writers seek an understanding, in different ways, of gender under patriarchal capitalism. Angel, Eltit, Parente Cunha, and others share poststructuralist interests in the theory of language, subjectivity, and power as knowledge production. Many of these writers have been engaged in a search for an *écriture féminine*.

Albalucía Angel, Diamela Eltit, Orietta Lozano, and several other women writers have published a series of radical fictions that contest the dominant power structure with different types of *écriture féminine*. Angel's personal and professional interest in a self-conscious feminist writing is most evident in her two novels *Misiá Señora* (1982) and *Las andariegas* (1984). These are also her most complex works. The protagonist of *Misiá Señora*, Mariana, is reared by a family of the landed aristocracy in the coffee-growing region of Colombia. She eventually finds herself caught between the expectations a patriarchal capitalist society holds for young women—marriage, mother-hood, and reproduction—and a more marginal but potentially meaningful existence. Her friendships with Yosmina and Anais offer an alternative to the established order.

The structure of *Misiá Señora*, divided into three parts, relates three chron-ological stages of Mariana's life. These parts are formally identified as *imágenes*. The first of these, titled "Tengo una muñeca vestida de azul" (I have a doll dressed in blue), deals with Mariana's childhood and adolescence. The second, "Antigua sin sombra" (ancient one without shadow), relates her courtship, marriage, her two children's births, and her weakening mental state, which results in a stay in a mental institution. The third *imagen*, "Los sueños del silencio" (dreams of silence), describes a series of dramatic visions that often relate her to important female figures-her mother and grandmother.

Coming to an understanding of gender differences in female identity is the central thematic thread of *Misiá Señora*. Much of the first *imagen* deals with different aspects of female sexuality. Mariana's childhood contains the theme of the constitution of gender identity and involves sexual harassment, initial experiences with machismo, and, later, the gradual discovery of her own sexuality. The sexual harassment is a vague and incomprehensible experience for Mariana as a child and yet one of the significant images that she remembers in adulthood. The expression of machismo involves a variety of abusive experiences, including the portrayal of the traditional Latin American male role model as the assumed ideal.

In *Misiá Señora*, gender issues are also associated with the ideology of the Catholic church and with class structure. The protagonist's experience with the Catholic church involves her indoctrination as a child that the body represents sin—for example, the lesson that looking at someone nude was a sin and that touching her own body was also a sin. She lives with the legends of sexuality and sin as related to her by Catholic women. Later, as an adult herself, she struggles to overcome the intellectual barriers of this ideological indoctrination in order to contest its reproduction of ideology. Her ideological awareness represents a first step in establishing a sense of her own sexual identity. When she loses her virginity, she thinks of all that the priests and monks had taught her as a child, and she feels the need to liberate herself from this past with the Church. Social class also affects the novel's presentation of gender issues: since Mariana belongs to the provincial aristocracy, she had been destined to become a passive and frivolous *niña linda* (pretty girl).

Misiá Señora is a novel whose feminism privileges the subjectivity of images and imagination, as defined by the work's tripartite structure. The protagonist, who occasionally assumes the role of writer, demonstrates a rampant imagination and proposes a search for a new feminine consciousness. As a child, Mariana's reaction to her identity crisis is to take refuge in her imagination. She pictures herself flying. As an adult, Mariana often interprets the concrete reality around her on the basis of her imagination. Consequently, in *Misiá Señora* the reader is presented a fictional world in which the line between reality and imagination is tenuous. One aspect of this highly imaginative experience is the creation of a new language—a feminine discourse—as part of Angel's feminist project.

Las andariegas is explicitly presented as a feminist work and is Angel's most radical experiment in fiction yet. It also represents a search for a an *écriture féminine* as well as an evocation of a woman's sense of courage. *Las andariegas* is a postmodern project in the sense that it is a self-conscious attempt at fictionalizing poststructuralist feminist theory. It begins with two epigraphs, a statement by the author that sets forth the feminist project, and then a third epigraph. The first epigraph is from *Les Guérrilleres* by Monique Wittig and refers to women breaking the existing order and to their need for strength and courage. The second epigraph is from *Las nuevas cartas portuguesas* by Maria

Isabel Barreno, Maria Teresa Horta, and Maria Velho da Costa, and refers to women as firm and committed warriors. These two epigraphs are explained by the author's page-long statement, the third prefatory section to appear before the narrative. Angel relates that her reading of Wittig's *Les Guérrilleres* inspired her to undertake this project with women warriors who advance "from nowhere to history." She uses images from stories of her childhood as a guide, transforming them into fables and cryptic visions. The final product of her search, according to Angel, is the hope for a better future that women have held throughout time. The third epigraph is from the mythology of a Colombian indigenous group, the Kogui, and emphasizes the role of the woman figure in creation.

The innovative language and experimental techniques of *Las andariegas* are an important aspect of its *écriture feminine*. Much of the narrative consists of brief phrases, often with unconventional punctuation. Rather than developing a consistent plot, these phrases often contain an image. The use of linguistic imagery is supported by visual images—a set of 12 drawings of women. Angel also experiments with the physical space of language in the text in a manner similar to the techniques of concrete poetry. The four pages of this type consist of a variety of circular and semicircular arrangements of the names of women famous in history. These four pages universalize the story of the constantly traveling women.

Las andariegas ends with a type of epilogue consisting of another quotation from Monique Wittig, comprising four brief sentences that call for precisely the undertaking that is the essence of Angel's last two novels: a new language, a new beginning, and a new history for women. The author expresses optimism for this new beginning with the final sentence: "Ellas dicen que el sol va a salir" [they (feminine) say that the sun is going to come out]. In summary, in her early work, Angel is concerned mostly with issues of class; in the later work she develops a postmodern *écriture feminine*.

Diamela Eltit's four novels constitute a radical and experimental feminist project and, like Angel and other contemporary feminists, Eltit is self-consciously forging an *écriture feminine*. She believes that the effects of feminism are only beginning to be discernible in Latin American literature, for women writers have been at the periphery of literary histories controlled by men. She maintains that women's writing can bring a new criterion for the orders and disorders of language. The first two novels, *Lumpérica* (1983) and *Por la patria* (1986) reveal a sense for the origins of the Latin language, the mother language of the later Romance language family, a family present in both novels. The discursive contexts change in the different fragments of *Lumpérica*, again, referring to Latin and with resonances of medieval Spanish and Italian.

These different historical languages coexist, in unresolved contradiction, with a more current masculine discourse subverted by other contemporary discourses—colloquial Chilean Spanish and feminine discourse. The juxtaposition of these languages could be seen as the "linguistic incest" in the language family that inhabits this novel. The entire situation in *El cuarto mundo* (1988) consists of degradation, commercialization, reification. The novel's last sentence is "La niña sudaca irá a la venta" [the *sudaca* girl will go up for sale]. The newly born child going up for sale belongs to the postmodern society of Jameson's late capitalism and Baudrillard's postmodernism, one in which abstract qualities like goodness and knowledge enter into the realm of exchange value. Truth also becomes degraded and meaningless in this *sudaca* world, as does language.

Angel and Eltit are among the most radical innovators among Latin America's postmodern feminist writers. Several other young women writers are engaged in a project of resistance, and Orietta Lozano's first novel, *Luminar* (1994), is comparable in several ways to the *Lumpérica* of Eltit and the fiction of Angel, as well as *The Bloody Countess* by Alejandra Pizarnik. Lozano's sense for the spectacle and the space of the urban night scene, in fact, is quite similar to the experience of *Lumpérica*. Both the writer Orietta Lozano and her alter ego in the text, Odette, are acutely aware of both their private and public space and the differences between the two; they are also interested in the writing of Pizarnik, as are several of the characters.

Feminists such as the Argentine Susana Torres Molina and the Puerto Rican Rosario Ferré, have feminist programs similar to those of cultural feminists in the United States.[4] Torres Molina is not as formally innovative as Angel and Eltit, but Torres Molina's set of stories *Dueña y señora* ("Owner and Lady") represented a major breakthrough in contemporary Argentine writing when it began to circulate in Buenos Aires in 1983. The lesbian encounters in *Dueña y señora* scandalized Argentina's conservative reading public as much as Enrique Medina's irreverent and sexually daring novels had a decade earlier. Never before had a woman Argentine celebrated the female body and lesbianism in such a fashion. Its shock value aside, Torres Molina's central focus is how gender relations are constituted, reproduced, and contested.

Dueña y señora consists of a prologue written by Martha Berlin, followed by nine stories told in the first person by Torres Molina. Several of the early stories question and subvert the traditional gender relations established by Argentina's patriarchal order, and many of the stories portray a woman's celebration of sexuality and pleasure. This feminist perspective is similar to the position of the cultural feminists in the United States.[5] The last story, "Impresiones de una futura mamá" (Impressions of a future mother), is a celebration of lesbianism. In her prologue, Berlin sets forth one of the key points of and constant concerns of this volume, pointing out that women have not had the opportunity to "nominar los espacios del goce" [name the spaces of pleasure]. Berlin also questions the ideological implications of the Argentine colloquial phrases *verdaderas mujeres* (true women) and *verdaderos hombres* (true men). In addition, she describes Torres Molina as a writer who is fully conscious of her ideological agenda.

These nine stories are not particularly "well written," either in the traditional sense of "well-crafted fiction" (*buen escribir,* in the Latin American tradition) or in the modern sense of being technically innovative. The language appears simple and colloquial; the style is clearly the most "antiliterary" of any of the writers mentioned in this chapter. Nevertheless, these fictions subtly undermine the traditional sense of gender relations, including much of the everyday and colloquial language intimately associated with traditional sex roles. In the first story, Torres Molina questions the Latin American tradition of the *piropo* (flirtatious catcalls). The female protagonist is harassed on the street by a male who delivers progressively more vulgar *piropos,* but in the end, she reverses the traditional sex roles and intimidates him in a surprising turn of events: she returns even more aggressive and vulgar *piropos* to him.

The publication of Torres Molina's *Dueña y señora* marked an important turning point for women's writing in Argentina and in Latin America: for the first time a woman had published a book with an explicitly lesbian content.[6] Torres Molina's writing functions along the lines of a cultural feminism that Mary Daly and Adrienne Rich have promoted as the ideology of a female nature or female essence reappropriated by women themselves in an effort to revalidate undervalued female attributes. In "Impresiones de una futura mamá," Torres Molina aligns herself with the cultural feminists, for she celebrates female biological difference. For the cultural feminists, the enemy of women is not merely a social system, an economic institution, or a set of backward beliefs, but masculinity itself and in some cases male biology. Torres Molina also questions the social system and its reproduction of patriarchal social codes. Like Angel, she is engaged in the analysis of gender-based power relations, for they are the primary focus of these stories.

Rosario Ferré has written a large volume of fiction and essays dealing with the marginalization of women and racial prejudice in Puerto Rico. In her novel *Maldito amor* (1986), she relates how several marginalized sectors of society revise and appropriate the history of Puerto Rico. In addition to the marginality of women and racial prejudice, Ferré's writing often focusses on female creativity, frequently by means of daring sexual language.

Helena Parente Cunha, a professor of literary theory at the Universidade Federal in Rio de Janeiro, published her first novel, *Woman Between Mirrors* (originally written in Portuguese) in 1983. Given her background in literary theory, Parente Cunha is more similar to Angel and Eltit in some ways than to Torres Molina. Previously unknown as a fiction writer in Brazil, Parente Cunha in this work demonstrates interest in psychoanalytic models of sexuality and subjectivity. *Woman Between Mirrors* is an experiment in privileging the subjective in constituting the meaning of a middle-aged woman's lived reality. The protagonist is a forty-five-year-old Brazilian married to an extraordinarily dominant Brazilian man. She also has three teenage sons. The narrative is her response to the otherness of female sexuality that has been repressed.

The woman begins by relating anecdotes from her youth. She tells her life story in a basically linear fashion, although she does alternate between the past and the present. In her earliest childhood memories, she recalls competition with her brother, who received more attention than she from her parents. As a child she always respected the patriarchal order, assuming a role inferior to her brother and being totally subservient to her father. She has played a similar role with her husband, an alcoholic woman chaser who eventually becomes a physically repugnant and boring figure for her. In addition to her multiple fantasies about the ideal lover, she actually has an affair—with the man whose wife is having an affair with her husband. By the end of the novel, the protagonist is successfully reworking the terms of her existence.

Woman Between Mirrors is an innovative work, and one of its most interesting technical devices is the constant presence of a voice identified as "the woman who writes me." This voice appears in italicized type in passages ranging from a sentence to several lengthy paragraphs. "The woman who writes me" is an oppositional voice that frequently questions the protagonist's thoughts, actions, and motives. In the early stages, this voice plays the role of an analytical psychologist, questioning the protagonist's true motives, even though the latter claims that she has invented and controls this fictional voice. The protagonist also states that the woman who writes her never gets out of her control. Nevertheless, the relationship between the two involves a constant power struggle.

In this novel, the act of writing functions as a paradigm of power relationships. The protagonist struggles with "the woman who writes me" just as she struggles with her husband. She gradually takes control of her entire situation, exercising power over both the woman who writes her and her husband. She also establishes identity by rediscovering the African culture of Brazil that had been forbidden when she was a child. (The image of the mango tree appears throughout the novel in association with this repressive childhood.) At the end of the novel she describes herself as whole and multiple.

Woman Between Mirrors is a heterogeneous and theoretically self-conscious work that is typical of some of the most engaging feminist novels written in Latin America in the 1980s. Parente Cunha has put into practice Hélène Cixous's admonition to "write yourself. Your body must be heard." Consequently, this Brazilian writer, like Torres Molina, also aligns herself with the cultural feminists in the United States who believe in an essence of female biology.

Sylvia Molloy and Clarice Lispector also are feminist writers with a self-conscious feminist agenda, and Molloy's *Certificate of Absence* (1981) has many direct parallels with *Woman Between Mirrors*. Molloy's narrator-protagonist is also engaged in an identity search related to her writing—what David William Foster has described as the topos of the prison-house of love.[7] *Certificate of Absence* deals with an Argentine woman who returns to an apartment in New England where she had once had an affair with another woman and where she writes a memoir about this experience. Like the protagonist of *Woman Between Mirrors*, she struggles with her expression, and her self-conscious rereading of her writing makes this novel comparable to much postmodern fiction.

Author of nine novels and six volumes of short fiction, Clarice Lispector is one of Latin America's most influential women writers. Many of her characters relate to issues of feminism. *A hora da estela* (1977) and *Un sopro de vida* (1978) characterize women in search of self realization and freedom. *A hora da estrela* ("The hour of the star") presents a woman who is both artistic creator and victim of contemporary society.[8] Lispector's constant focus is *nordestinas*, women from the Northeast of Brazil who are characterized as faceless beings who are disenfranchised. The new women writers in Brazil after the generation of Lispector include Lya Luft, Márcia Denser, Sonia Coutinho, Ruth Bueno, and Anna Maria Martins.

Women writers such as the Costa Rican Carmen Naranjo, the Uruguayans Armonía Sommers and Cristina Peri Rossi, the Mexicans Elena Poniatowska and María Luisa Mendoza, and the Venezuelans Milagros Mata Gil and Ana Teresa Torres have also made major contributions to women's writing in Latin America. In addition to *Diario de una multitud* ("Diary of a multitude," 1984) Naranjo's extensive work has included her novel *Sobrepunto* (1985), which explores the role of women in Latin American society. The feminist and postmodern work of Sommers and Peri Rossi is also vast. Poniatowska's fiction is generally more traditional in narrative technique, but her two recent novels, La "Flor de Lis" (1989) and Tinísima (1992) both deal with women. Mendoza's concerns for the causes of women have appeared in a broad spectrum of fictional and journalistic writings. The literary careers of Mata Gil and Torres are in their early stages in Venezuela, but both writers are engaged in significant feminist projects.

GAY AND LESBIAN WRITING

Susan Torres Molina and Sylvia Molloy are lesbian writers with an evident feminist agenda. In general, writers with gay themes have been increasingly visible since the 1970s, particularly since the publication of Manuel Puig's Betrayed by Rita Hayworth and Kiss of the Spider Woman; lesbian themes have surfaced noticeably in the 1980s. Before that, Lezama Lima's Paradiso (1966) had dealt explicitly with homosexuality, as had Bomarzo (1962) by the Argentine Manuel Mújica Láinez. Occasional works had appeared before that, as David William Foster has documented.[9] In his insightful study of gay and lesbian themes in Latin American literature, Foster proposes that homosexuality cannot be viewed as simply the psychological complex of specific individuals, but rather must be seen as an intrasubjective matter that has ultimately to do with the controlling social dynamic.[10]

Novelists with gay themes are generally more in evidence than those with lesbian issues, and some of the fiction expressing both themes demonstrates postmodern tendencies. Their narrative strategies are varied, however, and can be associated with the traditional, the modern, and the postmodern, according to each individual case. Contemporary writers who deal with gay themes include the Mexican Luis Zapata, the Cuban Reinaldo Arenas, the Argentine Oscar Hermes Villordo, the Colombian Fernando Vallejo, and the Brazilians Aguinalado Silva and Darcy Penteado. Writers who have articulated lesbian themes include Alejandra Pizarnik, the Brazilian Márcia Denser, and the Mexican Rosamaría Roffel.

Zapata had already published one novel with a gay protagonist (Las aventuras, desventuras y sueños de Adonis García, el vampiro de la colonia Roma, "The adventures, misadventures, and dreams of Adonis García, the vampire of the colonia Roma," 1979) when En jirones ("In bits," 1985) appeared. En jirones is not only a gay novel, but a metafiction with postmodern tendencies. It is a first-person narrative about the narrator's destructive gay relationship with a character named A. He writes in a cuaderno (notebook), ostensibly for A., but also as an attempt to find a language appropriate for the expression of his emotions.

Reinaldo Arenas and Oscar Hermes Villordo have published an entire body of fiction associated with the postmodern that also characterize gays suffering repressive political regimes. In *Arturo, la estrella más brillante* ("Arturo, the most brilliant star," 1984), Arenas deals with homosexuality within the context of a Cuban regime unwilling to recognize human rights for gays. Hermes Villordo's *La otra mejilla* ("The other cheek," 1986) contains scenes similar to those in Arenas's novel, with harassment and exploitation of homosexuals by the police, as well as intimidating violence.

Fernando Vallejo has published a trilogy of novels dealing with gay experience in the hypocritical social milieu of Medellín, Colombia. In *El fuego secreto* ("The secret fire," 1986), he recounts the narrator-protagonist's growing up gay in Medellín, moving in and out of its gay bars. He seeks a realm of personal freedom beyond the limits of conventional society. Foster notes that the protagonist's gauging of a personal identity gives this novel interest as an account of the discovery of an alternate social reality beneath the facade of public life.

Aguinaldo Silva and Darcy Penteado are two Brazilians with an explicit political agenda to accompany their gay themes. Following in the path of historical research of Fuentes's *Terra Nostra* and Piglia's *Artificial Respiration*, Aguinaldo Silva rewrites an episode of the Portuguese occupation of Brazil in *No país das sombras* ("In the country of shadows," 1979). Two young soldiers in a homosexual relationship murder the chief of their military garrison in order to avoid being transferred to separate military bases. The novel cites a variety of documentary sources, thus revealing different layers of historical truth. A postmodern turn of *No país das sombras* takes place when the narrator studies documents in the National Library and he is observed by a Borges figure named Luís Borges. Penteado's *Nivaldo e Jeronimo* ("Nivaldo and Jeronimo," 1981) deals with a gay engaged in guerrilla warfare, and confirms the author's belief that sexual liberation and political liberation are one and the same process.

Alejandra Pizarnik and Márcia Denser explore lesbian themes with a self-conscious writing. Pizarnik's *The Bloody Countess* (1971) is an Argentine rewriting of the story of the seventeenth-century Hungarian Countess Erzébet Bárthory, who tortured and killed over six hundred adolescent women in order to fulfill her erotic fantasies. At the end of this short novel, the narrator states that the Countess's career is yet another proof that absolute human liberty is horrible. Foster proposes that the text, particularly with this ending, "prefigures the worst abuses of power in the name of moral reconstruction in the 1970s."[11] As in *You Will Die in a Distant Land* of Pacheco, the postmodern reader of *The Bloody Countess* plays an ambivalent role of both critical observor and participant-voyeur. Denser's *Diana cacadora* ("Diana the huntress, 1986) characterizes a lesbian protagonist who is also predatory, but this one approaches *macho* males. This protagonist finds herself attempting to find meaning in a variety of situations, including the meaning of writing and the meaning of having to function in a series of passive situations with men.

Rosamaría Roffel published the first Mexican novel with lesbian themes, *Amora* (1989). Like the narrator-protagonists in *Woman Between Mirrors* and *Certificate of Absence*, the narrator in *Amora* is a self-conscious feminist well aware of feminist theory. This explicitly lesbian novel describes the vicissitudes of the narrator's relationship with a character named Claudia. It also contains a considerable amount of the self-conscious reflection typical of postmodern texts.

THE TESTIMONIO

On the surface, the Latin American writing least associated with the postmodernities of this study is the *testimonio*. With no exact equivalent in either the English language or Anglo-American literary production, the *testimonio* is closely allied to genres such as the American New Journalism or the faction of Tom Wolfe, Norman Mailer, Truman Capote, and the documentary novel. In Latin America, this *testimonio* has a broad range of practitioners, including such similar and disparate figures as Miguel Barnet, Gabriel Careaga, Elizabeth Burgos-Debray, Elena Poniatowska, and Rodolfo Walsh. In general, the different variants of postmodern fiction have in common distant and subversive positions toward truth; the *testimonio* tends to seek veracity and truth.

In her well-informed introduction, synthesis, and analysis of the *testimonio*, Elzbieta Sklodowska reviews a variety of formats for these books.[12] Frequently, there is an interaction between an interviewer and a witness, a special relationship between the editor and the interlocutor, an intellectual commitment and solidarity with the causes of the marginalized, a need of the marginalized to have a voice, and other factors.[13] In his *Biografía de un cimarrón* ("Biography of a runaway slave," 1966), Miguel Barnet engages in ethnographic research to tell the story of Afro-Cubans. *Me llamo Rigoberta Menchú y así me nació la conciencia* ("My name is Rigoberta Menchu and this is how my awareness was born," 1983) on the other hand, is the result of Elizabeth Burgos-Debray's interviewing the Guatemalan woman Rigoberta Menchú and then editing the volume. Within the genre of *testimonio*, Sklodowska also studies Rodolfo Walsh's *Operación masacre* ("Operation massacre," 1956), and Elena Poniatowska's *La noche de Tlatelolco* ("The night of Tlatelolco," 1971), two books covering historical events in a fashion comparable in ways to New Journalism. With respect to truth, Poniatowska recognizes the relativity of human truths.[14]

The Latin American *testimonio* is a genre generally distant from the innovative and experimental fictional production discussed in the previous chapters of this book. The *testimonio* is less formally innovative and more committed to the idea of truth than the postmodernities discussed here. In addition, the narrative strategies of *testimonio* writers tend to legitimate the authority of the main voice, rather than subvert it. Nevertheless, *testimonios* are heterogeneous texts, some of which attempt to give marginalized peoples a voice, as do some postmodern novels. Many postmodern novels question the very concept of the individual subject; many *testimonios* emphasize the community over the individual. Rather than novels, *testimonios* are closely aligned to postmodern ethnography.[15]

BRAZILIAN POSTMODERNITIES

Brazil initiated a self-conscious effort to modernize its culture by organizing a well-remembered Modern Art Week in São Paulo in 1922, a turning point in Brazilian literature. Modern Art Week brought the European avant-garde movements of the time to the consciousness of Brazil's intellectuals and literati. One offshoot from this process was the fiction of Oswald de Andrade, who was influenced by the cubists and futurists in the canonical novels *Memórias sentimentais de João Miramar* ("Sentimental memories of Joao Miramar," 1924) and *Seraphim Ponte Grande* ("Seraphim Ponte Grande," 1933). Contemporary fiction has taken a plethora of directions in Brazil, from highly experimental postmodern works to science fiction, pulp novels, murder mysteries and adventure narratives.[16]

Jorge Amado, Clarice Lispector, and João Guimaraes Rosa, each with a substantive body of fiction, have been the major modernist writers in Brazil in recent decades. The key precedent to postmodern fiction in Brazil, however, was Mário de Andrade's *Macunaíma* ("Macunaíma," 1928) a bold and fragmented narrative experiment that combines Brazilian legends, folk tales, popular culture, and Western literature. Writing in the Portuguese language in a nation located in South America, however, both the modernist and the postmodern writers of Brazil have tended to be relatively ignored or marginalized by both academics and the publishing industry in the remainder of the Americas. The turning point for experimental fiction in Brazil took place in the early 1970s, as it did in the remainder of Latin America. Ignácio de Loyola Brandao, Flávio Moreira da Costa, and Osman Lins published fiction in the early 1970s that marked this turning point. Lins belonged to an older generation, but his novel *Avalovara* ("Avalovara," 1973) was very important for postmodern fiction in Brazil. It is a work in the form of a series of narrative fragments and it contains many of the elements proposed by Morelli in Julio Cortázar's *Hopscotch*.

Leading exponents of postmodern fiction in Brazil have been Clarice Lispector, Ignácio de Loyola Brandao, Roberto Drummond, Rubem Fonseca, Ivan Angelo, and Flávio Moreira da Costa. Lispector, like Carlos Fuentes and Mario Vargas Llosa, was fundamentally a modernist writer who was affected by the postmodern later in her career. Her feminist work *A hora da estrela* (1977) is a metafiction that deals with the creative process and fictionalizes an active postmodern reader.

Loyola Brandao is one of the most experimental of the Brazilian postmodern writers. His novel *Zero* (1974) was one of the most innovative works to be published in Brazil in the early 1970s, and invites comparisons with Cortázar's *A Manuel for Manuel* and Piglia's *Artificial Respiration;* the relationship between a police interrogator and his captive is portrayed as a complex game to be deciphered only by the most engaged postmodern reader. Loyola Brandao's *Nao verás país nenhum* ("You will see no country," 1982) is a futuristic novel in which the author openly recognizes his literary masters, including Isaac Asimov, Ray Bradbury, and Kurt Vonnegut. With frequent black humor, Loyola Brandao communicates a sense of exhaustion for Brazilian society that has been observed in much postmodern fiction published since the early 1970s.

In *Sangue de Coca-Cola* ("Coca Cola Blood," 1983), Roberto Drummond appropriates the popular culture of the Mardi Gras carnival, carrying a performance comparable to Luis Rafael Sánchez's *Macho Camacho's Beat.* Underneath the beat of this popular music, however, is a rewriting of the recent history of Brazil under military dictatorships. Fonseca's *Bufo & Spallanzani* (1985) is a parody of detective fiction, with a character who is a compulsive writer in the process of creating a book—titled *Bufo & Spallanzani.* *A festa* ("The Celebration," 1976) by Ivan Angelo is experimental in technique and leaves the postmodern reader the task of rewriting official history. One critic has explained that *A festa* is conceived "with a free-floating narrative focus, a Cortázarian openness."[16] Moreira da Costa's *O deastronauta: OK Jack Kerouac nós estamos te esperando em Copacabana* ("The anti-astronaut: O.K. Jack Kerouac we are waiting for you in Copacabana," 1971) is a metafiction with the irreverent and rebellious attitude of the fiction of Gustavo Sainz and José Agustín in Mexico in the 1960s.

A Latin Americanist well acquainted with the literatures of several Latin American nations, David William Foster considers Brazilian literature "unquestionably the equal of any Western artistic production."[17] In a country of such vast and diverse novelistic creation, numerous other writers with postmodern tendencies could be mentioned. Márcio Souza is not generally as innovative as novelists such as Loyola Brandao or Piglia, but his novel *Mad Maria* (1982) is a political novel that one critic has described as an "ontological journey."[18] Souza, like many modernists in Latin America, searches to understand human relationships and truths, both of which find more substantive possibilities than in most postmodern fiction.

CENTRAL AMERICAN POSTMODERNITIES

The rise of modernist fiction in the Central American region was initiated in the 1940s and 1950s by the Guatemalans Miguel Angel Asturias and Mario Monteforte Toledo, the Costa Ricans Carlos Luis Fallas and Yolanda Oreamuno, and the Panamanian Rogelio Sinán. Asturias's *El Señor Presidente* (1946), affected by Surrealism and the European modernists, was one of the key novels in the rise of modernist fiction in Latin America in the 1940s. Asturias was awarded the Nobel Prize for literature in 1967. Nevertheless, the lack of large publishing houses and other factors have meant the relative marginalization of writers in Central America, including Toledo, Fallas, Oreamuno, and Sinán.

The Central American region has not been a center of postmodern fictional production. Nevertheless, writers such as the Costa Ricans Carmen Naranjo and Samuel Rovinski, as well as the Guatemalan Mario Roberto Morales and the Honduran Roberto Quezada, have published novels with some postmodern tendencies. Morales's *Los demonios salvajes* ("The savage demons," 1978) and Naranjo's *Diario de una multitud* (1986) were early manifestations of such tendencies. Since then, Sergio Ramírez's *El castigo divino* ("Divine punishment," 1988), Gioconda Belli's *La mujer habitada* ("The inhabited woman," 1988) and Quesada's *The Ships* (1988) are notable contributions to postmodern fiction in Central America.

Central America has become one of Latin America's most active producers of the postmodern ethnology identified in Latin America as *testimonio*. The best known of the Central American *testimonios* is Burgos-Debray's *Me llamo Rigoberto Menchu y así me nació la conciencia*. Sergio Ramírez's novel *¿Te dio miedo la sangre?* ("Did the blood scare you?" 1983) was an important precursor to the *testimonio*, and several Nicaraguans have published books in the *testimonio* mode. Omar Cabezas, a FSLN officer, published a *testimonio* about a young boy's *rite de passage*, *La montaña es algo más que una inmensa estepa verde* ("The mountain is something more than an inmense, green steppe," 1982), and followed with more guerrilla experience in *Canción de amor para los hombres* ("Song of love for men," 1988). El Salvador's Roque Dalton recounted the story of a Communist Party veteran in *Miguel Mármol* (1971). Manlio Argueta's *A Day in the Life* (1980) tells one day in the life of a middle-age peasant. Claribel Alegría's *No me agarrán viva* ("They won't get me alive," 1983) and *Luisa in Realityland* (1987) provide a woman's voice to the guerrilla war in El Salvador.

PARAGUAYAN POSTMODERNITIES

Asunción certainly is not one of the centers of Latin American postmodernism, and relatively little high quality fiction—be it traditional, modern, or postmodern—has been published in Paraguay. While Paraguay was under the dictatorship of Alfredo Stroessner, the conditions were not propitious for the writing and publishing of novels.

In the 1950s, Gabriel Cassacia and Augusto Roa Bastos published novels that represent the first efforts toward a modernist fiction in Paraguay. Roa Bastos's *Hijo de hombre* ("Son of man," 1959) and Cassacia's *La llaga* ("The sore," 1964) were important contributions toward the modernization of a relatively provincial literary scene in marginalized Paraguay.

The central figure for modern and postmodern fiction in Paraguay is Roa Bastos, who wrote and published in exile from the 1970s until the fall of Stroessner in 1988. Fundamentally a modernist writer of the Boom generation, his one work most visibly affected by the postmodern is *I, the Supreme* (1975); he later published *Vigilia del almirante* ("The vigil of the admiral," 1992). Other Paraguayan novelists to publish since the early 1970s have been Juan Manuel Marcos, Raquel Saguier, Guido Rodríguez Alcalá, Santiago Trías Coll, Augusto Casola, Santiago Dumas Aranda, Cristián González Safstrand, Eduardo Amatuna, Oleg Vysokolán, Gilberto Ramírez Santacruz, Mabel Pagano and Mario Halley Mora.

Roa Bastos's *I, the Supreme* is a historical novel dealing with the Paraguayan dictator Dr. Francia. Roa Bastos incorporates a multiplicity of historical documents in this complex novel. Much of this complexity is based on its multiple voices, some of which are not easily identifiable. *I, the Supreme* covers the period from the Colonial period to modern times, and the basic narrative is presented by a "compiler."

I, the Supreme contains a totalizing impulse and other characteristics of Latin American modernist fiction. This novel, however, bridges modernist and postmodern fiction, blurring the boundaries between genres, presenting knowledge as a construct, and questioning the concept of narrative authority. Truth is extremely difficult to establish in this text, although the complex series of texts and narrators leaves the possibility of establishing some truths.

The very heterogeneity of recent writing in Latin America makes the task of dealing with today's postmodernities an arduous and sometimes risky proposition. Certainly writers such as Eltit, Angel, Molloy, Zapata, and Loyola Brandao are postmodern writers as they have been described and analyzed in previous chapters of this book. Much of the contemporary writing in the margins described in the present chapter, however, is either fundamentally traditional or modernist in narrative strategies and is unrelated to the postmodern (or relates to the postmodern only tangentially, at best).

Much recent feminist, gay, and lesbian writing, as well as the fiction of marginalized writers in Brazil, Central America and Paraguay, shares the multiple political agenda of postmodern writers such as Fuentes, Piglia, and Pacheco. Some of these marginalized writers, perhaps not as innovative as Piglia and Pacheco, question the historical bases of dominant ideologies and search for methods to subvert literary and political traditions. In some cases, this writing reminds the reader, once again, that there is not always a clear dichotomy between many modernist and postmodern practices; the postmodern is a continuation of the modernist tradition. Writers of the generations of Roa Bastos, Fuentes, and Lispector, in fact, have written some predominantly modernist texts and others more in the postmodern mode.

Many of these writers in the margins, particularly the authors of *testimonios* and texts with gay and lesbian themes, tend to exhibit different attitudes toward truth than the experimental postmodern writers. With an evident political agenda and social commitment, the authors of *testimonios* often have much more confidence in the possibility of expressing truth than the postmodern fiction writers.

7

Conclusion

"Is there a story?" a character asks on the first page of Ricardo Piglia's *Artificial Respiration*, a novel published four decades after Jorge Luis Borges wrote several of his early stories without strong story lines, such as "The Library of Babel" and "Pierre Menard, Author of the *Quijote*" and several decades after Walter Benjamin lamented the end of storytelling in his celebrated essay "The Storyteller." Since Borges, (and perhaps despite "La Biblioteca de Babel" and Benjamin's lamentations), Latin America has seen the blossoming of a postmodern fiction both with a story and without much of a story at all. Some postmodern innovations, such as Carlos Fuentes's *Birthday*, the fiction of Salvador Elizondo, and Diamela Eltit's *Lumpérica* have been more mediations on space, literature, or theory than the telling of a story.

Obviously, there are numerous postmodern tendencies in contemporary Latin American fiction of the past two decades. These Latin American postmodernities can be identified following the rise of postmodern culture in the late 1960s in various sectors of this simultaneously premodern, modern, and postmodern society. One might be tempted to speak of a "light" postmodernism in the parody of *Aunt Julia and the Script Writer*, or the "heavy" postmodernism of Diamela Eltit and Ricardo Piglia. Once stated, however, exactly where does the fiction of a Manuel Puig fit in these simple categories, a fiction that is both "lightly" parodic and entertaining as well as "heavily" subversive? Fuentes's postmodern fiction also escapes categorization into either of these divisions. Once again, postmodern fiction escapes simple definition.

The discourse of truth, developed by Hans-Georg Gadamer, Paul Ricoeur, and others of the hermeneutic tradition, is placed under serious question by the postmodern novel in Latin America. Latin American society and culture have experienced the same crisis of truth that Jean-François Lyotard, Jean Baudrillard, and Fredric Jameson describe in the North Atlantic nations; this crisis of truth is manifested in the recent postmodern novel.

As has been amply discussed, Linda Hutcheon has proposed that the term *postmodern fiction* be reserved for historiographic metafiction. This postmodern fiction often reflects the problematic nature of the relation of writing history to narrativization, raising questions about the cognitive status of historical knowledge. Certainly some Latin American postmodern fictions, such as José Emilio Pacheco's *You Will Die in a Distant Land,* Fuentes's *Terra Nostra* and Piglia's *Artificial Respiration,* do enact this problematic nature of writing and of historical knowledge. The broad varieties of Latin American postmodernities, however, point to the limitations of Hutcheon's virtual definition of postmodern fiction. Postmodern writers such as Severo Sarduy, Luis Rafael Sánchez, and Puig have a variety of agendas other than raising questions about the cognitive status of historical knowledge.

For Fredric Jameson, Terry Eagleton, and several other neo-Marxist critics, postmodernism is just another commodity within the dynamic of the bourgeois for new markets. Even if one accepts this proposition, however, it seems questionable exactly which postmodernism Jameson is questioning. Of the postmodern fiction reviewed in this book, one can identify certain strains of highly innovative fiction in search of a new market. Experimentalism for the sake of experimentalism, however, seemed to reach its apogee in Latin America in the early-to-mid-1970s. The innovation market for Latin American fiction seemed to reach a nadir, yet Latin American postmodernities have mutated into various other forms. Contrary to Jameson's narrow view of postmodern fiction in general and often uninformed understanding of postmodern fiction in Latin America, the most significant postmodern projects of Latin America, such as those of Diamela Eltit and Ricardo Piglia, are, in fact, of relatively little commercial value today.

Despite the prognostications of Benjamin and the critical view of a very limited type of postmodern fiction that Jameson takes into account, postmodern fiction in Latin America is a culturally viable and politically responsive literary form. Several of the postmodern writers have engaged in a serious and profound search for cultural origins, a linguistic search. Consequently, *Por la patria* by Diamela Eltit, *Los felinos del Canceller* of R. H. Moreno-Durán, *Artificial Respiration* of Ricardo Piglia, *Terra Nostra* of Fuentes and *Cobra* of Severo Sarduy are all novels in which the search for origins involves a return to the origins of the Spanish language. Their concern for language, their confrontation with language, and their use of language in these novels are far more serious enterprises than the mere "play" with language that some critics have ascribed to a perhaps more frivolous type of postmodernism.

An epochal break is evident in the cultures of Latin America in the late 1960s. In the Latin American novel, this break is particularly evident from

1968 to 1972, a break that produced the highly influential *Betrayed by Rita Hayworth* by Manuel Puig, *Cobra* by Severo Sarduy, and other postmodern fictions. The postmodernities of Latin America play out in different forms in the different regions. The military dictatorships of Argentina, Chile, and Uruguay were major factors in the production of the particular type of postmodern fiction written by Piglia and Eltit under these repressive regimes. The drug industry of the Andean region has been a major factor in this region's postmodern society and culture, far more so than elsewhere. Mexico and the Caribbean, on the other hand, have been most directly and visibly affected by U.S. culture and First World postmodern writing.

The centers of postmodern literary production in Latin America are Mexico and the Southern Cone. After a first wave of irreverence toward modernist writing, manifested by the Onda in Mexico, a period of hyperexperimentation followed. Several novelists began radical experiments with space. With the return to storytelling, the Mexican writers pursued new avenues for questioning truth. In the Southern Cone, postmodern fiction often surfaced as underground allegories of resistance or a literature written in exile.

The cultural phenomenon of Buenos Aires and Mexico City, as well as the multiple postmodernities in other regions, are unquestionable evidence of a postmodern novel in Latin America, despite the critics of the postmodern. Never constituted to be a repetition or duplication of the Boom of the 1960s, this heterogeneous and political fiction marks several directions for the turn of the century, unlike the unified aesthetic and commercial agenda of the internationally recognized flourishing of Latin American culture in the 1960s. Indeed, there are many stories.

Notes

Preface

1. See Alex Callinicos, *Against Postmodernism*.
2. There has been a recent tendency among Hispanists, like those in other literary studies, to postmodernize writers from all periods. At a recent professional conference, a young academic presented a paper on the postmodernism of the Mexican novel *The Underdogs* by Mariano Azuela, a realist novel published in 1917. This type of looseness in the use of the term postmodernism is one of the principal sources of my own irritation. A difference between Callinicos's irritation and mine is that this looseness causes me to reject this particular reading of *The Underdogs;* it causes him to reject the entire concept of postmodernism.
3. See George Yúdice et al, *On the Edge*, 1.
4. See Fredric Jameson, *Postmodernism, or the Cultural Logic of Late Capitalism*.
5. See Fernando Calderón, "Latin American Identity and Mixed Temporalities; or How to Be Postmodern and Indian at the Same Time," in John Beverly and José Oviedo, editors, *The Postmodernism Debate in Latin America*.
6. See special issues *Nuevo Texto Crítico* (1991) and *Boundary* 2 vol 20, no. 3, (Fall 1993) for Hispanic approaches to postmodernism. The special issue of *Boundary* 2 is edited by John Beverly and José Oviedo, *The Postmodernism Debate in Latin America*.
7. Fredric Jameson has become more favorable in some of his attitudes about postmodern culture more recently, as can be observed in his *Postmodernism, or the Cultural Logic of Late Capitalism*.

Chapter 1

1. The bibliography on postmodernism in Latin America is substantive and growing, but recent important contributions include Santiago Colás, *Postmodernity in Latin America: the Argentine Paradigm;* George Yúdice, "Postmodernity and Transnational Capitalism in Latin America," in George Yúdice et al, *On Edge;* Alfonso de Toro, "Postmodernidad y Latinoamérica (con un modelo para la narrativa postmoderna)," 105-128.

2. Several factors have changed the status of Latin American literature in First World academia. The Cuban Revolution and Sputnik were important contributors to the rise of federally funded Latin American Studies programs in the 1960s. At the same time, the Latin American sections of Spanish departments began evolving from perhaps one or two token specialists in Latin American literature to larger, more representative sectors of these departments. Similarly, numerous new academic journals that specialize exclusively in Latin American literature, such as *Chasqui* and *The Latin American Literary Review* have become established since the 1960s.

3. The original version of this chapter, much abbreviated, was prepared for the Opening Forum on the topic "Discourse of Truth," organized by Mario Valdés at the annual meeting of the Modern Language Association, 27 December 1991. This presentation appeared as "Truth Claims, Postmodernism and the Latin American Novel," in *Profession* (1992), pp. 6-9. An expanded version, titled "Western Truth Claims in the Context of the Modern and Postmodern Latin American Novel," appeared in *Readerly/Writerly Texts* volume 1, no. 1 (Fall/Winter 1993): 39-64.

4. Hans-Georg Gadamer, *Truth and Method,* 222-223.

5. Ibid., 98.

6. Ibid., 173.

7. Ibid., 300.

8. Frank Lentriccia, *After the New Criticism,* 150.

9. Hans-Georg Gadamer, 276.

10. Ibid. 269.

11. Frank Lentriccia, *After the New Criticsm,* 151.

12. Hans-Georg Gadamer, 83.

13. Paul Ricoeur, *History and Truth,* 166.

14. Fredric Jameson, *Essays,* vol. 2, 119.

15. Paul Ricoeur, *History and Truth,* 174.

16. Ibid., 174.

17. Mario Vargas Llosa has explained his concept of fiction as lies in numerous publications. See in particular, *La verdad de las mentiras*.

18. Paul Ricoeur, *History and Truth*, 174.

19. Gabriel García Márquez, *One Hundred Years of Solitude*, 14.

20. Walter Ong has discussed this as being a typical manifestation of oral culture in *Orality and Literacy*, chapter 3.

21. Walter Ong delineates reactions such as hers as being typical of primary oral cultures in *Orality and Literacy*. See in particular chapter 3, "Some Psychodynamics of Orality." I have studied the residue of oral culture in *One Hundred Years of Solitude* in chapter 4 of *The Colombian Novel, 1844-1987*.

22. The first Colombian novel dealing with the 1928 strike was actually written by García Márquez's close friend, Alvaro Cepeda Samudio. See Alvaro Cepeda Samudio, *La casa grande* (1962). It appeared in English under the same title (Austin: University of Texas Press, 1991), with a preface by García Márquez.

23. Steven Conner, *Postmodernist Culture: An Introduction to Theories of the Contemporary*, 105.

24. Raymond Williams, *Politics*, 33.

25. See Walter Benjamin, "The Storyteller," in *Illuminations*, 83-110.

26. Frank Kermode, *The Sense of an Ending*, 91.

27. David Daiches, "Politics and the Literary Imagination," 197.

28. Jean-François Lyotard, *The Postmodern Condition*, 30.

29. Fredric Jameson, foreword, in Jean-François Lyotard, *The Postmodern Condition*, xvii.

30. Steven Conner, *Postmodernist Culture: An Introduction to Theories of the Contemporary*, 107.

31. Ibid., 107.

32. Steven Conner makes this point about First World modernism in ibid., 202.

33. In making this allusion to the "truth industry" of the Latin American novel, I refer to the major publishers of the Latin American novel of the Boom, such as Harper and Row in the United States and Seix Barral in Spain. Jean Franco has studied the ideology of the Boom in "The Crisis of the Liberal Imagination."

34. Fredric Jameson, *The Political Unconscious*, 236.

35. Fredric Jameson analyzes the strategies of containment to be found in Conrad and other modern writers in ibid.

36. Linda Hutcheon, *A Poetics of Postmodernism*, 36.

37. Ibid., 49.

38. Jean-François Lyotard, *The Postmodern Condition: A Report on Knowledge*, 37.

39. Ibid., 37.

40. Ibid., 18.

41. Ibid., 8.

42. As pointed out in the preface, one could cite an extensive bibliography of this debate, published in Spanish in Spain and Latin America. During the months of July and August of 1990, the Spanish translation of Lyotard's *The Postmodern Condition* was actually a best-seller in Buenos Aires. A set of Fredric Jameson's essays on the postmodern has been published in Spanish in Buenos Aires under the title of *Ensayos sobre el posmodernismo*. Nicolás Casullo has compiled a volume of essays on the postmodern debate containing essays by Habermas, Lyotard, Huyssen, and others: *El debate modernidad-posmodernidad*. Many of the theorists of poststructuralism and postmodernism have appeared in the Chilean journal *Revista de Crítica Cultural*, published in Santiago de Chile by Nelly Richard. *Boundary 2* and *Nuevo Texto Crítico* have published special issues on the topic of postmodernism in Latin America.

43. Jean Baudrillard, *Simulations*, 31.

44. Ibid., 44.

45. Ibid., 24.

46. Both Foucault and Derrida have been translated extensively into Spanish. Studies on Foucault in Spanish include *Lectura de Foucault* by Miguel Morey.

47. Linda Hutcheon, *A Poetics of Postmodernism*, 5.

48. Ibid., 47.

49. Ibid., 49.

50. Ibid., 93.

51. Ibid., 109.

52. Alex Callinicos, *Against Postmodernism*, 2.

53. As pointed out in note 1, a broad range of North Atlantic Latin Americanists and Latin American social scientists have been engaged in a dialogue on the viability of identifying Latin America or sectors of its society as "postmodern." See George Yúdice, Jean Franco, and Juan Flores, editors, *On Edge* and Herman Herlinghaus and Monika Walter, editors, *Posmodernidad en la periferia*.

54. Alex Callinicos cites Christopher Norris in *Against Postmodernism*, 94.

55. Hans-Georg Gadamer, *Truth and Method*, 389.

56. Linda Hutcheon, *A Poetics of Postmodernism*, 8.

57. Ibid., 41.

58. Fredric Jameson makes few references to Latin American writing when he writes of postmodern fiction, but he tends to limit his vision of postmodern fiction to the "light" variety, such as Mario Vargas Llosa's *Aunt Julia and the Script Writer*. See *Postmodernism or the Cultural Logic of Late Capitalism*, 373. Despite his limited vision of postmodern fiction in Latin America, Jameson's essays on postmodern culture are well known in that region. See *Ensayos sobre el posmodernismo*.

59. See Angela McCrobbie, *Postmodernism and Popular Culture.*

60. Linda Hutcheon, *A Poetics of Postmodernism,* 4.

61. See Nelly Richard, *La estratificación de los márgenes.*

62. Alex Callinicos, *Against Postmodernism,* 25.

63. See David Harvey, *The Condition of Postmodernity,* for a discussion of Van de Rohe and others on truth.

64. In *Postmodernist Culture* (p. 17) Steven Conner discusses this idea of Edward Said. See Edward Said, "Opponents, Audiences, Constiuencies, and Community," in *The Politics of Interpretation,* ed W. J. T. Mitchell (Chicago: University of Chicago Press, 1983), 7-32.

65. Alex Callinicos, *Against Postmodernism,* 15.

Chapter 2

1. I have discussed the Octavio Paz industry in Mexico in "The Octavio Paz Industry," *American Book Review,* vol. 14, no. 3 (August-September 1992): 3-10.

2. Cynthia Steel has studied the work of Poniatowska in detail in *Politics, Gender, and the Mexican Novel, 1968-1988.*

3. Roger Bartra, an influential cultural critic in Mexico, was skeptical about any use of the term *postmodern* with reference to Mexico when I spoke with him in December of 1989. Since then, he has published several articles and books that accept this term. See Bartra, *La jaula de la melancolía.*

4. One example of the type of article published on postmodernism in the Mexican popular press is Tetsuji Tamamoto, "El desplazamiento teórico de las ciencias sociales: una perspectiva japonesa," *Jornada Semanal,* 239, (January 9, 1994): 33-40.

5. Brian McHale, *Postmodernist Fiction.*

6. In a comprehensive study of the complete fiction of Carlos Fuentes currently in press, I delineate the modernist and postmodern fiction of Fuentes. He is a fundamentally modernist writer who has also been affected by the postmodern. His modernist works include the early novels *Where the Air Is Clear* and *The Death of Artemio Cruz.* His postmodern work includes *Holy Place, A Change of Skin,* and *Christopher Unborn. Terra Nostra* contains many qualities of the modernist and the postmodern, but Brian McHale describes *Terra Nostra* as part of the postmodern "transhistorical carnaval." See *Postmodernist Fiction,* 17.

7. Daniel J. Anderson, *Vicente Leñero: the Novelist as Critic,* 49.

8. Ibid., 50.

9. See chapter 1 of Brian McHale, *Postmodernist Fiction*.

10. Carlos Fuentes, *Zona sagrada*, 29.

11. Ibid., 65.

12. Ibid., 162.

13. Ibid., 16.

14. Brian McHale, *Postmodernist Fiction*, 11.

15. John S. Brushwood, *La narrativa mexicana, 1967–1982*, 47.

16. Carlos Fuentes, *Cumpleaños*, 65.

17. Carlos Fuentes, *Terra Nostra*, 765.

18. Carlos Fuentes prefers the term "Indo-Afro-Iberoamerica" to "Latin America." In *The Buried Mirror*, he explains that the term "Latin America" was coined by the French in the nineteenth century to justify their own colonial interests in the region.

19. See Charles Jencks, *What is Postmodernism?*

20. McHale discusses the double coding of postmodern fiction in *Postmodernist Fiction*, chapter 1.

21. Jorge Luis Borges, *Ficciones*, 53.

22. See González Echevarría, "*Terra Nostra*: Theory and Practice."

23. Jorge Luis Borges, *Ficciones*, 53.

24. Michel de Certeau, *L'écriture de l'histoire*, 4.

25. Michel Foucault has discussed imitation and repetition in the Renaissance in *The Order of Things*, 300-307.

26. See Roberto González Echevarría, "*Terra Nostra*: Theory and Practice" and Lucille Kerr, *Reclaiming the Author: Figures and Fictions from Spanish America*.

27. Carlos Fuentes, *Una familia lejana*, 200.

28. Ibid., 128.

29. Carlos Fuentes, *Cristóbal Nonato*, 14.

30. Joseph and Shizinko Muller-Brockman, *History of the Poster*. (Zurich: ABC Editions, 1971).

31. Raymond Leslie Williams, "Novel as Poster," in *José Agustín: Onda and Beyond*, edited by June C. D. Carter and Donald L. Schmidt. (Columbia, Missouri: University of Missouri Press, 1986): 68-77.

32. Stephen Bell, "Postmodern Fiction in Spanish America: the Example of Salvador Elizondo and Néstor Sánchez."

33. Jesús Salas Elorza has studied the metafictional qualities of Pitol's fiction in his doctoral dissertation "La narrativa de Sergio Pitol y el proyecto dialógico de Mijail Bajtín," University of Colorado, 1992.

34. John S. Brushwood has discussed the relative accessibility of the Mexican novel of the late 1970s and early 1980s in *La narrativa mexicana, 1967–1982*.

35. See David Harvey, *The Condition of Postmodernity*, chapter 4.

Chapter 3

1. See Fernando Calderón, "Latin American Identity and Mixed Temporalities; or How to Be Postmodern and Indian at the Same Time."

2. George Yúdice, *On Edge*, 2.

3. These observations on the visibly postmodern transformation of Pereira, Colombia, were part of my personal experience in a visit to Pereira in August of 1994.

4. Fernando Calderón, "Latin American Identity and Mixed Temporalities; or How to Be Postmodern and Indian at the Same Time," 55.

5. As I have indicated in the preface, a working assumption of this book is that different sectors of contemporary Latin American society are simultaneously premodern, modern and postmodern.

6. For an in-depth study of the rise of the modern novel in Colombia in the 1940s, see Yolanda Forero-Villegas, *Un eslabón perdido: la novela colombiana de los años cuarenta (1941-1949) primer proyecto moderno en Colombia*.

7. Gabriel García Márquez has been a celebrity figure and cultural icon in Colombia since he was awarded the Nobel Prize in literature in 1982. Before achieving this status as celebrity and icon in 1982, he was often the recipient of strident criticism in Colombia, criticism that came from both liberal and conservative press. The reasons for the attacks were multiple, but often referred to García Márquez's public support of leftist movements in Colombia and Latin America. In the 1970s, García Márquez was the director of the leftist journal *Alternativa* in Colombia.

8. Raymond Leslie Williams, *The Colombian Novel*, 25.

9. Ibid., 26.

10. R. H. Moreno-Durán, *Los felinos del Canceller*, 29

11. Peter Elmore has studied *La casa de cartón* in the context of Peruvian fiction in *Los muros invisibles: Lima y modernidad en lanovela del siglo XX*.

12. In *Vargas Llosa Among the Postmodernists*, Keith M. Booker identifies *The War of the End of the World* as postmodern, but I consider it a work that grows out of Vargas Llosa's modernist impulse. Booker seems to force the issue with *The War of the End of the World*, stating "This text appears on the surface to be a relatively traditional realistic novel, but if what makes a postmodernist text is a postmodernist reader, then we should have no trouble finding postmodernist elements there"(Booker, 74). I consider Vargas Llosa's fundamentally modernist work to be *The Time of the Hero, The Green House, Conversation in The Cathedral, The War of the End of the World*, and *The Storyteller*. His postmodern gestures are *Captain Pantoja and the Special Service, Aunt Julia and the Script Writer, Who Killed Palomino Molero?*, and *In Praise of the Stepmother*.

13. Keith M. Booker, *Vargas Llosa Among the Postmodernists*, 37.
14. Ibid., 42.
15. Fredric Jameson, *Postmodernism or the Cultural Logic of Late Capitalism*, 373.
16. Keith M. Booker, *Vargas Llosa Among the Postmodernists*, 54.
17. For a further discussion of historical fiction in the Andean region and Latin America, see Raymond D. Souza, *La historia en la novela hispanoamericana moderna* and Seymour Menton, *The New Historical Novel*.

Chapter 4

1. See Bernardo Subercaseaux, "Nueva sensibilidad y horizonte 'post' en Chile."
2. Ibid.
3. Héctor Libertella, *Las sagradas escrituras*, 212.
4. Hugo Achúgar has discussed postmodern Uruguay in "Fin de siglo: reflexiones desde la periferia," in Herman Herlinghaus and Monika Walter, editors, *Posmodernidad en la periferia*, 233-255.
5. Ibid.
6. John S. Brushwood, *The Spanish American Novel: A Twentieth-Century Survey*, 310.
7. Julio Ortega, "Diamela Eltit y el Imaginario de la Virtualidad," in Juan Carlos Lértora, editor, *Una poética de literatura menor*, 53.
8. Ibid., 53.
9. Diamela Eltit, *Lumpérica*, 98
10. Ibid., 105.
11. Ibid., 8.
12. Jean Baudrillard, *Simulations*, 54.
13. Diamela Eltit, *Lumpérica*, 19.
14. Ibid., 20.
15. Sara Castro-Klarén, "La crítica literaria feminista y la escritora en América Latina," 99.
16. Julio Ortega, "Diamela Eltit y el Imaginario de la Virtualidad," 53.
17. Linda Hutcheon, *A Poetics of Postmodernism*, 119.
18. Julio Ortega, "Diamela Eltit y el Imaginario de la Virtualidad," 53.
19. Diamela Eltit, *El cuarto mundo*, 23.
20. Ibid., 30.
21. Ibid., 87.
22. Ibid., 95.
23. Ibid., 128.
24. Guillermo García Corales, "La deconstrucción del poder en *Lumpérica*," 111.

25. John S. Brushwood, *The Spanish American Novel*, 304.

26. Ibid., 313-321.

27. Lucille Kerr, *Reclaiming the Author: Figures and Fictions from Spanish America*, 24.

28. Jonathan Tittler, *Manuel Puig*, 129.

29. Lucille Kerr, *Reclaiming the Author: Figures and Fictions from Spanish America*, 244.

30. Linda Hutcheon, *A Poetics of Postmodernism*, 119.

31. Seymour Menton, *The New Historical Novel*, 127.

32. Ibid., 127.

33. Daniel Balderson, "Latent Meanings in Ricardo Piglia's *Respiración Artificial* and Luis Gusman's *El corazón de junio*," 212.

34. Ricardo Piglia, *Artificial Respiration*, 21.

35. Ibid., 212.

36. Daniel Balderson, "Latent Meanings in Ricardo Pigilia's *Respiración artificial* and Luis Gusman's *En el corazón de junio*," 211.

37. Ricardo Piglia, *Artificial Respiration*, 55

38. Ibid., 187.

39. Ibid., 146.

40. Ricardo Piglia's *Prisión perpetua* contains one additional story not included in his earlier volume *Nombre falso*; the latter also contains one story not included in the former.

41. In addition to the problem of the "mother tongue" as read in Spanish, these problematics are compounded for the reader of this text in English, which is not the "mother tongue" of Piglia either.

42. Ellen McCracken, "Metaplagiarism and the Critic's Role as Detective: Ricardo Piglia's Reinvention of Roberto Arlt," 1077.

43. Sandra Garabano has discussed this matter in her doctoral dissertation "Reescribiendo la nación: la narrativa de Ricardo Piglia" University of Colorado, 1994.

44. Sandra Garabano has discussed the "paranoiac tale" in ibid.

45. Sandra Garabano has discussed this issue in ibid.

46. See Ricardo Piglia, *Crítica y ficción*.

47. Héctor Libertella, *Las sagradas escrituras*, 122.

48. Ibid., 44.

49. For a further discussion of this matter, see Balderson, "Latent Meanings in Ricardo Piglia's *Respiración artificial* and Luis Gusman's *En el corazón de junio*."

50. Personal interview with Híber Conteris, New York, October 1994.

51. See Santiago Colas, "Un posmodernismo resistente: *El diez por ciento de la vida y la historia*."

52. Santiago Colas cites Elaine Scarry in ibid., 176.

Chapter 5

1. Doris Sommer and Esteban Torres, "Dominican Republic," 272.
2. Aníbal González "Puerto Rico," 567.
3. Aníbal González sets forth and synthesizes this matter in ibid.
4. Antonio Benítez Rojo, *The Repeating Island: the Caribbean and the Postmodern Perspective*, 11.
5. Ibid., 1.
6. Ibid., 29.
7. Ibid., 29
8. For a further discussion of the fiction of Novás Calvo, see Raymond D. Souza, *Lino Novás Calvo*.
9. Roberto González Echevarría, "Alejo Carpentier," 103.
10. Ibid., 106.
11. John S. Brushwood, *The Spanish American Novel*, 292.
12. Ibid., 292-294.
13. Raymond D. Souza has discussed this stage of Cabrera Infante's writing in *Guillermo Cabrera Infante: A Creative Odyssey*, forthcoming, University of Texas Press.
14. Roberto González Echevarría, *La ruta de Severo Sarduy*, 243-253.
15. Ibid., 167.
16. Ibid., 173.
17. Ibid., 184.
18. René Prieto, "The Ambivalent Fiction of Severo Sarduy," 50-51.
19. Ibid., 52.
20. Roberto González Echevarría, *La ruta de Severo Sarduy*, 227.
21. Aníbal González, "Puerto Rico," 566.
22. Ibid., 566-577.
23. Carlos Alonso, "*La guaracha del Macho Camacho*: the Novel as Dirge," 348.
24. Joseph Chadwick, "'Repito para consumo de los radiooyentes': "Repetition and Fetishism in *La guaracha del Macho Camacho*," 66.
25. Luis Rafael Sánchez, *La importancia de llamarse Daniel Santos*, 5.
26. Carlos Alonso, "*La guaracha del Macho Camacho*: the Novel as Dirge," 350.
27. Doris Sommer and Esteban Torres, "Dominican Republic," 276.
28. Ibid., 284.

Chapter 6

1. Linda Hutcheon, *A Poetics of Postmodernism*, 16.
2. Carlos Alonso has discussed this matter in detail in *The Spanish American Regionalist Novel*.
3. Jean Franco, "Apuntes sobre la crítica feminista y la literatura hispanoamericana," *Hispamérica* 15 (December 1986): 31-43.
4. Linda Alcoff has set for the concept of "cultural feminism" in "Cultural Feminism versus Poststructuralism."
5. Linda Alcoff has discussed cultural feminism in greater detail in ibid.
6. David William Foster has discussed in the importance of Torres Molina's fiction in *Gay and Lesbian Themes in Latin American Writing*, 131-136.
7. Ibid., 111.
8. Robert E. Di Antonio, *Brazilian Fiction: Aspects and Evolution of the Contemporary Narrative*, 172.
9. David William Foster has documented a vast bibliography of these works in *Gay and Lesbian Themes in Latin American Writing*.
10. Ibid., 3.
11. Ibid., 98.
12. Elzbieta Sklodowska, *El testimonio hispanoamericano: historia, teoría, poética*.
13. Ibid., 50-51.
14. Ibid., 159.
15. The idea of a postmodern ethnography does not appear in the general studies on postmodernism used in this study. In the field of anthropology, however, written personal accounts of cultural experience are often called "postmodern ethnography."
16. Robert E. DiAntonio points to the numerous directions of the contemporary Brazilian novel in *Brazilian Fiction: Aspects and Evolution of the Contemporary Narrative*.
17. Ibid., x.
18. Ibid., 83.

Selected Bibliography

Many of the writers cited in this book have yet to become as well known (and distributed) in the United States as the generation of the Boom. University Presses are beginning to publish the writings of some of these authors; Ricardo Piglia's *Artificial Respiration* is published by Duke University Press and Diamela Eltit's *El cuarto mundo* is forthcoming from the University of Nebraska Press. For those readers with a knowledge of Spanish, most of the novels cited in this book can be ordered from international bookstores in New York, Miami, Chicago, Los Angeles, and other major cities. They are also readily available in most university and college libraries.

Fiction Cited

Borges, Jorge Luis. *Ficciones.* Edited with an introduction by Anthony Kerrigan. New York: Grove Press, 1987.

Cepeda Samudio, Alvaro. *La casa grande.* Translated by Seymour Menton. Austin: University of Texas Press, 1991.

Eltit, Diamela. *Lumperica.* Santiago: Ediciones del Ornitorrinco, 1983.

Fuentes, Carlos. *Cristóbal nonato.* Mexico: Fondo de Cultura, 1987.

———. *Cumpleaños.* Mexico: Joaquín Mortiz, 1976.

———. *Holy Place,* translated by Suzanne Jill Levine, in *Triple Cross.* New York: Dutton, 1972.

———. *Terra Nostra.* Mexico: Joaquín Mortiz, 1975.

———. *Una familia lejana.* Mexico: Ediciones Era, 1980.

———. *Zona sagrada.* Mexico: Siglo Veintuno, 1977.

García Márquez, Gabriel. *One Hundred Years of Solitude.* Translated by Gregory Rabassa. New York: Harper and Row, 1970.

Moreno-Durán, R. H. *Los felinos del Canciller.* Bogotá: Planeta, 1987.

Pacheco, José Emilio. *You Will Die in a Distant Land*. Translated by Elizabeth Umlas. Coral Gables, Florida: North-South Center, University of Miami, 1991.

Piglia, Ricardo. *Artificial Respiration*. Translated by Daniel Balderson. Durham: Duke University Press, 1993.

Sánchez, Luis Rafael. *La importancia de llamarse Daniel Santos*. Hanover: Ediciones del Norte, 1989.

Critical and Theoretical Works Cited

Achúgar, Hugo. "Fin de siglo. Reflexiones desde la periferia," in Hermann Herlinghaus and Monika Walter, editors, *Posmodernidad en la periferia*. Berlin: Langer Verlag, 1994, 233-255.

Alcoff, Linda. "Cultural Feminism versus Poststructuralism: the Identity Crisis in Feminist Theory," *Signs: Journal of Women in Culture and Society* vol. 13, no. 3: 405-436.

Alonso, Carlos. "*La guaracha del Macho Camacho*: the Novel as Dirge," *MLN*, vol. 100, no. 2 (March 1985): 348-360.

———. *The Spanish American Regionalist Novel*. Cambridge: Cambridge University Press, 1990.

Anderson, Daniel J. *Vicent Leñero: the Novelist as Critic*. University of Texas Studies in Contemporary Spanish American Fiction. Volume 3. New York: Peter Lang, 1989.

Balderson, Daniel. "Latent Meanings in Ricardo Piglia's *Respiración Artificial* and Luis Gusman's *En el corazón de junio*," *Revista Canadiense de Estudios Hispánicos*, vol. XII, no. 2 (Winter 1988): 207-219.

Bartra, Roger. *La jaula de la melacolía: identidad y metamorfosis del mexicano*. Mexico: Enlace/Grijalbo, 1987.

Baudrillard, Jean. *Simulations*. New York: Semiotext(e), 1983.

Bell, Stephen. "Postmodern Fiction in Spanish America: the Example of Salvador Elizondo and Néstor Sánchez," *Arizona Quarterly*, vol. 42, no. 1 (1986): 6-15.

Benítez Rojo, Antonio. *The Repeating Island: the Caribbean and the Postmodern Perspective*. Translated by James E. Maraaniss. Durham: Duke University Press, 1992.

Benjamin, Walter. *Illuminations*. New York: Schocken, 1968.

Booker, M. Keith. *Vargas Llosa Among the Postmodernists*. Gainesville: University Press of Florida, 1994.

Brushwood, John S. *The Spanish American Novel*. Austin: University of Texas Press, 1975.

———. *La narrativa mexicana, 1967-1982*. Mexico: Enlace/Grijalbo, 1984.

Calderón, Fernando. "Latin American Identity and Mixed Temporalities; or How to Be Postmodern and Indian at the Same Time," *Boundary* 2, vol. 20, no. 3 (Fall 1993): 55-64.

Callinicos, Alex. *Against Postmodernism*. New York: St. Martin's Press, 1989.

Castro-Klarén, Sara. "La crítica literaria feminista y la escritora en América Latina," in Patricia González and Eliana Ortega, editors, *La sartén por el mango*. San Juan: Ediciones Huracán, 1985: 27-46

Casullo, Nicolás, ed. *El debate modernidad-postmodernidad*. Buenos Aires: Puntosur, 1989.

Chadwick, Joseph. "'Repito para consumo de los radioyentes': Repetition and Fetishism in *La guaracha del Macho Camacho*," *Revista de Estudios Hispánicos*, vol. 21 no. 1 (January 1987): 61-83.

Colás, Santiago. *Postmodernity in Latin America: the Argentine Paradigm*. Durham: Duke University Press, 1994.

————. "Un posmodernismo resistente: *El diez por ciento de vida* y la historia," *Nuevo texto crítico* 7 (1991): 175-196.

Conner, Steven. *Postmodernist Culture: An Introduction to the Theories of the Contemporary*. Oxford: Basil Blackwell, 1989.

Daiches, David. "Politics and the Literary Imagination," in Ihab Hassan, editor, *Liberations: New Essays on the Humanities in Revolution*. Middletown, CT: Wesleyan University Press, 1971: 100-116.

De Toro, Alfonso. "Postmodernidad y Latinoamérica (con un modelo para la narrativa postmoderna)" *Revista Iberoamericana*, número 155-156 (abril-septiembre 1991): 441-467.

DiAntonio, Robert E. *Brazilian Fiction: Aspects and Evolution of the Contemporary Narrative*. Fayeteville: University of Arkansas Press, 1989.

Eagleton, Terry. *Theory of Literature*. Minneapolis: University of Minnesota Press, 1983.

Elmore, Peter. *Los muros invisibles: Lima y la modernidad en la novela del siglo XX*. Lima: Mosca Azul Editores, 1993.

Forero-Villegas, M. Yolanda. *Un eslabón perdido: la novela colombiana de los años cuarenta (1941-1949) primer proyecto moderno en Colombia*. Bogotá: Editorial Kelly, 1994.

Foster, David William. *Gay and Lesbian Themes in Latin American Writing*. Austin: University of Texas Press, 1991.

————. *Handbook of Latin American Studies*. New York: Garland, 1992.

Foucault, Michel. *The Order of Things: An Archeology of the Human Sciences*. Translation of *Les Mots et les Choses*. New York: Vintage Books, 1973.

Franco, Jean. *Plotting Women: Gender and Representation in Mexico*. New York: Columbia University Press, 1992.

————. "The Crisis of the Liberal Imagination." *Ideologies and Literature* 1.1 (December 1976-77): 5-24.

————. "Apuntes sobre la crítica feminista y la literatura hispanoamericana," *Hispamérica* 15 (45) 1986: 31-43.

Fuentes, Carlos. *The Buried Mirror: Reflections on Spain and the New World*. London: Andre Deutsch, 1992.

Gadamer, Hans-Georg. *Truth and Method.* Second Revised Edition. Translated and revised by Joel Weinsheimer and Donald G. Marshall, 1990. New York: Crossroad, 1990.

Garabano, Sandra. "Reescribiendo la nación: la narrativa de Ricardo Piglia," Doctoral Dissertation, University of Colorado, 1994.

García Corales, Guillermo. "La deconstrucción del poder en *Lumpérica,*" in Juan Carlos Lértora, editor, *Una poética de literatura menor: la narrativa de Diamela Eltit.* Santiago: Editorial Cuarto Propio, 1993: 111-126

González, Aníbal. "Puerto Rico" in David William Foster, editor, *Handbook of Latin American Studies.* New York: Garland, 1992: 555-582.

González Echevarría, Roberto. "*Terra Nostra*: Theory and Practice" in Robert Brody and Charles Rossman, editors, *Carlos Fuentes.* Austin: University of Texas Press, 1978: 132-145.

————. "Alejo Carpentier," in William Luis, Editor, *Dictionary of Literary Biography.* Detroit: Gale Research, 1992: 96-109.

————. *La ruta de Severo Sarduy.* Hanover: Ediciones del Norte, 1987.

Harvey, David. *The Condition of Postmodernity.* Cambridge, Mass: Blackwell Publishers, 1989.

Hassan, Ihab. *The Dismemberment of Orpheus: Toward a Postmodern Literature.* Second edition. Madison: University of Wisconsin Press, 1982.

————. *The Postmodern Turn: Essays in Postmodern Theory and Culture.* Columbus: Ohio State University Press, 1987.

Herlinghaus, Herman and Monika Walter, Editors, *Posmodernidad en la periferia.* Berlin: Langer Verlag, 1994.

Hutcheon, Linda. *A Poetics of Postmodernism: History, Theory, Fiction.* New York: Routledge, 1988.

————. *The Politics of Postmodernism.* New York: Routledge, 1989.

Jameson, Fredric. *Ensayos sobre el posmodernismo.* Buenos Aires: Ediciones Imago Mundi, 1991.

————. *The Ideologies of Theory: Essays 1971-1986.* vol. 2: *the Syntax of History.* Minneapolis: University of Minnesota Press, 1988.

————. *The Political Unconscious: Narrative as a Socially Symbolic Act.* Ithaca: Cornell University Press, 1981.

————. *Postmodernism or the Cultural Logic of Late Capitalism.* Durham: Duke University Press, 1991.

Jencks, Charles. *What Is Postmodernism?* London: Academy Editions; New York: St. Martin's Press, 1986.

Kellner, Douglas. *Jean Baudrillard: From Marxism to Postmodernism and Beyond.* Stanford: Stanford University Press, 1989.

Kermode, Frank. *The Sense of An Ending.* London: Oxford University Press, 1966.

Kerr, Lucille. *Reclaiming the Author: Figures and Fictions from Spanish America.* Durham: Duke University Press, 1992.

Lentriccia, Frank. *After the New Criticism.* Chicago: University of Chicago Press, 1980.

Lértora, Juan Carlos, editor. *Una poética de literatura menor: la narrativa de Diamela Eltit.* Santiago: Editorial Cuarto Propio, 1993.

Libertella, Héctor. *Las sagradas escrituras.* Buenos Aires: Editorial Sudamericana, 1993.

Luis, William, editor. *Dictionary of Literary Biography. Volume 113: Modern Latin American Fiction Writers.* Detroit: Gale Research, 1992.

Lyotard, Jean-François. *The Postmodern Condition: A Report on Knowledge.* Theory and History of Literature, vol. 10. Minneapolis: University of Minnesota Press, 1989.

McCracken, Ellen. "Metaplagiarism and the Critic's Role as Detective: Ricardo Piglia's Reinvention of Roberto Arlt," *Publications of the Modern Language Association,* vol. 106, nos. 4-6 (1991): 1071-1082.

McHale, Brian. *Postmodernist Fiction.* New York: Methuen, 1987.

McRobie, Angela. *Postmodernism and Popular Culture.* New York: Routledge, 1994.

Menton, Seymour. *The New Historical Novel.* Austin: University of Texas Press, 1993.

Morey, Miguel. *Lectura de Foucault.* Madrid: Taurus, 1983.

Newman, Charles. *The Post-Modern Aura: The Act of Fiction in an Age of Inflation.* Evanston: Northwestern University Press, 1985.

Ong, Walter. *Orality and Literacy: The Technologizing of the Word.* London: Methuen, 1982.

Piglia, Ricardo. *Crítica y ficción.* Buenos Aires: Extensión Universitaria, Serie Ensayos, 1986.

Prieto, René. "The Ambiviolent Fiction of Severo Sarduy," *Symposium* vol. 39, no. 1 (Spring 1985): 49-60.

Richard, Nelly. *La estratificación de los márgenes.* Santiago de Chile: Francisco Zegers, 1989.

Ricoeur, Paul. *History and Truth.* Translation and Introduction Charles A. Kelbley. Evanston: Northwestern University Press, 1965.

Salas Elorza, Jesús. "La narrativa de Sergio Pitol y el proyecto dialógico de Mijail Bajtín," Doctoral Dissertation, University of Colorado at Boulder, 1992.

Sarlo, Beatriz. *Escenas de la vida posmoderna.* Buenos Aires: Ariel, 1994.

Sklodowska, Elzbieta. *Testimonio hispanoamericano: historia, teoría, poética.* New York: Peter Lang, 1992.

Sommer, Doris and Esteban Torres, "Dominican Republic" in David William Foster, editor, *Handbook of Latin American Literature.* New York: Garland Publishing Company, 1992: 271-286.

Souza, Raymond D. *Lino Novás Calvo.* Boston: G. K. Hall, Twayne World Author Series, 1981.

————. *La historia en la novela hispanoamericana moderna*, Bogotá: Tercer Mundo Editores, 1988.

Steele, Cynthia. *Politics, Gender, and the Mexican Novel, 1968–1988.* Austin: University of Texas Press, 1992.

Subercaseaux, Bernardo. "Nueva sensibilidad y horizonte "post" en Chile," *Nuevo Texto Crítico* 6 (1990): 135-145.

Tamaoto, Tetsuji, "El desplazamiento teórico en las ciencias sociales: una perspectiva japonesa," *Jornada Semanal* 239 (January 9, 1994): 33-40.

Tittler, Jonathan. *Manuel Puig.* Boston: G. K. Hall, 1993.

Vargas Llosa, Mario. *La verdad de las mentiras.* Barcelona: Seix Barral, 1990.

Williams, Raymond. *The Politics of Modernism.* London: Verso, 1989.

Williams, Raymond Leslie. *The Colombian Novel: 1844–1987.* Austion: University of Texas Press, 1991.

————. "The Octavio Paz Industry," *American Book Review* Vol. 14, No. 3 (August-September 1992): 3-10.

————. "Western Truth Claims in the Context of the Modern and Postmodern Latin American Novel," *Readerly/Writerly Texts* Vol. 1, No. 1 (Fall/Winter 1993): 39-64

————. "Truth Claims, Postmodernism and the Latin American Novel," *Profession* (November 1992): 6-9.

————. "Novel as Poster," in June C.D. Carter and Donald Schmidt, Editors, *José Agustín: Onda and Beyond.* Columbia: University of Missouri Press, 1986: 68-77.

Yúdice, George. "Postmodernity and Transnational Capitalism in Latin America," *On Edge: the Crisis of Contemporary Latin American Culture.* Minneapolis: University of Minnesota Press, 1992.

Yúdice, George, Jean Franco and Juan Flores, editors, *On Edge: the Crisis of Contemporary Latin American Culture.* Cultural Politics, Volume 4. Minneapolis: University of Minnesota Press, 1992.

Index